"THE MEDICINE HORN is a story of the time when the frontier began in the East, and the frontiersman was just reaching out to become the Mountain Man of the West. A well-crafted tale that every buckskinner and blackpowder shooter will enjoy, told by one of our own."

— Don Coldsmith, author of the SPANISH BIT SAGA

"Jory Sherman catches the westering impulse that formed our nation. He evokes an era, plunging us into the 1790's, when adventuresome people poured over the Appalachians and into forested Kentucky to build new lives. In the hands of this master storyteller, we are right there, living in a time of muzzle-loading rifles, one-bottom plows, and mule-drawn wagons."

— Richard S. Wheeler, author of the SKYE'S WEST series

"With THE MEDICINE HORN, Jory Sherman has created the first part of a rousing saga. Journeying through perilous territory, the skillfully drawn characters and their adventures fit perfectly into this earthy and violent era of America's frontier past."

— Dee Brown, Author of Bury my Heart at Wounded Knee

"In THE MEDICINE HORN, Jor̲_____ ___ ___ ⁣_es us to a time few authors have explored—th_____ _____ American republic when the west was _____ ____ng beyond was barely a dream. He bri___ ___ ___ ____ls who will dream the dream, the m___ ___ ___ ___ bound by fate to cross the Missouri ____ ___ _____ _____ient. They don't know their future v___ ____ ___ ___ ll wait impatiently for the promised s_____ ____ ___es of this trilogy called The Buckskinners."

— John Byrne_ _____ _uthor of South of the Border

By JORY SHERMAN
from TOM DOHERTY ASSOCIATES

THE MEDICINE HORN

BOOK ONE OF
THE BUCKSKINNERS

Jory Sherman

A TOM DOHERTY ASSOCIATES BOOK
NEW YORK

This is a work of fiction. All of the characters, organizations, and events portrayed in this novel are either products of the author's imagination or are used fictitiously.

THE MEDICINE HORN

Copyright © 1991 by Jory Sherman

All rights reserved.

A Forge Book
Published by Tom Doherty Associates
175 Fifth Avenue
New York, NY 10010

www.tor-forge.com

Forge® is a registered trademark of Macmillan Publishing Group, LLC.

ISBN 978-1-250-30506-0

Our books may be purchased in bulk for promotional, educational, or business use. Please contact your local bookseller or the Macmillan Corporate and Premium Sales Department at 1-800-221-7945, extension 5442, or by email at MacmillanSpecialMarkets@macmillan.com.

First Edition: March 1991
Second Mass Market Edition: October 2018

Printed in the United States of America

0 9 8 7 6 5 4 3 2 1

For Terry C. Johnston

Middle Mississippi Valley and Adjacent Areas, 1793—1843

THE
MEDICINE
HORN

1

Lemuel Hawke slipped the harness reins from his shoulder, wiped his broad, sweat-beaded forehead. The last of his boyhood freckles had faded during the winter; he was growing through them so fast since his marriage that the few that were left seemed like they would wash off in the next rain. His muslin shirt, streaked with soil, clung to his lean hard frame. He watched the rider leave the freshly plowed field, his horse switching its tail like a metronome. There was a taste in young Hawke's mouth like brackish water, a tightness in his chest. He felt closed in, caught like a rabbit in a box trap, choking on his own breath.

"Damn you, Dan'l Brown," Hawke muttered. "Damn tax collector." He crumpled the scrap of paper in his hand, shoved it in the pocket of his trousers. Sometimes he wished he'd never learned how to read and write.

Daniel Brown stopped at the road, turned his mottled gray mare with a light touch of the reins. The mare swung sideways, jerked to a halt, stood there hipshot.

"I'll be back, Lem. You have that money for me."

Hawke compressed his still boyish lips into a tight frown. A drop of sweat dripped from his brow, struck his eye with a crisp saline sting. He blinked involuntarily, rubbed his eye and brow. Beyond a low hill, a lark stammered a lyrical trill, the notes bright and saucy as dandelion wine. The late afternoon sun beat down on him, a distant seething flame shimmering like an orange mirage rising out of mist. The air steamed, heavy with humidity, but the sky was cloudless, a vast blue void that stretched from horizon to horizon.

"Go on, Dan'l," said Hawke, too low for the tax collector to hear, "less'n you aim to take your dole in sweat."

Brown touched blunt spurs to the mare's flanks, drifted down the road through watery waves that distorted the animal's image into a quivering gray blur. The earth, fecund with moisture, gave off the dank aroma of decay and compost in air as cloying and vaporous as steam. The hard rains of March had come, bringing with them the tax collector, as inevitable as the first robin in the piedmont. The assessor, Lemuel knew, rode all the trails connecting the scattered farms that lay along the courses of the Hazel and Thornton rivers west of the Rappahannock. This was Brown's district, the northern half of Culpeper County, extending from the tidewater over the red loam hills through the stands of thick hardwood and evergreen timber to the precipice of the Blue Ridge.

Lem gathered up the harness, unhitched it from the single moldboard plow. The plow tilted to one side, leaned at an angle over the worm-threaded furrow, and the jenny brayed softly. He took the harness off the mule, left only a tattered rope halter. He pulled a short rope from his pocket, attached the narrow-gapped hook to one of the D rings.

"Come on, Goldie," he said. "You done plowed your last Virginny pasture." The jenny's hide, glazed sleek with sweat, twitched with ropy tremors, the ripples striped with blood where the horseflies had gotten to her with needled teeth. Hawke slung the tangled harness over his shoulder, pulled Goldie across the field toward the house and barn. The sun stood just above the horizon, framed by the gentle, forested hills adance with the bobbing heads of spring flowers. After weeks of rain, the land had dried out enough to plow, but he knew he was in the fields early. He had to squeeze time from a year's growing like water from a stone.

"The worst thing, Goldie," he said to the mule as he came up to the ramshackle barn, "was Dan didn't even put your sad spavined carcass on the tax rolls. Just the horse and two mules." One of the mules, grazing in the short pasture behind the house, lifted its head from a thatch of emerald grass as if it had overheard. The other mule switched its tail at the interminable swarm of flies and continued to graze, its shaggy chestnut hide burnished by the sunglint until it shone like oiled rosewood.

He hung up the harness in the tack room, grained the jenny in a stall, forked some hay into the trough, saw to it that Goldie had water in the wooden bucket hanging from a pitchfork tine he'd driven into the wood like a nail. Lemuel slopped the hogs before he washed up at the wooden pump and went into the house. The sun furred the fresh-turned earth with the liquid gild of wild honey and he turned to look at the field for a moment. He could smell the soil, fresh and loamy, exuding a musky nourishment for crops he would probably never plant.

When he slammed the door, his wife Roberta called out to him as if she knew for sure the noise was his doing, no other's.

"Lem, you take them boots off before you come traipsin' through the house." Her voice still chirped with adolescence, tiny, lyrical as feathered dulcimer music.

Lem shucked the dirt-encrusted boots, left them sagging forlornly on the small porch. He padded barefoot into the kitchen, the boards groaning under his weight. The house was under a spring siege by carpenter ants and termites. He had seen the little white devils marching under the porch logs only yesterday. Given time, they would eat the cabin to dust and there would be no trace of man's intrusion.

"Feet're dirtier'n the boots," he said. He smelled the aroma of last year's turnips boiling on the woodstove, waded through a thin cirrus of steam that misted into his sinuses.

"I'm in the front room," called Roberta.

"I hear you," he said. He hated turnips, but they were down to grubbing for their vegetables now. They'd eaten the last of the dried beans last week. Turnips. The thought of them made his stomach tauten like a drumhead.

"I'm going to fry squirrel for your supper," she said.

"It won't brighten me none." He had shot three squirrels that morning. They were small, thin from the winter's den, but he dearly loved fried squirrel, the lean gravy Roberta made with pork fat, buckwheat flour, and goat's milk.

Roberta sat in the one halfway comfortable chair they owned. He had whipsawed the frame from oak, stuffed the dyed burlap upholstery with hog bristles. The bristles had worked through the fabric like small black wires that stung like the needles of mosquitoes. When he sat in it, he felt like a pincushion. The chair wouldn't last another winter. It no longer rocked, but sat crooked on its broken arches, a hopeless cripple. She looked up from the dress she was sewing, a piece of dark thread dangling from her mouth. Roberta seemed always to be making new clothes for herself, while his were in tatters. Even now, he thought, she was dressed almost as if she were going to church. She kept the house well, he gave her that. Never mind that she always looked as if she was going to a ball. This was hard country, and they had few visitors. None put on special clothes for visiting. Roberta, he mused, had ideas about life and such as if she were in the center of a grand painting hanging on a museum wall for everyone to ogle. She always told him that he should dress as if he was going to die and be seen by strangers.

Lem thought such talk was nonsense. If you are dead, you are dead, he always told her, and your shame is only in the shroud they wrap about your rotting corpse.

He loved her; he loved her deeply. It was just that she always pretended that they were gentry, when in truth, they were churchmice, scurrying in the aisles for crumbs. He looked at her delicate hands, cringed at their redness. Lye soap did things to a girl's hands, burned them harder than the sun on the plow-crimped hands of a farmer.

"You got a sour look on your face. I saw Dan'l Brown snoopin' around."

Lem sank wearily into another chair he had cut and hammered to shape, braced with elk sinew, latticed with cowhide. The resin that held it all together had long since lost its gleam. The chair creaked with his weight. He tapped his shirt pocket. He hadn't had any tobacco for a month, but the habit was still with him, like skin. He had been smoking since he turned thirteen, trying so hard to be a man he got the habit quicker than he grew.

"Yair, Dan says he's goin' to take them two hosses for taxes. Says they be the only things we got what's worth a tupenny." His voice was soft, low, laden with the slow vibrato of his Virginia accent, an accent filtered down from the singing voices of his coal-mining ancestors in Wales and Scotland, blended with the English lowborn, altered only slightly in the last hundred years of living in the New World, cultivating Virginia-grown latakia tobacco.

Roberta plunged the needle into a pincushion that had once resembled a cloth tomato. She leaned down over the dress and cut the thread with her teeth.

"Dan'l's goin' to tax you? He didn't last year."

"Probably felt sorry for us." He paused, wishing he had some tobacco left. "I work, damn it all, from sunup to sundown and got nary a thing to show for it."

"Ain't no call to curse, Lemuel Hawke. You've got grain and tobacco, cattle and hogs. More'n some folks."

"Hah! Dan Brown wants more shillings than I have. Pay up, he says, or he'll take the mules. We got to leave here, Roberta, or I'll be in the poorhouse. I owe ever'body and his brother as it is. Dan'l takes my mules, that'd put me afoot and nothin' to work with 'ceptin' Goldie. She's plumb tuckered."

"Leave here?" Roberta asked, as if the notion had stuck there in her mind like a flame in a storm lamp.

"Yes. Get out from under these damned bone-crushing debts." When he got angry, his voice rose in pitch, squeaked like a choirboy's going through the puberty.

"Where would we go? What would we do?"

He sensed the growing panic in her tone, as if she was teetering on the edge of that craziness that made a female wail and screech and rip at her hair like someone hanging onto the edge of a cliff in a high wind. He didn't understand such caterwauling behavings. Scared him halfmost to sobriety, into turning Christian witness.

"Kentucky." The moment he said it, he knew it had been on his mind all along. All winter, leastways. Something in him wanting to move on, to get away from people and laws and government. Get out from under the yoke. He knew what it was, but he had never voiced it aloud before. It was a yearning, a yearning to leave the yoke of civilization and venture into the frontier of a new land. It was more than a yearning. He knew that now. It was a hunger, the hunger of a man to go westward, a burning to see and touch and feel what was beyond the boundaries of this rented Virginia land. It was a lust in the heart to push beyond the isolation of a plot of ground, the walls of another man's house, the frontiers of an earthbound soul.

"Kentucky," he said again. "Rent some good bottom land. I hear tell Lexington's got some fine folks there. Kind of folks you like, fancy and such. Place to wear your pretty dresses. Lots of folks already gone there, folks in predicaments same as us. Good green land, good as any, better'n Virginny."

"I don't know, Lem. I'm plumb leery of just movin' with no place to go. No sure place to go. You been talkin' to that Silas again?"

"No'm," he said, puzzled by her question.

"He come by today. Again. Gives me the chilblains. Looks in the winders. You didn't see him? No, I speck not. He come up to the back porch and like to scared me out of my wits. Old man like that."

"Silas ain't old. He can't be more'n twenty-five or thirty."

"Old, and scaresome. I don't like him."

"He don't mean no harm. Fact is, he was the one tolt me about Kentucky. He talks about other places too. Good places for a man to go."

"A woman needs roots, Lem. Kids. I want to raise my kids in a good home, a fine home, on land we own. This Kentucky, it's wild, full of Indians and renegades. We ought to raise us some kids here, in Virginia."

"We're gonna raise us kids, you say. Hell, we ain't nothin' more'n kids ourselves. You want 'em to grow up like us, poor and dumb as bumpkins? Kentucky's a new state. A promised land. Good weather, they say, good land, plenty of it. Woods full of game to feed a man and his family until he can bring in a good crop. We can drive what cattle we got, butcher the hogs and smoke 'em, or sell 'em on the hoof. Start over fresh. No debts. No tax collector a-houndin' me, no money-grubbin' creditors breathin' down my neck."

Roberta set her dress on the arm of the chair, rose and walked to the hand-wrought maple cabinet set along the wall. She stooped, opened the door and pulled out a tin box, its paint worn off from use, battered from travel.

She opened the box. Lem heard the paper rustle, the clink of coins.

"We have only a few pounds," she said, her voice dropping into a lower register. He could almost measure the deepness of her despondency. She was pretty low, he thought. They had been into court at least four times, dragged there by creditors. He had given the bloodsuckers almost everything he had. His crops were promised out to them for at least two more seasons. What was the sense of it? Earning money you would never see. Working for people who didn't give a damn if you broke your back pushing a plow. As long as they got paid. All wanting their shylockian pound of flesh. It didn't matter to the creditors if he starved, as long as he paid on time. That was all that mattered to them, the bloodsuckers, the leeching sonsofbitches.

"Money don't mean much, if you're free," he said stubbornly.

"I want a family," she said, just as stubbornly.

He leaned forward in the chair, his intensity burning into her, scorching the very room.

"But not here, Roberta. Not here. In the promised land. Kentucky."

"Promised land, indeed. Why, there is no such thing except in the Bible, Lemuel Hawke. One must pay for what one obtains."

"There you go, actin' like your mother, talkin' uppity as if you were gentry."

"I pride myself on my education," she said stiffly.

"Haw, you ain't got much more'n me. My pa read me Shakespeare and lots of books and I don't try and talk like none of 'em. Neither does anyone I know. You're always tryin' to be something you ain't, like you had more brains than anyone else. It's pure common sense to go on to Kentucky. That's somethin' you might try and get more of, 'stead of puttin' on airs like you was a fine lady."

"It's that damned Silas," she said. "He's the one turned your mind."

"No," he said, "it's seein' us breaking our backs on the land here, and it's knowin' there's somethin' better a-waitin' for us."

He rose, moved to her, opened his arms.

"Yes," she said, and he kissed her softly on the mouth. He held her to him as the only dear thing he possessed, as the only thing nobody could take away from him. Roberta was beautiful, and he thanked the stars a hundred times a day that he had such a woman for his wife.

Lem loved her, had known her since he was twelve. They had married when he was fifteen, a year ago. She was but thirteen, yet she was comely, with fine brown hair, brown eyes, like his, soft skin, a pretty chin, and sweet soft lips, and those sweet tender hands that were scorched raw from washing his clothes, the pots and pans and dishes, the woodwork. But her lips were what he cherished most. They were rubied now, from the force of his kiss. Her cheeks flared with pale crimson, flamed like a pair of autumn sumac leaves. She was not shy like him, but bold in her lovemaking, and this always startled him. He was still scrawny, lean as a whip, with dark hair, eyes brown as coffee beans, lighter than hers, perhaps. Dreamer's eyes, she called them, set in a face chiseled angular. She loved his face, she told him. Loved to touch the wide high cheekbones, stroke the narrow chin, rub the wide forehead. She laughed at him sometimes when he talked. He knew why; his Adam's apple bobbed up and down in his throat every time he spoke. It seemed sharp enough to cut through the skin of his neck.

"Lem, don't," she said, and there was a dry husk in her voice, like a cat purring in season.

He touched one of her breasts, drew her to him again.

"You really don't want me to?" he asked.

"It's full daylight."

"That's what it means to be free," he said. "Loving day or night."

"Oh, you; you're wicked, Lemuel Hawke."

"With a wicked woman to love me."

When he kissed her again, she fed on his lips eagerly and they spoke no more as he lifted her in his arms, carried her easily to the bedroom.

She giggled brightly as he lay her on the bed. He threw up her skirts and her complexion flared with a rose flame.

"My," she said.

He turned away from her, heard the rustle of cloth as she slid out of her clothes. Sometimes he couldn't understand her cockeyed modesty. She did not want him to see her shuck out of her dress, but in a moment they would both be as naked as Adam and Eve. It didn't make any sense to him, but it was part of her mystery. When he turned back to her, her eyes opened wide.

"You can see how it is, woman."

He slid onto the bed, took her in his arms. It would be slow. She liked it slow, the beginning part, the loving part. The kissing, the hide-and-seek, the exploring.

"Yes, yes," she said, when he entered her and the sunlight streaming through the window made her hair shine, made the light in her eyes dance like flames in the winter hearth.

The rifle was a Virginia-made flintlock, wrought by a German smith living in the Shenandoah Valley. The low-combed butt-stock had a pronounced drop to it; the four-piece brass patchbox in a golden flourish rendered a touch of elegance to the rifle's clean, graceful lines. The rifle was 57 inches long, rifled, in .53 caliber. Its heavy octagonal barrel was browned to a smooth rust, adorned with an open V for the rear sight, a dovetailed blade for the front. Like the patchbox, the buttplate, heelplate, keyplate, trigger guard, and ramrod were all of brass. The lockplate was flat-faced with a detachable, iron-faceted pan, flat-faced goose-neck cock, and roller on frizzen. There were no maker's markings on the barrel, but Lem knew that a man named Samuel Steinbach had built it for his son, who had taken sick and died before the rifle was proof-shot. Hawke had traded three hogs for it two years ago and thought he had gotten the better of the bargain.

He stood behind a sturdy hickory, the pan primed, frizzen

pitched upward at an angle. Inside the barrel, a patched ball, .526 in diameter, sat atop 90 grains of double fine black powder. Lem wore buckskins, carried a powder horn and a possibles sack filled with patches and balls he had molded himself. A wide-bladed skinning knife, sheathed in cowhide, with a buckhorn handle, graced his belt.

The doe had been moving up the gully between two ridges, feeding on mast, nibbling on shoots of grass along the seasonal stream that arrowed the hollow. Lem felt the slight breeze against his face, knew that if it did not shift, the deer would not scent him. He had listened to her for fifteen minutes, knew she was very close. Now, he saw the tips of her ears, knew she would come under his sights in a few moments. He held the trigger down, pulled the hammer back, snugged the frizzen down tight. The lock made only a small sound as the sear engaged, but he completed the action while the deer moved past a clump of noisy brush.

He held his breath as the doe ambled behind a stand of sassafrass. He brought the rifle slowly up to his shoulder, braced it against the bark of the hickory tree. He sighted along a path just to the right of the sassafrass cluster. The doe was moving higher, would be in full view when she emerged from the brush. He did not want his ball to deflect when he fired. Carefully, he looked down the barrel, sighting along the invisible path the ball would travel. There were no obstructions.

It seemed to take forever before the doe stepped out from behind the slender shoots of the sassafrass. The step was only tentative. She raised her head, frozen for a moment in midstride. Her ears twisted to pick up any sound. Her eyes, like giant magnifying glasses, scanned the slope of the ridge where Lem stood. He had the feeling that she was looking straight into his own eyes. He did not flick an eyelash, stood breathless as a statue for an eternity.

Only her forequarters, front legs, chest and head, showed.

The air in Lem's chest turned hot, yet he dared not expel it. Not yet. Finally, the doe finished her stride, stepped into the open. She dropped her head to the ground, wrenched at a clump of grass.

Lem picked a spot behind her right foreleg. He expelled his breath, drew in another, held it. When the doe raised her head again, her ears flirting at the slight shift of breeze, Lem squeezed the trigger, caressing it in a steady pull. The hammer popped forward, the flint striking the plate, showering the fine powder in the pan with sizzling sparks. The rifle bucked against his shoulder. A cloud of white smoke billowed out from the muzzle, followed by a burst of orange flame. The ball hissed through the air, struck the doe just behind her shoulder. She hunched down, but was too late. The ball kicked up a puff of dust from her russet hide and she staggered sideways, blown into the opposing slope by the force of ninety grains of powder pushing the lead ball through her flesh. The ball flattened on impact, slammed into her heart, hammering it into bloody pulp.

It was a clean hit, Lem knew. When the smoke cleared, he saw her lying against the hillside, struggling to regain her feet. He dropped the rifle from his shoulder, grasped it just in front of the trigger guard and raced down the slope at a dead run. He hurdled the ditch, drew his knife. The doe bleated softly, but its eyes were glazed, its tongue lolling from its gaping mouth. He slashed the throat quickly, stepped back as the blood spurted onto his moccasins. The doe quivered and her eyes frosted over with the mist of death.

Hawke panted for breath. Time stood still as he looked down on his kill. The doe would dress out to better than a hundred pounds. Out of habit, Lem measured out ninety grains of powder, poured it down the barrel of his flintlock. He wet a precut patch of pillow ticking, placed a ball in the center. He pushed the patch and ball down the barrel with the short wooden starter, then took his ramrod and seated the ball on the powder.

He did not prime the pan, but he could do this quickly by pouring very fine powder out of a small horn hanging from his neck by a leather thong.

He propped the rifle in the fork of a sturdy sassafrass and drew his skinning knife, took a length of rope from his possibles pouch. He turned the doe over on its back, tied one leg to the trunk of an uphill beech, spread the other one. He drew his knife, made the cut, began to dress out the doe as deftly as a surgeon. In less than ten minutes he was finished. He roped a tree limb, hoisted the deer up in the air. He began to skin it out from the neck down.

Lem almost missed the movement. A leaf jangled silently twenty yards from where he knelt. He froze, peered intently into the brush. He gripped the knife more tightly. The handle and his fingers were slippery with blood.

The bushes moved again and this time they made noise. A buckskinned man stepped through them, shunting branches aside with the barrel of his long rifle.

"Silas," said Lem, breathing a sigh of relief. His hand loosened its grip on the skinning knife. He sank to his haunches, waited for Silas to come up.

"Fair shot, Lemuel," said Silas Morgan, coming to a halt. He stabbed the butt of his rifle into the hillside, leaned on it for support. A lean wiry man, Silas stood five foot seven, wore a coonskin cap over his shock of curly dark hair, hair that was slashed with streaks of steeldust. His friendly smile showed that he had teeth missing. His hooked nose bent over a brushy moustache that dripped over his upper lip like shaggy moss. His blue eyes crackled with the cool blue fires of cut diamonds. He spat a stream of tobacco juice onto the ground. Viscous droplets clung to his moustache, glittered like gobs of amber resin.

"Old Smokey shoots true," said Lem, glancing at his rifle.

"That she does."

Silas set his rifle down, squatted next to Lem. He pulled a bundle from his bulging possibles pouch, lay it on the ground. Lem stopped his skinning, looked up at Silas.

"What you got there?"

"Made yer some mokersons."

"What for?"

"Might be yer gonna wear out them you got."

"Might. Silas, what you got in your craw, 'sides terbaccy?"

"Haw! Son, I seen you sellin' off your stock to ever' Tom, Dick and Benedict Arnold. Smokehouse burnin' hick'ry shavin's night 'n day, hog bristles stenchin' up the air. You ain't hauled that plow in a week. Grass is high enough 'long the trails for you to be settin' out. Kentucky, I reckon."

"We're fixin' to leave, all right. Didn't think nobody knew but us."

"Tax collector knows. He's been makin' noise, gettin' him together some cronies to come out and grab what you got left."

"Dan Brown? He'd do that?"

"You got maybe a week."

Lem put the skinning knife to work again. He used the blade deftly, separating the hide from the flesh, sliding the point along the fat layer with smooth strokes. He would have hung the deer up by the hind legs, but that would have taken too much time. He made an incision around the deer's throat, just below the head, and started peeling the hide downward.

Then, he switched to the deer's hindquarters, skinned the hind legs, cut the tail at the base and stripped the hide down to the place where he had stopped. He severed the rest of the hide, laid it out and began to quarter the deer. It was hard work.

"Reckon I'll leave tomorrow," Lem said, puffing at the end of the sentence.

"Might not be too soon." Silas opened the oilcloth, shook out the moccasins. He held them up for Lem to see. There was nothing fancy about them. He had stitched two sturdy chunks of leather for the soles, fringed the tops. "You take these along."

"Thanks," said Lem. "I'm mighty obliged."

"Wish I was goin' with you."

"It's you what told me about Kentucky, how it was."

"I been there. Goin' on meself, way out yonder." Silas waved an arm in a westward arc. "Heard tell of good huntin' beyond the line." The "line" was something Lem had heard about for years. The British had set a boundary line, but many settlers had pushed beyond it, and the "line" had kept changing for years. No one really knew where the "line" was anymore. It was imaginary; it was where restless men like Silas went to get away from civilization. It was always a place to cross; a frontier meant to be conquered.

"Wherebouts you goin'?" asked Lem. He cracked a hind leg, sliced the tendon. "Didn't you get your tailfeathers singed enough?"

Silas showed no visible sign of emotion. Lem stared at his impassive face and wanted to bite his own tongue for bringing up Morgan's past like that. Everyone knew the story; everyone talked about the Morgans and their troubles during the Indian wars, when Silas and some of his kin were ranging. Fifteen years before, in 1778, when Silas was in his late teens, he was hunting with his older brother, Virgil, in the Clinch River valley. Virgil was a ranger, had been fighting against the British in the east, the Indians in the west.

Their father was plowing that morning, accompanied by their little brother, Lucas, who was only ten years old. Silas and Virgil waved to them, entered the woods. They heard shooting coming from the field. Virgil broke into a dead run, Silas at his heels. Some Delawares had slipped through the outlying ranger patrols and had surprised their father, Benjamin, as he turned the plow horse at the end of a row. Silas watched in horror as his father was cut down, scalped in the field. Little Lucas never made it to the stockade in the settlement. He was shot as he tried to climb over the split-rail fence surrounding the field.

Virgil shot two Delawares before they charged him as he was stuffing a ball down the barrel of his rifle. They broke one of his legs with tomahawks and Virgil went down, screaming in pain. Silas's rifle misfired and he was swarmed over by a half-dozen Indians. They dragged him to where Virgil lay stricken. Virgil was still alive, but they broke his other leg. He did not scream this time, but glared at the chief, cursed him.

The chief of the Delaware band, Iron Lance, reached down, picked up a handful of dirt. He stuffed the dirt into Virgil's mouth.

"You want our land, I give it to you."

Then, as Silas watched, Iron Lance drove his tomahawk into Virgil's skull, splitting it in two.

The Delawares kept Silas as their prisoner. They also captured his mother, raped her repeatedly as he watched. They sold her to some Wyandottes. Silas finally escaped from the Delawares and ransomed his mother from the Wyandottes, but she was never the same after that. She had died the year before, in 1792, and was buried someplace in the woods that only Silas knew about.

"There's a big river out west, bigger'n any in the whole world," said Silas, as Lem finished dressing out the deer. "I aim to go on beyond it. They say they's mountains out yonder make the Smokies look like anthills."

"How do you know about this river?" He broke the doe's backbone just below the ribs, put pressure on the knife to work through a pair of vertebrae.

"I heered talk, seed a map."

"Somebody's pullin' your leg, Silas."

"Maybeso. I aim to find out. Might be I'll see you out there someday."

"Roberta won't go. Kentucky's far enough for her."

"Welp," said Silas, rising to his feet, "luck to you."

"Take the heart and liver, Silas," said Lem. "You want a haunch?"

"I'll take the vittles and gladly. You keep the rest."

Silas wrapped the liver and heart in fresh leaves, stuck the organs in his possibles pouch. Lem had seen the man eat such meats raw more than once.

The frontiersman picked up his rifle. In a few moments he was gone, a stillness of green leaves in his wake, like a curtain hanging in an airless room.

———•———

Roberta fought the smoke, retrieved a ham from the little wooden shed out back of the house. The wood smoke spooled a tangy fragrance into the air. She plopped the ham into a wicker basket at her feet. She picked up two chunks of hickory soaking in the wooden vat outside, placed them on the smouldering fire. Picking up the basket, Roberta started for the house. Something caught the corner of her eye and she stopped. She saw Lem emerge from the woods, wave to her. She set the basket down, rescued a vagrant wisp of hair from under her nose, brushed it back. She waved back.

Lem grinned when he came up to her, cocked a thumb to show her the deerhide on his back, all bundled up with the meat inside.

"I'll bone her out and smoke her tonight," he said.

"I've a ham here."

"Yes. I saw Silas Morgan. He's headin' out too."

Roberta frowned. A shadow seemed to cross her face and her eyes dulled as the gaps between the lids narrowed. Her long, carefully tended eyelashes veiled the dark look in her eyes. She looked at her husband's blood-smeared hands, at his blood-streaked face, turned away in disgust.

"You better wash up," she said. She lifted the basket, trudged away, as if to carry her feelings with her, hide them in a closet where her husband could not see them.

"Silas ain't goin' with us," Lem said. "He's goin' far away, to the west."

Roberta stopped, turned around. Her eyes now were thin inscrutable slits, but the sun glinted off her hair, turning it auburn. The fine strands shimmered like fine copper wire spun from a magic loom.

"What do I care?"

"I thought you might be mad if you thought—"

"If I thought Silas Morgan was a-goin' with us to Kentucky," she said coldly, "I would not go at all."

"Why? Why don't you like him? What's he ever done to you?"

"I don't know. I just don't like him," she said, a quaver in her voice mirroring the fear she could not define, could not quell. Something inside her rebelled against such men as Silas Morgan. They were rootless, ungentlemanly, wanderers without substance. Deep down, she knew she was afraid that Silas would infect her husband with his wanderlust. Indeed, he already had. In Lemuel, she sensed the same wild, free spirit. Lem cared nothing for fine clothes, grooming, the elegance of a fine home in a prosperous community, the comradeship of well-to-do gentry. She yearned desperately for such things. She thought of herself as a bright graceful flower, an orchid, perhaps, blooming in a dank and neglected cellar, hidden from the sun and every admiring eye. She dreaded becoming an ugly toadstool pushing up through mud, destined to live and die in a drab darkness of the soul, unknown and unsung. This was more than fear, she realized. This was terror, stark and raging, frightening as an unexpected eclipse at noon. She could not express this fear to Lemuel, nor to anyone. This was the secret she carried in her bosom, in her heart, and sometimes it emerged and engulfed her, smothered her until she could not breathe, could not speak.

"You done something to your hair," he said.

Her heart froze and the panic made her heart pump hard until she could hear its pounding in her temples.

She turned and tramped away from him.

"I washed it," she said, blurting it out so that he would not question her, would not know that she had spent some of their money on henna and vermilion, yardage for a new dress to wear someday when they lived in a town manor, gentry at last. She had bought these things that morning from a passing drummer, paying the exorbitant prices not only in shillings, but in guilt and shame.

These were some of her secrets, locked away, like the dress material, the beads, the henna, vermilion, rouge and lace, all of the other things she had been hoarding, from the prying eyes of her husband.

"Looks nice," said Lemuel and she almost stopped again so that she could turn slowly in the sun and let him see how beautiful she was. For a moment she did feel beautiful and she wanted to bask in his praise, tell him how she felt, tell him everything. The moment passed, and she knew that the beauty was only superficial and temporary. Inside, she felt the drabness of their existence pulling on her, pulling her back down into the cellar, into the mud of anonymity and neglect. She went on, toward the house, without saying more, the secret of her yearning safe once again, safe only in her silent terrifying prison.

3

In the dark before dawn, Roberta packed the wagon with foodstuffs, cooking and kitchen utensils, clothing, Lem's farming tools. Lem hitched up the team of mules, saddled his horse, a six-year-old sorrel gelding he called Hammerhead for its blunt nose, short ears. There was a moment when he felt his stomach turn queasy. The scent of fresh-plowed fields, the heady musk of dewy soil assailed his nostrils, tugged at him with a longing for the home he was leaving. A lump clogged his throat and he had to swallow hard to wrench it loose. He wondered if Roberta felt as he did, homeless and lost, edgy over the coming journey. He fought off the feelings by dreaming of the new land, steeling himself to walk away from their first home. The lump in his throat returned, nevertheless, as he poked Hammerhead's belly, drew the cinch up tight. The gelding had a way of swelling out so that he could carry the saddle with a loose cinch.

A sniffing wind rose out of the highlands, prowled the piedmont, crept through the valley like some dark Arabian rider swathed in dark linens. A curious sound, the wind in the darkness; it made the dead things seem alive: a shutter creaked on the empty house, the leaves of a maple rustled in conspiratorial whispers, a skeletal leaf from the previous fall crabbed across the stony road. From far off, he heard the lonesome sound of a cowbell, a disembodied clanking from a neighboring farm that he continued to hear long after the sound had ceased. The gelding shook its head, snorted. One of the mules rattled its traces. Even the animals were impatient to be on the trail, Lem thought.

"You ready, Bobbie?" Lem said to Roberta. It was a name he called her in private.

"Lem, it's dark as pitch."

He caught the impatience in her voice, the frustration of being uprooted.

"We got to get going," he said. "Dan Brown catches us, he'll take it all. Maybe us too. We'll take turns driving the wagon. I'll spell you whenever you want."

She sighed heavily and he made out her form by the wagon. He walked over to her, helped her up on the seat. Her skirt got tangled on the brake and she kicked at it. He heard the sound of cloth ripping.

"Damn! My petticoat," she exclaimed. "You ruined it, you clod."

"Bobbie, hey. I didn't do anything."

She sagged onto the seat, muttering something under her breath. He wondered at the things she kept inside her. She was not a talkative person. When she did say anything it was usually a complaint or telling him something to do. Still, he loved her. That was just her way. The German in her, maybe, from her parents. Folks said Germans were hardheaded, stingy with talk. Just like Roberta was most times.

"We'll start out slow," he said, to mollify her. "It'll be light right soon."

She turned to him, then.

"I feel like a criminal," she said. "Why couldn't we leave in daylight, hold our heads up proud? We could have gone with the Pilchers, or the Stamps, had some company. 'Stead, you steal away in the dead of night like a thief. I don't see the sense of going all that far and taking our poorness with us. You don't have to quit."

It was true. Others had left Culpeper and Stafford counties, days before. Roberta had wanted to go with them, have company on the journey. Well, there were hundreds of others leaving Virginia. It was likely they'd run into other families along the way.

"Bobbie, Bobbie," he said, soothingly, "don't you see? Here, we're nothing. We're dirt. Less than dirt. If we don't own land, we can't vote and the guv'mint can just run right over us, plow us under. We got to go. We got to find a life for ourselves."

"Oh, Lemuel, don't whine."

"I ain't whinin', Roberta, dammit. I'm just tellin' you whichaway the wind blows. Give me a chance, will you?"

"Or what? You'd run off and just leave me, wouldn't you?"

That surprised him. He stepped back, filled his lungs with a raunch breath. The air tasted like wet tree bark, like hickory.

"Why, I don't rightly know. I always thought you would go 'long with me, wherever I went. You're my wife and—"

"And I got to obey you," she said, her tone razor-edged, dicing.

"You put it hard," he said.

"I'm only saying what's so," she replied, sulking, and he saw her as shadow, dark and brooding, pulling away from him into that private world of hers where he could not venture. Just a shadow, he thought, and not the laughing shy girl he had watched curiously at Arbor School, helped pick berries in the green spring of yesteryear when the sun played in her hair and pebbled her face with freckles. He felt that same ache again,

recalling those first days of seeing her, watching her, wondering
about her as he wondered about the sky and the clouds, the
growing trees, the vast migrations of wildfowl blacking out the
sun for days on end.

"We'd best get on," he said lamely, because there were no
words to argue with her, to tell her how sad he was inside, how
he felt the sadness growing like the shadows that hid her face,
blurred her eyes to hollow sockets. He shambled away, crushed
by something hard in her silence, shattered by something in her
eyes he could not see, could only feel knifing at his heart like a
surgeon's cold blade.

He mounted Hammerhead, heard the cowhide saddle creak
under his weight. He clucked to the horse, laid the right rein
against his neck. The horse turned, moved ahead of the wagon.

"Don't forget to take the brake off," Lem said as he passed the
blackened hulk on the seat. She released it with a snap and the
wagon lurched forward on freshly oiled wheels, the through
braces groaning under the strain of the load. Everything they
owned, he thought, and food enough to feed them for a time.

In the cool of morning, when the light brought everything to
life again, they headed for Swift Run Gap in the Blue Ridge
Mountains. The lilting chromatic trill of a lark floated over a hill
greening up like a raw emerald. Roberta sat on a shabby pillow
she had brought along, seemed to take no notice of their
surroundings. But Lem Hawke felt the morning in his bones,
felt the heat of the sun warm him, brighten his spirits as if he had
taken whiskey into his belly.

Long slow dreamy miles of riding through magical country,
the dew turning to steam each morning, pockets of mist clinging
to the hollows of the earth like fairy gauze and the earth giving
up its scents as the larks tweedled in the hedgerows, crows
cawed raucous from the forest fringe. Down into the Shenandoah Valley to the settlement at Rocktown they went, wending
their way wide-eyed with the wonder and beauty of a land

hemmed in by graceful hushed hills. They turned southwest, taking the Great Valley Road, felt it rise steadily under them as the Shenandoah Valley rose gradually out of the bottoms, preening in the sun.

They met other families going their way, heading for Kentucky and Tennessee, bundles piled high in their wagons, driving hogs and cattle ahead of them, making but a few miles a day. People waved and greeted them with fervor, asked questions: "Where do you hail from?" and "Where are you bound?" Lem and Roberta rode through the parted waves of people, but sometimes grazed the horse and mules with others who had stopped by the wayside.

The trough through the mountains was long and fertile, and they lingered one long afternoon in a meadow. Lemuel pitched their tent, set stones in a circle for a cookfire. At sunset, another wagon pulled up, set up camp near theirs. There was good water in the brook, and the people settling in for the evening waved to the Hawkes. One of them walked over to Lem's campfire shortly after dusk. He was short, lean, with curly red hair, a thin, bony wedge of a nose, a soft, fleshy jaw, cheekbones round and smooth as knee sockets, flashing blue eyes. His buckskins showed him to be a man of the woods as well as the trail. He carried in his hands a pouch of tobacco, his pipe.

"Smoke?" he said to Lem. His small crooked slit of a mouth looked as if it was carved out of his skull with a knife. The ragged, reddish moustache plastered his upper lip like a makeshift bandage.

"Set," said Hawke. "I'd be much obliged." He fished out his empty pipe, held the bowl upside down and laughed.

The stranger sat on a downed log that Lem had dragged over from the stream. It was dry and shimmering in the light from the fire. Roberta looked at him closely, but he seemed not to notice.

Lem dipped his bowl into the tobacco pouch, tamped it down. He handed the pouch back to the stranger.

The road was empty and they heard only the clatter of pots and pans from the other camp across the greensward. A light breeze rippled through the grasses, ruffling them like feathers on a chick.

"Name's Lemuel Hawke, what's your'n?"

"Barry O'Neil. Where you headed?" He stuck a twig into the fire.

"Kentucky."

"I be going back to Lexington, myself."

"You been there, then?" Lemuel leaned forward, the pipe in his mouth as O'Neil held out the flaming twig. He sucked on the pipe, drew the flame through the tobacco. His cheeks collapsed into two large dimples.

"Been there a year. Come back for my brother and his family."

Roberta cleared her throat with a discernible rasp.

"Barry, this here's my wife, Roberta. You married?"

O'Neil turned his head. He fixed his gaze on Lem's wife. His mouth crinkled in a warped smile.

"Glad to meet you ma'am," he said.

"You married?" asked Hawke again.

"Nope." O'Neil's gaze didn't waver. He lit his pipe, drew on it as he continued to stare at Roberta. She did not turn away, but regarded him boldly, an almost wistful look in her eyes.

"We been married a year," said Lemuel, filling his lungs with the smoke from Virginia-grown tobacco. The faint aroma of apples wafted to his nostrils. "Mighty fine terbaccy," he added.

"My brother growed it," said Barry. "Landlord took most of it for hisself. James won't have to do that no more in Kentucky. He aims to grow barley and wheat, corn, make his own whiskey."

"Tell me about Lexington," said Roberta, moving close to the fire. The water for the dishes had not yet boiled. The fire-blackened pot hung on the irons, flames licking its bottom. "Is it nice there?"

"Mighty nice, ma'am. It is like a pretty flower blossoming at the end of a long stem. That stem's got its roots in Virginia, mostly. There's maybe three or four hundred homes there, all clustered around the courthouse. It stands in the middle of a wide plain like Philadelphia."

"How about the land thereabouts?" asked Lem. "Can it be bought cheap?"

"Land aplenty," said O'Neil. "Sells for about seven shillings the acre."

"Oh," said Lem, crestfallen. He brooded behind the smoke from his pipe.

"What about the town?" asked Roberta. "What industry have they there?"

"Oh, there's much dealing to do in Lexington, ma'am. We got smiths and shoemakers, brewers and wagon-makers, hatters and clothiers. It is the center of Kentucky, the anvil on which all commerce is forged."

"You sure do talk pretty," said Roberta, and Lem detected a new tone in her voice, a softness that had not been there in a long while. He looked at her across the fire, but could not see her eyes. They were filled with shadows and only her face stood out, daubed with soft orange flames. She looked mysterious and exciting, as if the bloom of love-making had rouged her face.

"Thank you, ma'am," said O'Neil and he smiled wide, showing his teeth for the first time. He was in his twenties, Lem figured, certainly older than they were.

Roberta asked Barry a lot of questions about Kentucky and he answered her politely and noncommittally as far as Lem could tell. He let the talk wash over him, drift in and out of his mind like the vagrant smoke from the campfire and his pipe. He thought about the land in Kentucky, wondered how he would ever be able to buy any. No matter, he would lease some good bottom land and that would be almost the same as owning it.

The sound of Roberta's laughter jarred Lemuel out of his reverie. He had missed whatever it was that the redheaded man had said to make his wife laugh.

". . . you make it sound so romantic," said Roberta. "That's the trouble with most men. They have their nose to the grindstone and can't smell the flowers."

"Well, I don't know about that," said O'Neil, laughing with her. "A man has to pay his own way."

"All work and no play . . ." said Roberta, her voice trailing off as she angled a glance at her husband.

Barry's low chuckle rattled in his throat, the sound of a stick rapping a rolling wagon's spokes.

"Welp," said Lem, "I'm ready to turn in." He knocked the dottle from his pipe against the heel of his boot. "Bobbie?"

"I want to set by the fire a spell, Lem. You go on."

"Long one tomorrow."

"I'll be there by and by," she replied.

"O'Neil. 'Night. Thanks for the tobacco."

"I'll leave a few pinches with the missus," said O'Neil.

"Much obliged."

Lemuel walked to the tent, dropped to his knees and crawled inside. He pulled off his boots, kicked them to one side of the tent. He crawled atop the blankets, lay down on his back. He felt the tiredness seep through him. A feeling of drowsiness shut down his senses. He closed his eyes, listened to the distorted garble of voices out by the fire. He couldn't make out the words. They were soft-toned, so low he couldn't do more than separate Roberta's from Barry's. He heard a low laugh which turned into a girlish giggle.

The lassitude set in like mortar hardening and Lem rolled over on his side, sank into the soundless sea of sleep, the drone of voices fading away in the dark of his mind.

He didn't know how long he slept. Some sound outside startled him, jarred him awake. For several moments he lay there in the tent, disoriented, confused. At first he thought he was back home in Virginia, in his own bed. He shook out the tangled threads of dream and sleep, sat up. He felt beside him.

Roberta was not in the blankets. He groped around the pitch tent.

"Bobbie?" he whispered, but he knew there would be no answer.

He heard the faint tinkle of laughter, then. It was the sound he had heard in his dream, the same sound that had awakened him.

Lem strained to hear the laugh again, but his ears only buzzed with the small whispers of silence like the faint vacant roar in a conch shell.

A moment later he heard the padding of feet across the greensward. He reached for his rifle, but did not pick it up. The sounds were not furtive. The tent flap rustled and he saw a shadow as it opened.

"Bobbie?"

"Lem," she gasped. "You awake?"

"I just woke up. What are you doing out there?"

She crawled onto the blankets, shook out her hair. He touched her dress, felt the reassuring contour of her thigh. It seemed to him that she flinched, drew away from him, but it was only an impression. Perhaps his touch had startled her. She sighed deeply, shook out her hair.

"I—I was heeding a call to nature," she said, her voice weak, breathless.

"You went out there in the dark? You should have used that old oak bucket I brought along."

"I—I couldn't, Lem. It wasn't just one thing I had to do."

"I didn't hear you come to bed, Bobbie."

"You were dead to the world."

"Hmm. Maybe so."

"Go back to sleep. I'll get into my night clothes."

But he couldn't go back to sleep. He listened to her in the dark, felt her moving around, riffling through the carpetbag, slipping out of her clothes, pulling her nightgown over her head, settling in under the blankets. When he drew close to her, she curled up.

"I want you," he whispered, close to her ear.

"Lem. Not now. I'm awful tired."

"Christ."

"Don't curse," she said.

"Hell, I don't know what you're doin', wanderin' around in the night. You always used to be scairt of your own shadder."

"Mmmph. Let me sleep, Lem."

"Oh, all right. Go to sleep, Bobbie."

He turned over, away from her. He lay there for a long time, unable to go under, until he heard her breathing slow down and grow even. His thoughts crowded in on him, but he pushed them away with other thoughts. He didn't want to think that Bobbie might be a bad woman. He had to trust her, didn't he? She probably had to go real bad, like she said, and wanted privacy.

He shut down his thoughts, thought only of sleep. The faint burble of the creek worked a soporific spell on him and he drifted back down into sleep and, later, into dream. The dream was complex and he could make no sense of it, then or when he awakened in the morning.

4

The barred owl woke Lemuel early the next morning. Mucus that had dried and turned gritty sealed his eyes shut. He rubbed the "sand" free as the owl's throaty baritone sounded again.

He shivered in the chill, tried to pull the blanket around him. But Roberta, her back to him and still asleep, jerked it back. She lay curled into a ball, her hair a-tangle on the pillow. Lem sat up, pulled on his boots, groped around for his coat, a light sheepskin-lined buckskin he had made himself. The buttons were made of deer antlers, with hand-drilled holes, sewn to the garment with sinew.

He crawled outside the tent, blinked in the pale, mist-gauzed light. He looked across the creek toward the other side of the meadow, steaming wisps of ground fog. The other wagon was gone. He hadn't heard them leave. Usually folks made some noise when they packed up. Strange. They left mighty quiet. But why?

Lem stood up, rubbed his eyes. A light mist hung over the

31

valley. The fire was out. He poked it with a stick, found some small coals. He drew his hunting knife, made from an old leaf spring, a staghorn handle that was rough enough to give him a good grip. He kept it sharp, used it now to shave a stick. He placed the dry shavings on a cluster of coals, made a cone with larger trims from the same stick. He leaned close, blew on the coals. The shavings bristled as they caught fire. The larger pieces caught and Lem added kindling to the blaze until it was large enough for bigger chunks of wood.

When he had the fire going well, he made a circle of the camp. He prowled the fringes of woods, looking for sign. He wouldn't put it to words in his mind. Just sign. Hated himself for doing such a thing behind Roberta's back. But, a man had to know, he told himself. Why? He just had to know. Had to know what? Things. Dammit, just things.

Lem knew how to read tracks, how to tell if a foot had mashed grass down and if that foot was human or animal. Since he was a boy he had felt a profound kinship with nature. His curiosity had compelled him to study all sorts of tracks in all kinds of weather conditions. He had watched animal footprints over long periods of time, watched how they aged from fresh to cold, watched what the wind did, and the rain.

He found a place on the other side of the meadow that wrestled his attention. A large swatch of grass was mashed down. Blanket marks in the soft earth between the blades where they poked out of the ground. It might not mean much, he reasoned. It wasn't far from where the other wagon had been moored overnight. Mashed grass between the wagon and the flat spot.

He took another look at the woods near his own tent. He could find no place where Roberta had heeded a call to nature during the night. He might have missed it, though. His sense of smell was good, but he could have missed it. Something tightened in his stomach and his jaw line hardened without conscious thought.

He sat by the fire, looked into the flames for a long time as the sun came up, a swirling ball of fire hanging in the risen mist like a disk hammered in bronze, fired in a kiln and plunged into cloud. It didn't hurt his eyes to look at it for a few seconds. The rising sun, a dark steamy red, made him feel good, and when the birds started singing he felt even better. There was a fresh green smell to the morning and his stomach growled with hunger. He drank from the creek, lying flat, holding his head sideways. His buckskins were slick with dew when he got up and the sun had cleared the ground fog, shimmered yellow as goldenrod now, fatally blinding to any man's stare.

He called to Roberta as he approached the tent, two woolen blankets he had sewn together in a rectangle. Half a blanket for the backside, the other half slit and buttonholed for the front. String tied to wooden stakes kept the sides apart; longer stakes held up the inverted V of the roof.

"Mornin' Bobbie," he said when he drew near. "Time to get crackin'."

"Let me sleep," she argued, her voice muffled in the blankets.

It took him twenty minutes to bring her out of her stupor, and she took her time dressing. Lem tended to the stock, watering the horses, putting them in harness. He folded up the tent while she stood by the fire, embracing herself as if she was still cold.

"One morning, couldn't we just sleep late?" she asked.

"Some morning, maybe. Not this 'un."

"Lem, there's never going to be any grass grow under your feet."

"In Kentucky, there will."

She made a face, crinkled her nose at him.

Lem laughed.

"You going to cook anything or do you want to eat on the trace."

"We've got broth and yesterday's flour biscuits. Let's just go."

He soaked the fire with water while Roberta sat on the wagon seat tying on her bonnet. He shouldered his rifle and climbed into the saddle, tapped his heels to the horse's flanks. They left the meadow behind, gained the road. Roberta fought the ruts all morning until Lemuel spelled her and she rode his horse until they nooned at the road junction market town of Staunton.

Lemuel looked for O'Neil's wagon, but saw no sign of it, or him.

Roberta came out of her grumps after they ate roasted ears of corn they bought from a farmer for a few pence, sliced ham wedged between the hardened biscuits, washed it down with dandelion tea. After eating their humble meal, Roberta ladled honey onto a spoon for Lem.

"To sweeten your tongue," she said.

He gave her a peck on the cheek and she looked around, blushing. She spoke to some of the other women while Lem helped a man fix a loose spoke on his wagon wheel.

In the days that followed, the Hawkes followed the other migrants in a slow stream southwestward, going through the small Virginia settlement of Lexington, a few days later through Hans Meadow. They gazed raptly at the natural bridge over Cedar Creek. At Radford, they crossed the natural divide between the waters flowing to the Atlantic and those spilling into the Ohio. At Ingles' Ferry, they forded the New River, too poor to afford the float.

Lemuel's spirits perked up, there was a spring in his step, a boil of wings in his belly when they got beyond New River. There, the road turned almost due west and the country was less populated between old Fort Chiswell and the new settlement at Evensham. He had sought campsites well off the trail in days past, but now it was not so difficult to avoid the company of people. Roberta was sick most every morning and he knew it embarrassed her. He didn't know what was wrong with her and she never told him.

"Why can't we travel with other folks?" Roberta asked him,

after they got gone nearly 275 miles from home. "You always stay away from their camps when we stop for the night."

"Maybe I like to keep you for myself in private."

"What's that supposed to mean?"

His lips creased in a lewd smile.

"You know."

"Oh, Lem," she said, "is that all you think of?"

"Mostly," he grinned. They had made love almost every night, and sometimes at dawn when he was most hungry for her. It seemed better, somehow, with no people about. He still had not seen Barry O'Neil, but he knew the man was somewhere along the road, either ahead or behind them. He didn't care if he never saw him again. He was sure, though, that Roberta wouldn't do more than flirt with the man. He had been wrong to doubt her. In the dark of their tent, she was willing enough, passionate as ever. He wasn't so sure how she'd be with other folks as camping neighbors.

Five miles later, some thirty miles west of Abingdon, they came up on the blockhouse near the Holston River.

"Yonder it lies," said Lem, stopping to spell the horses before taking them down to the river to drink.

Roberta looked in the direction where Lem's extended hand pointed.

"All I see is a passel of trees and a bridle path," she said.

Lem laughed.

"That path is the Wilderness Road, darlin'. Hell on a wagon, they say, and thick with painted redskins, b'ars and such."

"You oughten not to scare me, Lemuel Hawke."

"Aw, I didn't mean nuthin', Bert. It'll be mighty slow goin', but I reckon we ain't in no big dither to get to Kentucky."

"You had red ants in your britches back home," she snapped. "That way looks real bad, Lem. Why the trail's nary wide enough for a horse, much less this wagon."

"You foller. I'll find us a way."

There was no real road through the wilderness. Sometimes, they were able to follow the rough path, but when it narrowed, Lem left the trail and blazed trees so Roberta could follow. The small branches lashed at her face, raised rude welts on her face. The going was slow and tortuous and often she thought they might be lost. Sometimes she got sick and they had to stop until she finished throwing up her breakfast. But Lemuel Hawke forged on, keeping his bearings by the sun, finding his way by dead reckoning. Always, he used the narrow trail as his guide, crossing and crisscrossing it several times in the course of that first day in wild, untamed country that made his heart sing with its savage rhythms. They made camp by a small melodic stream that night. The tiredness seeped through them on silent runners when they finally stopped long enough to catch their breaths. They ate a cold supper of roast ham, corncakes, washed down with cool water, and retired early, closed in by centuries of growing things, things green and timeless, like the eternal stars floating above the dark treetops in a dark and endless sea.

They came upon the frightened families late the next afternoon. In a clearing just off the main trail, men and women huddled around a ring of wagons and carts. Snuffle-nosed children herded hogs and goats and cattle away from the grown folks, their eyes wide with wonder and shadow-laced with fear. One man was fixing a wheel broken on the dry, rocky streambed that crossed the path at right angles.

Two men on guard at the edge of the clearing leveled rifles in Lem's direction, until they saw he was a traveler like themselves.

"Sorry," said one as Lemuel waved his hand at Roberta, ordering her to hold back. "We thought you might be a Injun."

Lem saw a man lying in the shade of another wagon, his face bloody, a sleeve torn from his muslin shirt. A woman dabbed at his face with a wet cloth, trying to clean away the blood. The man winced every time she touched him.

Three men were wrestling with another man, trying to prop

him up against the wheel of a two-wheeled cart. A woman sobbed as she watched them. They placed him upright, but the man toppled over and Lem saw the fist-sized hole in the back of his head, the gore on the back of his shirt like flung barn paint. Roberta gasped.

"Stay here," he said softly. "I'll see what they're about here."

Lem walked over to one of the guards, whispered to him.

"What happened?" he asked.

The lean, bony man, his face charred with three days of beard stubble, squinted, shoved a chaw of tobacco to one side of his mouth, nudging it up from between his lower teeth in the front.

"We heered some hollerin', women a-screamin', wagons a-rumblin' like a slide o' rock and come up on this clearin' where they was a couple of buck savages terrorizin' these folk. I reckon the men come up on the Injuns fust and got into a tangle with 'em. The redskins run off when we struck 'em some flint sparks."

"You reckon there's more out there?" Lem asked, looking beyond the clearing.

"Can't rightly say. Me'n Orm here told the folks to calm down and we'd set with 'em a while. That's our wagon over yonder under that water oak. We got women too and we don't want to see 'em get to Kentucky in widderhood."

The man speaking said his name was Dick Hauser. His traveling partner was Ormly Shield. Six of the pasty-faced children were theirs, but Dick didn't say which. There were a dozen kids, their eyes big and black like prunes sunk in the pudding of their faces, keeping the stock bunched up.

Lem told them his name.

"You goin' after 'em?" asked Lem.

"After who?" asked Ormly, speaking for the first time. He stood a half-dozen inches over six feet, as unshaven as Hauser, with a razor-sharp Adam's apple puncturing the tight skin of his throat. He was lean as a slat, carried a rifle that must have had a barrel length of 65 inches or so. Both men wore dirty linsey-woolsey shirts with the sleeves cut off above the elbows. Their arms were the color of tanned leather from the sun.

"The Injuns."

"I reckon not," said Hauser. "We'll just set her out, wait for more folks to come up. You got a fusil?"

"I do."

"Best check yore powder," said Dick. He glanced over at the dead man. They had him laid out now. The woman put a blanket over him, crumpled up when she covered his face, fell on his body, sobbing so hard it hurt Lem to watch her. He saw Roberta set the brake and climb down from the wagon. She walked over to the woman, squatted down next to her. She put a hand on the woman's shoulder, just to give her comfort.

"We could be here for days, waitin' for folks," said Lem.

"At least our hair wouldn't be danglin' from no buck's sash," said Ormly. "They's red niggers all through these woods."

"You been here before?" asked Lem.

Orm nodded.

"What kind of Indians was they?"

"I make 'em to be Tuscarory," replied Hauser.

"Weren't Cherokee, ner Shawnee, neither," affirmed Shield.

Some of the men broke shovels out of their wagons. They walked around, testing the ground. Some distance from the stream, one of them started digging. He tried to be quiet, but Lem could hear the shovel strike stone. The other man started digging about six feet away.

"Sounds godawful, don't it?" said Hauser.

"Which way did them Injuns go?" asked Lem.

Orm pointed a long arm to the west of the clearing. Lem turned on his heel, went back to his horse. He slipped the rifle from the blanket sheath tied to his saddle's D rings. He poured fine powder into the pan, blew it thin. The rifle was loaded with powder and ball. He checked his possibles pouch, weighed the

powder horn in his hand. It was almost full. Satisfied, he walked
back over to where Hauser and Shield were standing.

"I reckon I'll do some tracking, see what I run across."

"Lemuel, is that your name? You're either plumb crazy or you
got a set of nuts big as cannonballs. They was at least two of
them sneaks, and by gum, I'd bet more's jest a-waitin' out there
for fresh white meat. You'd best take your woman into the shade
and set a spell."

"I can't set," said Lem.

He walked over to Roberta. She was sitting down on the grass,
holding one of the grieving woman's hands.

"I'm goin' huntin'," Lem said. "Likely we'll spend the night
here."

"Lem, is that all you think about?"

"I got to go," he said awkwardly. "Ma'am, I'm real sorry you
lost your man."

The sobbing woman looked up at him with red-rimmed eyes.
He turned away.

"I'll be back directly," he said to Roberta. She speared him
with a look that made a lump form in his throat. He padded
away, his head down, already reading sign in the flattened
grasses, the barely visible furrows made by footsteps only
moments before.

Lem melted into the forest. The sounds of the digging faded
away. He stepped carefully, looking harder than he ever had for
sign. His pulse throbbed in his ears and he drew deep slow
breaths to calm his heart. He saw the crushed grass, the blades
just starting to creep back upright.

Something came over him when he entered woodlands. A
change that he recognized, a change in him, in his senses. It was
as if he became a different person, entered a different world. All
of the references changed for him. He shifted his senses to the
stimulus of the forest. He became part of it, blending into its
lush growth, its furtive sounds, letting it all penetrate deep into

him, letting himself soak it all in until he was part of it, part of its pulse, its faint heartbeat. It was a thrilling experience and it worked faster and better if he was alone. He felt at home in the woods, felt part of a larger world, a secret world that was shared by animals and trees and birds, even the fish in the streams. It was a powerful feeling. It made his muscles feel sleek and tireless, it made his step light, his hearing and sight acute. The forest changed him and he exulted in the magical world of his own senses, the opening of secrets that always followed once he left civilization and its trappings behind.

His stomach fluttered, but he was on the trail.

It was better than sitting back there with strangers, waiting for something else to happen. He marked the sun's position. He followed bent twigs, ground broken so slightly it strained his eyes to see the tracks, but they were there. He moved slow, stopping often to listen behind a tree. He put a kerchief to the ground and put his ear to it. He heard no sounds, but he had often heard deer moving around by doing just that. It was something he had learned from old Silas Morgan back in Virginia. He wished Silas was with him now. Lem had never hunted Indians before. He didn't know what he'd do if he found one. Would he shoot him? It was something to study, all right. Shooting a man, that was something he hadn't figured on. But, he knew Silas would, after what had happened to his kinfolk.

He thought about the dead man back there at the camp. That was reason enough to kill an Indian. Maybe he would think about that man if he ran across any redskins. Maybe that would help him pull the trigger when it came time to take a man's life.

The birds stopped singing suddenly. It grew quiet as a graveyard. Lem's senses perked up as if he'd been stung in the eye.

The stillness seeped through him, but he resisted its sleeping-powder allure. He listened, as always when it was so quiet in the woods, for the sounds beneath sounds, the faint stirrings of leaves, the quiver of a sapling's branch, the muffled tread of a footfall. Lem held his breath, strained his ears to pick up the undertones that would warn him of another human's presence in the forest.

He heard it then, a low wheezing sound, the whispery prattle of a sapling brushed in passing—by an animal, a deer, maybe, or a man. He put his ear to the ground and listened as a surgeon would listen to a man's chest for a heartbeat.

Lem crept forward, careful to step softly and avoid brushing his buckskins against a leaf or bare branch. He moved when he heard sound, froze when the forest steeped itself in stillness once again. His ears tracked the direction of the sounds. As near as he could figure, there were two men, or two deer, stepping carefully through the woods. He guessed he had found his Indians because he would have expected even a wary deer to make more noise, to crack a dry twig or overturn a stone. He heard none of these sounds. Instead, they were as furtive as any noises he'd ever heard.

The two sounds drifted apart and he knew the Indians, if that was who was making the sneak, had split up. This made his tracking more dangerous. Lem hunched low, held his rifle slanted in front of him, frizzen closed down tight, thumb on the hammer.

He moved closer, towards the last sound he had heard. He crept as silently as a panther, his eyes narrowed to shut out the sunlight. He heard a grunt and froze.

That's when he saw the feathers, dangling from a man's scalp lock. He saw only part of the back of a head, and the feathers.

And a single bronze arm glistening sleek in the sun.

5

Lem felt his blood surge out of his brain fast as rain down a waterspout. He felt lightheaded, giddy as a kid sipping fermented cider. His temples drummed with a rapid thunder.

His heart turned wild as a flushed timberdoodle, seemed as if it would jump from his chest cage. The Indian, standing next to a scaly bark hickory, was so gaudy with feathers and orange roach, Lem had the almost uncontrollable urge to rub the bright pigments from his eyes.

The tip of his nose began to itch from an unseen irritation. A gnat discovered the glassy water of his eye, flew at it like a miller against a lighted windowpane.

The Indian seemed part of the tree, part of the forest. Lem stretched his neck and more of the savage came into view. Still, he could see only the bare bronze of the Indian's back, the bright plumage dangling like a gutted ringnecked pheasant from his stiff roach, the long rifle in his hand studded with brass tacks along its stock, a single goose feather twirling on a thong attached to the frontplate. The Indian wore a breechclout over his deerskin leggings, a knife in a beaded leather sheath. An iron tomahawk jutted from a wide, colorful cloth sash that girded his midsection.

A bird called. Lem didn't move. Another bird answered with a short melodic trill. This call was closer, and Lem saw the Indian's head move slightly. That's when Hawke saw the other Indian, forty-some yards beyond, crouched behind a grassy mound, ferns and saplings sprouting profusely in emerald fountains over its surface.

In the distance, Lem heard a heavy pounding, a clang of metal against wood. He realized that he had been tracking in a wide arc, returning to his starting point along a ragged half-circle. The settlers' camp could not be far away. The Indians, he was sure, meant to double back and do them harm. The prickle in his nostril increased to a maddening degree.

Lem wriggled the tip of his nose, willing the itch away. The gnat stung the corner of his eye, stuck in the viscous fluid. Finally, it freed itself and Lem's eye swam as his tear ducts flowed to soothe the irritation.

Two of them, his mind whispered.

Both Indians carried long rifles. They had a pair of shots to his single. If he shot one, the other could shoot him. Fear strangled Hawke's thoughts, twisted his innards into knots. It was one thing to track them; another to see them so close, alive and breathing and armed. His lungs ached until he realized he was holding his breath. He let the dead air out slow and batted his eyelids. Slowly, his normal vision returned, but the one eye itched worse than his nose.

Maybe there were more than two, he thought. Maybe there was a whole band of them sneaking up on the travelers, ready to pounce on them. His nose started to run. He dared not sniff nor blow to clear it. Sweat trickled down his chest underneath his buckskins. A thousand little annoyances plagued his flesh and he was powerless to attend to the least of them.

The Indian farthest away moved into the underbrush, disappeared. A few moments later, Lem heard the *toowit tweet tweedle* of another artificial bird call. The Indian closest to Hawke replied with a replica of the same call.

It was then that Lem heard the singing.

The hackles rose on the back of his neck. The Indian, too, seemed startled. He slid around in back of the tree, exposing more of his body to Lem.

The settlers' voices were lifted in song. Lem could just make out the words.

"We shall gather at the river," they sang, and Lem could picture them in his mind, all standing around the fresh grave, with their Bibles and their hymnals, oblivious to the danger in the forest, just singing away as if they was in church back in Virginia or at a Sunday arbor meeting down by the creek.

Lem wondered if he should shoot the Indian. He could see all of him now. That would bring the other one a-runnin', and by God, he'd have to load and prime real fast, faster than he ever had before. Someone, maybe his pa, had once told him that during the Revolutionary War, the British soldiers could load a musket in twelve seconds. That was powerful fast. He had tried it a time or two, counting seconds, and the closest he could come was nearly twice that. And that was by himself, with nobody a-runnin' at him fixin' to kill him dead. If one of those Indians came after him, he didn't think he could reload inside of twenty-five seconds or so. He would probably be so scared he'd shake to death before the other buck could come up on him. But, at least the settlers would hear the shot and maybe a couple of the men would have sense enough to pick up their rifles and get the kids and womenfolk hid out.

What if he missed? He was so scared now, he didn't know if

he could hold his barrel steady. That redskin was so close he could smell him and he looked oversized and fierce with all that paint and feathers, those glistening muscles rippling under his ruddy skin.

Lem held still, knowing that if he fired his rifle, it might be the last thing he ever did. He wasn't afraid of missing, not at this range. He figured he might not have time to reload before that other Indian came up out of the brush and shot him or brained him with his iron tomahawk. It was a decision he made suddenly, not out of fear so much as from practicality. Maybe this Indian would join the other one and he could sneak up behind them both. Knowing there were at least two Indians and one of them out of sight tilted the odds in the redskins' favor.

The Indian took the decision out of Lemuel's hands.

The buck turned, looked straight at Hawke. Lem felt the redskin's eyes boring into him like a pair of fire-tipped skewers.

The Indian raised his rifle before Lem could recover from the shock of being discovered. The motion was so smooth and flawless, Hawke just stood there as if he was mired in wet clay. It seemed to take the Indian no time at all. One minute he was looking the other way, the next he had a long rifle pointed straight at Lem. Hawke felt his stomach sink four feet past his belt line, clear down to the tips of his boot moccasins. His head floated a foot above his shoulders.

Lem heard the click of the cocking hammer. It seemed as if he could hear the sear engage inside the massive lock on the rifle. He heard the report, saw an orange flame spew from the barrel, blossom into a bright, hideous flower. He heard the thunk of the ball as it smacked into the bark of the tree next to him, heard it rip wood like a crosscut saw. Chunks of bark spanked the side of Lem's head; slivers and splinters sliced into his face and forehead. He closed his eyes involuntarily, flinched at the sharp suddenness of the pain.

The Indian was obscured by a cloud of white smoke when

Lem opened his eyes. Then, he heard the underbrush crash with the flail of the buck's body as he charged straight toward Hawke.

Lem lifted his rifle, knowing there was no time to get off a shot. The Indian dropped his spent rifle, drew his tomahawk. He leaped over bushes, smashed through tough young saplings like a man splashing across a shallow creek. As Hawke brought his rifle up to his shoulder, thumb poised to hammer back, the Indian loomed less than five yards away, his lips flayed back from his carious wolf teeth, his face a painted, scarifying mask, more animal than human.

In that single terrifying moment, time fractured into chunks like mud flying off a wagon wheel. Lem saw everything happen in pieces, isolated fragments that seemed separate yet were all part of the same thing. It seemed as if he had no power over himself, that his movements came from outside himself. He did not think of what he must do. His body worked like something magical. His hands and feet moved of their own accord. There was no thinking at all. His mind was frozen in time, locked on that horrible face. Only his body was free and it performed as if it had been trained for just one single task: to kill a man.

Lem brought his rifle up, but it seemed to weigh more than a hundred pounds. It was so heavy and moved so slowly, some part of his mind knew he would never make it. There was no time to cock the hammer back. The Indian bounded over that last five or six feet like a bolting deer with its tail afire.

Hawke felt the rifle sting his palms as the Indian swung his tomahawk like a flailing scythe. The rifle spun out of his hands, the lock rattling with the dry metallic sound of shot in a tin cup. Lem's right hand shot downward in a spearing dive for the knife in its sheath. He crouched as he jerked the blade free, turned the sharp tip toward the charging savage.

Lem lunged, shoving the knife forward. The Indian tried to bring the tomahawk back to a striking position, but his right flank was exposed. Hawke shoved the blade of his knife into the soft flesh beneath the buck's ribs. He brought up his left hand and grasped the Indian's throat, throttled him.

The redskin grunted and twisted free of the knife. Lem felt blood spurt over his knuckles, warm and slick as oil. He squeezed the Indian's neck, his fingers tightening in a vise-grip as both fell to the ground, mashing the brush down with the weight of their bodies. The Indian rolled, trying to break free of the white man's grip. Lem drove the knife into the small of the brave's back, hammering it home to the hilt with a powerful thrust. The Indian kicked out, tried to capture Lem's legs in a scissor-lock. Lem twisted the knife, pushed hard to cut across the gristle of the buck's back muscles. He felt the red man thrash as he tried to escape the skewering blade, free Lem's grip on his throat.

The knife would not move. Lem jerked it from the Indian's back, swung it back over the man's belly. He slammed it hard into the buck's diaphragm, drew it toward him. He sliced through to the warrior's intestines, felt the coils pour over his hand like a clutch of water snakes. A terrible stench, mindful of a disemboweled hog, assailed Lem's nostrils. He felt the Indian shudder, his body go slack. He squeezed the throat again, but felt no response. He kicked away from the dead Indian, pushing him away as he rose unsteadily to his feet.

Panting, Hawke looked down at the limp body of the Indian. Excitement thrummed his veins, a giddy exhilaration smothered him until he managed to draw a deep breath into his lungs. He wiped the bloody blade of his knife on the right legging of his buckskins, sheathed it without thinking. He retrieved his rifle, flipped open the frizzen, checked the coating of powder in the pan. He clamped the frizzen back down and crouched there in the brush, listening, trying to hear above the booming throb of his heart.

He squeezed the trigger slightly, thumbed back the hammer. The lock made the faintest tink as the sear engaged at full cock.

Hawke waited, strangling on the fear clotting his throat. He looked at the dead brave again in disbelief. The Indian lay there with his innards covering his groin in shiny gray coils. Flies peppered the intestines like miniature vultures. He heard their annoying buzzes as they fed on the offal from a knife-torn section of gut.

Lem crawled slowly to a position behind a tree, some ten or twelve yards from the slain Indian. He looked at his bloody hands, swiped his forehead with his sleeve as sweat stung his eyes. There was a bloodstain on the front of his buckskins, bright as a new swatch of cloth.

Lem dug a round ball from his possibles pouch, fished out a round patch pre-cut from a small bolt of mattress cloth. He centered the ball on the patch, tucked both in his mouth like a wad of tobacco.

Then, he heard the bird sound.

Toowit tweet tweedle.

Hell, thought Lemuel. *I can do that.*

He pursed his lips, gave the whistle.

It sounded just like the other Indian's call, he thought.

A strange calm came over him. He knew, somehow, that the other Indian would come. He knew, also, that there were only two. Only one now. Lem readied his rifle, peered in the direction of camp, where he had heard the last fake bird call.

But the other Indian didn't come in from that direction. He had circled to Hawke's right, and if he hadn't made a noise, Lem would never have heard him.

The Indian called out in a low, gutteral voice. A moment later, he whistled another bird call. Lem swung around silently, brought his rifle up halfway to his shoulder. He waited, alert to any sound.

The Indian crept forward, hunched over. He struck an unerring path to the place where the dead Indian had been. He seemed intent on finding his companion. This Indian was some younger than the one Lem had killed. He was no less fearsome.

Lem brought his rifle up, seated the butt in the hollow between his shoulder and chest. Then, he puckered his lips and gave a similar low whistle.

The Indian stood up full-length, his orange roach bristling like a Hampshire red hog's hackles.

Lem dropped the sights on the Indian's chest, cradled the trigger with his finger. When the front and rear sights lined up, Hawke took a shallow breath, held it, then caressed the trigger, drawing it gently toward him. The hammer struck the frizzen plate, showering the pan with golden sparks. There was a puff of smoke, a sound like someone blowing on a dandelion. The fire exploded through the touchhole, igniting the main powder charge in the chamber. The rifle bucked in Lem's hands as 90 grains of coarse black powder exploded. A cloud of white smoke rushed out behind the rocketing flash of orange sparks.

Hawke heard a low grunt, jerked himself up to his feet, clawing for his powder horn. Frantically, he poured powder down the rifle barrel, just guessing at the measure. He spat out the ball and patch, thumbed them into the muzzle. He pulled the short starter from his belt, started the ball down the barrel with the long end, pounded it with the heel of his palm. He jerked the ramrod from its mooring, rammed it down the barrel. He jerked it downward with both hands, then pushed it against the tree to seat the ball. He pulled the ramrod free, let it drop to the ground. Quickly, he primed the pan with a small horn, blew away the excess grains, slammed the frizzen shut.

When the smoke cleared, Lem stood behind the tree, ready for another shot.

There was no sound.

Lem whistled.

No answer.

He whistled again, louder this time.

Still no answering toodle. He stepped out from behind the tree. Wisps of smoke drifted skyward like torn shreds of gossamer, like the conical shrouds of webworms.

A crashing of brush drew his guarded attention. He stepped toward the spot where he had drawn bead on the younger Indian. He heard white men's voices. *Christ,* he thought, *they make a lot of noise.*

The Indian was not dead, but blood and foam bubbled out of a hole in his chest. The warrior lay flat on his back, staring up at Lem with a venomous look of rage in his black eyes. The ball had entered just to the right of the Indian's thorax. Splinters of a rib bone jutted through the blue-black hole.

As Lem looked down at him, the mortally wounded Indian shuddered as if gripped by a sudden pain. His mouth opened wide and he seemed to be trying to breathe in more air. A fleeting shadow passed across the Indian's face. His eyes closed for a moment, opened again, glazed with that same wet patina Lem had seen in the eyes of wounded animals. The dying man was in pain, he knew. Pink foam, blood saturated with air bubbles, oozed from the chest wound.

The Indian couldn't have been much older than Lem himself. Perhaps, he thought, the other warrior was this one's father. There was a resemblance, beyond their costumes, their painted markings. Their noses were built out of the same mold, their faces shaped the same. Brothers, maybe. One much older than the other, anyways.

The brush crashed and Lem turned toward the sound for a moment.

"Hawke!"

Someone was calling his name.

"Over here," yelled Lem. He turned back to the wounded Indian.

The redskin's eyes flared and he lifted both his arms. He struggled to rise. Halfway up to a sitting position, he fell back and a low sigh escaped from his lips. His eyes bulged with one last look, then the glow in them faded like dead coals turning to ash. His body went slack and the blood stopped leaking from the hole in his chest.

"Jesus Gawdamighty!" hollered Ormly Shields as he bounded gangly as a wobbly-legged colt through the leafy undergrowth toward Hawke. He carried his rifle at the ready. "You get 'em, boy?"

Behind him, Dick Hauser scrambled to keep up with his long-legged partner, rifle held across his chest at a slant, possibles pouch and powder horns slapping against his buckskins.

Ormly stopped where the first Indian lay dead. He wet his lips, looked long and hard at the knife wounds. Then, he looked at Lem with something like raw wonder in his eyes. His gaze lingered over the bloodstains on Hawke's 'skins. He chewed at a nonexistent cud in his mouth.

"That the other'n?" he husked.

Lem nodded, eased the hammer of his rifle back down off of cock. He leaned against a water oak, swabbed sweat off his forehead with a swipe of a bloody finger.

Hauser halted in his tracks, stared down at the dead Indian Lem had knifed.

"You gut him like that?" he asked Hawke, that same distant rasp in his voice.

"He come at me," said Lem. "No time to shoot him."

Ormly walked over, inspected the other Indian. He leaned down, turned him over. There was a hole in the young buck's back the size of a sugar beet. A pool of blood lay beneath the body, already growing a skin as it dried.

"Hoo de haw," breathed Ormly. "You got him good. Both'n of 'em. Judas, I never seed such doin's."

Dick looked at the younger Indian as Ormly stepped back, drew his knife. He let out a low whistle.

"Them is prime bucks," he said.

"Those the ones you saw?" asked Hawke.

"I reckon," said Hauser. "They all look pretty much the same to me."

"You want their rifles, Hawke?" asked Shield.

"What for?"

"Why, you can brag on 'em, or sell 'em."

Hawke's stomach turned over like a griddle cake. It didn't seem right robbing the dead. He wanted nothing to do with the Indians. He'd see them enough in his dreams, day or night. The young one, the way he had looked at him, well, he wouldn't forget the glare in his eyes for a long time. He felt a queasy swirl in his stomach.

"Naw, you keep 'em."

"What about their hair?" asked Hauser.

"Huh?" asked Lem.

"Why, looky them orange bristles, proud as peacocks. Braggin' fodder what to carry on yore belt."

Ormly grinned, drew his knife. He knelt down and started cutting through the young buck's scalp. Lem knew he was going to be sick if he stayed there.

"You cut them nut bags off, Dick," said Ormly. "Hoo de haw, we done got us some prime souvenirs."

"One of them scalps is mine," said Hauser.

Lem walked away, the sounds of the scavengers' grisly banter fading as he made his way back to the wagons.

He couldn't make sense out of it. Which of them, the Indians or the white men, were the savages?

6

Emma Hauser, Dick's wife, gasped when she saw Lem enter the clearing, the front of his buckskins covered with blood, rifle over his shoulder. The others peeked from hiding places behind their wagons. Snouts of rifles dropped from view, or tilted toward the sky as Lem walked across the sward.

"Look at the blood. He's been shot!"

Lem saw a woman standing behind a wagon wheel, pointing at him. He looked around for Roberta. There was no sign of her. His wagon was gone.

"Poor man."

"Where's my Dick?" screeched Emma Hauser.

"And Ormly. Where's Ormly?" Lucasta Shield came running toward Hawke, awkward as a goose, her skirt billowing about her short stocky legs, her bonnet and its sash flapping like wounded swans. She looked like a washerwoman's clothesline in the swirling zephyrs of a dust devil. "Have they kilt my man?"

"Them two's out in the woods yet," said Lem. "They ain't been kilt."

"We heard a shot," said a boy crawling out from under one of the wagons, his rifle pointed carelessly at Lem.

"Son, you better p'int that fusil in another direction," said Lem. The boy, his face sanguine with embarrassment, pulled the rifle toward him, laid it under the wagon.

"Did you see any Indians?" asked another boy, peering from behind a flour barrel.

"A couple," said Lem. He saw his horse, Hammerhead, tied to a tree just inside the fringe of woods. He turned to the woman who had rushed out to question him about Ormly Shield. "Where'd my woman go?" he asked.

"Why, her brother come and got her," said Lucasta Shield. "She went on ahead with him."

"Her brother?"

"Why, yes. I believe his name was Barry. He come riding up on a mule just after you went a-huntin'. They seemed in an all-fired hurry. Didn't even stay to help us bury poor Mr. Dowell. He said somethin' about their sister-in-law bein' ill."

Lem looked at the fresh grave.

"I'm right sorry, Ma'am. Was he kin to you?"

"No. Ormly Shield's my man. You say he—he's in no fix?"

"I reckon not."

He heard the brush crackle, turned to see Ormly and Dick emerge from the woods. Their arms were full with booty taken from the Indians: rifles, knives, moccasins, sashes, beaded pouches—and a pair of bloody scalps. The kids rushed forward, passing the women and men who had emerged from hiding. Hogs grunted; sheep bleated. Hammerhead whickered, switched his tail.

Lem felt the ground quiver and fall out from under him. A fleeting giddiness temporarily addled his thoughts. What was

Barry O'Neil doing back here? And why did Roberta tell these people he was her brother? Why had he taken her away? None of it made sense to him. He regained his balance, staggered toward Hammerhead. The horse eyed him with a baleful look of suspicion.

Roberta hadn't left him much. He searched through the saddlebags. At least she hadn't taken anything. His canteen hung from the saddle horn. He had powder and ball, plenty of flints. Not a scrap of food.

The murmur of voices seemed distant to him as he sagged against a tree, rested his rifle on its butt. The dizziness left him, but his gut swirled with fear. He couldn't imagine Roberta riding off like that, not even saying good-bye. She must have had a pretty good reason. Maybe Barry O'Neil's sister-in-law was ailing and that's why she had left. Lem remembered Barry saying something about traveling with his brother and his family. But why did she tell it that Barry was her brother? That didn't make no sense at all. Seems like she would have told someone where he'd gone so he wouldn't worry none.

He thought of Barry O'Neil. He had never expected to see the man again. He was just someone they had come across along the trail, like a lot of others. Except there was something different about this one. He pestered a man like a fruit fly. Persistent as dust in a spinster's parlor.

Lem heard his name mentioned, turned to look at the people milling around Ormly and Dick. Dick pointed his way and everyone looked at him. Ormly beckoned to him.

"Hawke," said Shield, "we got something to put to you."

Lem walked over, leaving his rifle leaning against the tree. The people's faces swam like tethered buoys. He was beginning to feel sick over Roberta leaving like that, just up and following O'Neil like a puppy after a stranger with grub in his pocket.

"Yeah?" Lem said.

"We want you to lead us on to Kentucky," said Hauser. "Everybody's agreed. The way you took care of those two redskins."

"We'd be much obliged," said Mrs. Hauser, her face shaded by the brim of her bonnet.

"I reckon I got to go on by myself," said Lem. "My wife . . ."

"Surely, she'll wait for you up ahead," said Emma.

"Uh, well, she may need me," Lem said awkwardly.

"We're ready to go," said Ormly. "You lead the way."

Lem saw the anticipation in their faces. Even the children looked at him oddly, their faces scrooched up quizzically, eyes squinted against the sun. He felt very uncomfortable, itchy uncomfortable, like a man facing a jury, awaiting their verdict. The man who had been hurt now seemed to be all right. He, too, was standing there with his mouth open, his wife hanging on to him as if she were afraid he'd up and leave her. The other men seemed to be standing in their wives' shadows, taller than their children, but still little boys.

"I want to see the dead Indians," said a small boy, breaking into the silence.

"Yes, Pa, I want to see 'em too," said another, looking up at Dick Hauser.

Other children picked up the refrain and their voices rose in chorus. Hauser and Shield began to retreat as the children surged toward them, all clamoring at once. Their mothers raced after them, but they slipped out of each woman's grasp like tadpoles.

"We want to see the dead Indians!" the children screamed over and over, and finally their mothers threw up their hands and gave in. Boys tugged at their fathers' buckskins and dragged them toward the woods. Ormly escaped the clutches of three children and ran to a wagon, depositing his booty inside. Dick Hauser gave his Indian rifle to his wife, and Emma scurried away toward her wagon.

Lem watched as the travelers bunched up and headed across the sward, determined to see the two butchered Indians. Hawke shook his head and turned away from them.

"Look, Hawke, we got to let the kids see them two redskins or they won't give us no peace. You come too. Take your mind off your troubles."

Lem looked at Ormly in total bewilderment. He heard the words, but he could not digest them. Hawke shook his head.

"Suit yourself, Hawke. We'll likely catch up to you by the by."

Lem strode to Hammerhead, grabbed up his rifle. He heard the voices fading as he swung up into the saddle. He laid the rifle across his legs, turned the horse into the clearing. He saw Ormly running to catch up to the crowd disappearing into the woods. In a moment, he was gone. He heard the children gabbling like a flock of gray geese long after he rode away from the wagon stop, and then there was only the susurrus of the afternoon humming in his ears above the steady clop of Hammerhead's hooves on the rutted trail to Kentucky.

——·——

His kisses flared on her bare neck like a heat rash. She writhed in his torrid embrace, her breasts swelling in his sweaty palms, the nipples hardening at his touch, heating up like walnuts in a roasting pan.

"Stop it, Barry. No! Get your hands off me!"

"Too late for that, woman. You got me in a rut."

Roberta slapped at him, struggled to crawl out from under his crushing weight.

"My dress is going to be smeared with grass stains," she said incongruously.

Barry laughed and tugged at the bodice of her dress, exposing more of the flesh of her breasts. She tried to roll away from him. His fingernails clawed the soft skin of her breast. Roberta shrieked, began to kick wildly.

"What's the matter with you, Roberta? You wanted it bad enough the other night."

"No, no I didn't," she sobbed breathlessly. "I—I was just . . ."

How could she tell him? It sounded so silly, so stupid in the light of day. She had entertained his attention, his affections, but she never thought it would lead to this—this attack in broad daylight. She had let him kiss her and caress her, but she never dreamed she'd ever see him again. He said he and his brother and their family were leaving in the morning. There was no need to give any more of herself to him than she had. It was nice to be held and hugged and kissed, but she had not wanted to violate her marriage vows. It was wicked enough just letting Barry go as far as he had. Now, she realized that he expected more. And, he had lied to her. There was nothing wrong with his sister-in-law. They were probably way ahead and once Barry had his way with her, he would leave.

"You teased me," he husked, his mouth breathing hot in her ear.

"No, I didn't mean to. Barry, let me go. If Lemuel catches you . . ."

"He'll what? He'll laugh, Roberta. He knows what I know. You want it. You want it from every man you meet. I saw it the other night. I saw it today. I knew you wanted me and your husband couldn't satisfy you."

Anger boiled inside her, tore at her heart with razor-sharp talons. Barry O'Neil had no right to say those things about Lemuel. Yes, she had been infatuated with the stranger, but she didn't think a little harmless flirtation would turn him into a savage. He had brought her to this glade off the trail under false pretenses. He had lied to her, and now he was attacking her husband.

She jerked away from him. She felt her bodice rip, but she broke his clutch on her breasts, at least.

"I'm having his baby!" she cried hysterically. "He's my husband." She broke into sobs. She knew that what she said made no sense. But anything, anything to get Barry to leave her alone. "Liar, liar, liar!" she screamed.

She kicked him away from her, tugged at her torn blouse. Tears glazed her cheeks, soaked through her closed eyelids.

"Look what you've done to my dress," she sobbed. "What will my husband say?"

She stared at Barry, at the squinch of his face, the little powder-duster moustache, the greedy eyes, the slash of his mouth, and wondered at herself. She wondered at her brazen behavior, the submerged lust inside her that he had drawn out, first in the darkness of a firelit meadow and now in the harsh, glaring light of day.

It seemed to her that this was happening not to her, but to someone else. This was not she squatting soiled in a great forest, her dress smeared with grass stains, her bodice torn open, her breasts exposed to Barry's hungry eyes. Yet, she could feel his hand burning on each of her breasts, feel the burn of his kisses on her neck, the scratch of his moustache on her face.

"Go away," she pleaded. "Leave me alone. I—I hate you. I never want to see you again."

"Yes, you do," he gruffed. "You want it, Roberta. You want me to do it to you."

"No," she said, and buried her face in her hands, buried her face in shame. "Just go away."

She heard him, then. Heard him chuckle to himself, heard the rustle of leaves as he rose to his feet. She knew she could not face him again. She clutched her shorn bodice to her breasts and heard her heart thump hollow in her ears as if it was going to tear through her chest and punish her for being a fool. She deserved to die, she thought at that moment. She deserved to have her heart break open like a melon and gush its blood like a fountain.

She heard his footsteps as he walked away; heard him mount

his mule. She heard the rustle of leather as he slapped the reins against the animal's neck. She heard the soft pad of the mule's hoofbeats on grass.

"You come see me in Lexington," Barry called to her. "You come see me when you grow up, Roberta."

And then his laughter, soft and disembodied, shredding the empty ocean sounds in her ears, kneading the thump sound of her heart until it quieted.

She pulled her legs up close to her, wrapped her arms around them for steadiness. She held her eyes tightly closed until she no longer heard the mule's plodding footpads, no longer heard the echoes of her heart's pounding.

Lemuel rode up on her. She heard him coming, raised her head. She looked to see him guide Hammerhead over to her. She saw the bloody stains on his buckskins and looked for the deer across the saddle. She saw no game, even when he dismounted, tied his reins to a sapling, laid his rifle down as he knelt beside her.

"You been cryin'," he said.

She sniffed, avoided his gaze. She just couldn't look at him. Not now, with the shame inside her. He could probably see it blooming on her face like some wicked flower, like a huge red flower with bright red petals. She heaved with a sudden, involuntary breath and it caught in her throat like a bone, choked her for a moment.

"Well, I come after you," he said after a moment and he sat down beside her as if it was the most natural thing in the world and she stole a glance at him to see if he was angry, to see if he was going to slap her. "They said you went off with that Barry feller and I come after you, Bobbie."

"Yes, Lem. I—I'm glad you did."

"Did he run off?"

"I told him to go. I hate him."

She looked at him, then, let her eyes meet his just to see if he was angered, just to see if he meant to beat her with his fists.

"I hate him, too," Lem said softly.

She felt something dark inside of her brighten. It seemed, then, as if Lemuel was the sweetest, most understanding husband in the world. She reached out, touched his arm. She needed that steadiness just now. She needed to weld the sudden bond between them.

Her fingers clasped his wrist, tightened. He laid his other hand atop hers and patted her reassuringly.

"You tore your dress," he said.

She looked down at her breast, expecting to see Barry's finger marks all over it. But the skin of her breast was white and smooth and the nipple had lost its tumescence, had flattened into its round nest like a nightjar setting on eggs, all brown and sleepy in the sun.

"Oh, Lem. He—he was so mean. I—I kicked him. I hit him."

"You want me to fetch your sewing things?"

"No. I'll put on something else." She pulled the dress up with her free hand, covered her breast. She didn't want Lem to look at it. She didn't want him to think about Barry seeing her like that.

"We can set here long as you want," he told her, and it seemed to her that he was saying he wouldn't accuse her of being bad, that he was not going to punish her for running off from him like that. "There ain't no hurry, really."

"Lem," she said, something breaking down in her, breaking apart without her being able to stop it, "I'm scared. Scared of myself, scared of you, scared of everyone and everything. Do you—do you know what I mean?"

"Sometimes we all get scared of things. Mostly things we can't see, don't know nothin' about. Mostly things we can't put a name to."

"Yes, that's what it's like. You do understand. I'm scared of something I can't see, something deep inside me that I can't find."

"And no name to it," he said, looking off beyond her, beyond the sunlight in her hair, the look of terror in her red-rimmed eyes.

"I don't know what it is," she said, squeezing his arm, pulling on him as if to draw herself inside him where it was safe.

"Be better if you could call it out in the open. Take a look at it, maybe. Put a name to it."

"Your ma tell you that?"

"My grandma. When I was a kid, afraid of the dark and all kinds of boogers. My grandma was real sick and I guess that's what I was afeard of. Afeard she was goin' to die and I couldn't tell anyone about that because I was scared if I did she really would die. My grandma told me it didn't make any difference what I said or didn't say. She was going to die anyways, and she did. But I got so I wasn't afeard of the dark no more."

"I'm still afraid of the dark," she said. "It's easier when you're there with me, but I always had to see a candle burning or have the lamp lighted before I could close my eyes and sleep."

"You got to get over that, Bobbie. Ain't nothin' can hurt you, 'less you let it."

"Grandma?"

He laughed.

"No, my grandpa told me that, after my ma run off. We was poor and he worked for a rich man. This rich man had a kid what made fun of me and called me a beggar boy and it hurt so much I used to bawl my eyes out ever' night until my grandpa got on me about it."

"Then your grandpa died," she said.

"He died. Mule kicked him in the head and he died and I went and beat up that rich kid, knocked the ticking out of him."

"Why?"

"I wanted him to know I wasn't no beggar boy. I buried my

grandpa next to my grandma and run off. I kilt that mule, too. The one what kilt my grandpa."

"I remember," she said, and laughed. "That's when I saw you. Hiding out from the sheriff."

"Well, we ain't hidin' out no more," he said, heaving a sigh. "We ain't got nothing to be afeard of, Bobbie. Not when we get to Kentucky. Not never again."

She felt her stomach swirl as a feeling of hope surged through her heart. Maybe, she thought, Lemuel was right. Perhaps there was no longer anything to fear. It might be that they could make a new life for themselves in Kentucky.

"Could we live in a city?" she asked. "In a clean and elegant house like decent folks? Could we ride in carriages and wear fine clothes? Maybe we could settle in Lexington and you could learn a trade, become a gentleman, and buy me French lace and china and take me to dine in places where they have linen tablecloths and silver knives and forks, candlelight and wine. We could buy a big house and there would be servants in livery where merchants could call and show us their wares, where I could invite my friends for tea in the afternoons, with a parlor and a sitting room. I would wear jewelry and gowns and bright ribbons in my hair . . ."

"Bobbie," he interrupted. "I'm a farmer. I got to find land to lease and work. We got to buy stock and raise it for market. Where did you get these fool notions?"

She jerked her hand away from Lem's arm and covered her mouth. She saw the look in his eyes and knew that she had gone too far. She had said things to him that were secret, that were so private she had never expressed them to another human being.

"I know," she said, tightly, her lips pressed together so hard they were bloodless. "I know what you got to do. But, we don't always have to live poor, do we?"

"No. We can make a life for ourselves. We got a new chance now. Just let us get to Kentucky with no more trouble."

The space between them filled up with silence. Lem tore off a sprig of grass, stuck it in his teeth. Roberta fiddled with her torn bodice as if trying to bond it back together with pressure from her fingers. Lem sucked on the grass stem, looked at the light playing in his wife's hair.

"Yes," she said, after a moment, but the tightness was still in her voice. She looked again at his buckskins, then at his hands with blood caked on them like rust. "Did you kill something when you went huntin'?" she asked.

"Almost the other way around," he replied. "Saw me two real Indians out in the woods. They was fixin' to jump them people again."

"What happened?"

"Oh, I got into some fur-pullin' with 'em. One come at me with a knife. The other'n I shot."

"You killed two Indians?"

"Well, I didn't dance with 'em, Bobbie."

She looked again at the dried blood on his buckskins, at the flakes on his hands. She looked at his knife in its sheath and tried to imagine what Lem had done. A sense of horror filled her, struck her mute.

There he sat, she thought, sucking on a blade of grass and he had just killed two men. He no longer looked like a boy who was still wet behind the ears. There was something hard and distant about him, something terrible and unexplainable inside him. She knew Lem wasn't a braggart. If he said he'd killed two Indians, then she believed him. Two Indians lay dead in the woods and he had killed them with his own hands. He had broken one of the commandments. He had taken a human life and it didn't seem to bother him at all. He showed no signs of remorse or repentance.

Roberta shuddered inwardly, quelled the feeling of panic that rose up in her. Her stomach twisted as if had been wrenched from its moorings. She felt it swimming around inside her abdomen. She knew she was going to be sick.

She stood up, ran to the wagon. She fell against one of the wheels and held onto the side. Her stomach turned over, then, and she began to retch. Nothing would come up, and yet her stomach kept contracting.

Lem came to her side, grabbed her shoulders.

"You sick?" he asked.

She squeezed a spoke of the wagon wheel, draining her knuckles of blood.

"Yes," she gasped. "I'm sick. I'm sick of men, sick of you, sick of everything. God, I'm sick."

"Is there somethin' I can do?"

"Take a bath," she spat. "Wash your filthy skins. Leave me alone."

"Christ, Bobbie . . ."

"And quit swearing like a dock walloper," she said, pulling herself to a standing position. She held her stomach, staggered to the front of the wagon. She climbed up, began to rummage through the bags. In a moment she pulled out a dress, began to stretch out the wrinkles.

"Well, what are you waiting for?" she asked. "Get yourself cleaned up. I can drive the wagon after I get changed. I'll meet you up ahead somewheres."

"I reckon I'll have to scout me up a creek."

"What's wrong with the one back there? Can't be more'n an hour's ride."

Lem shrugged. He started for his horse, stopped dead in his tracks.

"What's that?" Roberta asked, looking back up the road.

"Shh!" he said, holding up his hand.

The popping sounds seemed to come from just around the bend in the trail. They sounded like Chinese firecrackers.

Then, they heard the sound of human voices. Men yelling, kids and women screaming. The hideous screeches of Indians.

The firing lasted for several seconds then stopped as abruptly as it had started.

The last thing they heard was the most terrible of all. A man screamed and screamed until they thought he would never stop. He kept yelling: "No, Jesus God, no! Please, God!"

The stillness hardened over them like a pane of coffin glass.

Lem turned around, looked at Roberta. She stood in the wagon, clutching the wrinkled dress to her breast. She was shivering as if she had taken chill. Her teeth chattered and her eyes stared up the road, fixed on nothingness, fixed on the echoes of that last scream.

"I'm really scared now, Lem," said Roberta.

"I got to go back yonder, Bobbie."

"It's them people, ain't it?"

"Couldn't be nothin' else," he said.

"It's none of our business, Lem. We ought to go on. Get away from this place."

"Might some of 'em need help. You go on if you want. Or wait here."

"Don't leave me alone," she said, and sank down on a carpetbag in the wagon.

"You better get to changin' or sewin', Bobbie. I got to find out what all the ruckus was about back there."

"Wait—I—I'll go with you."

"Well, don't be dawdlin' none."

He listened to the stillness, the murmuring saw of insects, the empty-headed twitter of birds. He didn't look at Roberta as she changed her dress. He heard her, though, heard the restless shuffle of the mules in harness, the faint tap of leather against hide, the tink of metal bits and D rings.

He wondered what he'd find when he rode back up the trail. Those people hadn't ought to have lingered, he thought. They oughtn't to have gone into the woods to look at those dead bucks. Their curiosity might have cost 'em. Might have cost 'em dear.

"Lem, do we have to go back there? Can't we just go on about our own business? Please."

Hawke twisted at the waist, looked at Roberta. She had changed into the wrinkled dress, but stood in the wagon like a child afraid to climb down from a barn loft. Her face was shadowed by leaves, but he could feel her fear.

"I'll hobble them mules," he said, and walked over to the wagon. He reached into the bed, got the rope hobbles from a box of spare harness. Roberta climbed down as he tied the last knot, stood nearby all pouted up as if to begin whimpering.

"What do you think happened?" she asked, her voice quaky.

"I think them folks got into some bad trouble," he told her.

"Indians?"

"Likely. I won't know till I look, Bobbie."

"I don't want—I can't—look at them if—if'n they're dead."

"Me neither. But, we can't just ride off as if none of this ever happened. We got to find out."

He stood up and she heaved a deep, quavering sigh. He wondered if she was going to make up her mind on her own. He could see that she was wrestling with it. People didn't scream like that less'n they was bein' got after. Kids didn't cry out for no reason. If he rode on, though, he'd always wonder what had happened to those folks. He'd always hate himself for not helping them what needed help. If any of them was still alive.

"We wait much longer, we might end up in misery worse'n them," he said, and if that didn't convince her, he was going on back by himself.

"All right. But, I don't want to look. Don't make me look at nobody dead, Lem. I seen one die already and that was just horrible. Just to see him die like that. One minute alive, the next they was puttin' him in the ground."

Lem wanted to slap her, but said nothing. He took Roberta's hand and led her over to Hammerhead. He helped her up into the saddle, grateful that she had stopped yammering like an idiot child. He climbed up behind her, snugging his crotch up under the bony cantle. He rode over to the tree, leaned over to snatch up his rifle.

They rode back up the leaf-shadowed trail, neither of them speaking. He felt Roberta's shoulders tremble against his arms. Hammerhead balked just before they rounded the second bend in the trail. Lem thumped the horse's flanks with the heels of his moccasins.

The horse almost stepped on the goat. The dead carcass lay alongside the trail, its head nearly severed from its body. Hammerhead sidestepped the carcass, began to bristle as a shiver coursed its spine.

At first, the Hawkes saw only the scattered garments. The clothing looked as if it had been blown from a drying line, or hurled against the brush, tossed into the branches of the trees. A woman's bonnet flapped silently from a quivering bush. A child's pale blue shirt hung from a sapling's thin limb; a man's hat, the crown crushed, lay in the center of the trail surrounded by kerchiefs and undergarments in disarray. Boxes and trunks and crude wooden toys littered the grass for fifty yards like flotsam in a ship's wake.

Lem reined in Hammerhead when he saw the first human body.

"You better wait here," he said, swinging a leg down.

"What is it?"

"I just saw something."

He helped Roberta dismount. He held on to her for a moment when her knees buckled and gave way. He felt her trembling. He wrapped the reins around a low limb, checked the rifle's pan for primer. An eerie stillness clung to the spot, spooky, like the silence of a graveyard.

Lem didn't recognize the woman at first. Her face was caved in, her brains leaking from a massive hole in the top of her skull. His stomach lurched and he fought to keep the bile from gushing up into his throat. The woman was lying face up, her dress rumpled up around her waist exposing her naked privates. There was a hole the size of a man's fist in her chest. Part of a breast had been blown away by the exiting rifle ball. Shreds of cloth from her dress clung to the wound. He recognized her as Dick Hauser's wife by her dress. They had driven part of a tree limb up into her womb and it stuck out of her obscenely.

He turned away from the woman and began to see them all, parts of them, in the grasses, hanging from the wagons, lying among the dead horses and cattle. The Indians seemed to have slaughtered everything that was alive. Sheep and hogs, cows and horses, chickens and goats, all lay within a radius of a hundred yards from where Lem stood in stunned disbelief.

He saw a man, what was left of him, sitting under a bloody tree, his teeth knocked out, his eyes gouged from their sockets. They had sliced away all signs of his manhood and stuffed his bag and penis in his mouth. There was a large patch of hair missing from his scalp. Flies ragged the torn spot like ants at the grease pail.

Lem stalked the killing ground, finding children and dogs, pigs, goats, along a line of flight that resembled an abattoir. He had never seen so much blood. It streaked the grass, spattered the leaves in the brush like barn paint. The attacking Indians had spared no one, it seemed, although Lem didn't count or try to identify every corpse. Some of the horses were gone, perhaps some of the stock. What they hadn't taken with them as booty, they had slaughtered.

One faceless man's body reeked of urine. Both of his hands had been cut off. His genitals, too, had been carved away, and his heart had been cut from his chest. Lem could no longer hold down the sickness. He caved in against a tree and heaved up the hot bile.

"Lem, are you there?" He heard Roberta calling him and he knew he had to get her away from this place. He couldn't even bury these poor people. There were arms and legs strewn through the brush, ears and heads all around him like garbage in a pigsty.

His stomach contracted as he staggered away from a young man's mutilated body. He could no longer look at the women. So far as he could tell, they were all dead. The Indians had probably not taken any captives. Maybe that was the only mercy they had showed, finally. He shuddered to think of a woman alive with such men. He looked at an eye lying in the open and his mind shrieked with outrage. It might have been a child's eye, it was so small and hideous, strangely bloodless in the impassive flicker of sunlight through the leaves.

"Christ," he swore, and stumbled back toward Roberta, who stood by the horse, her eyes covered with her hands. He wondered how much she had seen.

"Lem?"

"Don't look," he said. "I'll help you get back on the horse."

"Wha—what are you goin' to do?"

"We got to get out of here, Bobbie. Ain't nothin' we can do for these folks no more. Jesus, they're all dead. Every god-damned one of them."

For once, Roberta said nothing about his swearing. When he helped her aboard the horse, she began to whimper. She had held it in long enough, God knows, Lem thought. He pulled himself up behind her and swung Hammerhead in a tight circle. The last thing he saw when he left the place of ambush was a man's head sitting on a broken keg, mouth propped open with a chunk of striking steel jammed in so that he appeared to be grinning.

———•———

Lem and Roberta drove the wagon along the trail until well after dark. Roberta didn't ask him about what he had seen back there and he was grateful. He could get none of it out of his mind. Every time he tried to think of something else, a hideous image would bob up in his mind unbidden. He recalled things he didn't remember seeing. Little things, like a split-open sack of coffee beans piled on the ground like buck droppings, a woman's broken parasol, a child's wooden play-toy, a hobby horse broken in two, a crushed milk pail lying next to a dead horse, a man's glove with the hand still inside it. He hadn't seen a rifle or a knife, nor the scalps Hauser and Shields had taken from the two braves he had killed.

That must have been what angered them, Lem thought. Finding those scalps on the white men. The savages had swept through the travelers like a storm, killing everything in a blind rage.

The trail was no longer easy to follow in the darkness. It seemed to Lem that they had topped a ridge and that was the place to stop. He directed Roberta to pull the wagon off the dim trail. He helped her from the seat and put a finger on her lips. They stood there listening for a long time. Finally, satisfied, he whispered to her.

"Make as little noise as possible. I'm going to hobble the stock. Be real quiet."

Roberta made a bed for them beneath the wagon. She shivered

in the chill of the mountain air. Lem returned but she did not hear him come up, so quiet he was. He crawled under the wagon and she felt the stock of his rifle brush against her leg. His powderhorn rattled his knife until he grabbed it.

"I ain't hungry," he said. "You get what you want to eat and don't worry none about me."

"What are you going to do?" she whispered.

"Stand guard as long as I can."

"You think they'll come after us?"

"No. You get some sleep, Bobbie. I'll wear the worry cap."

"Wake me when you get tired. I can listen well as you."

He started to laugh, but he knew the sound would travel. It was quiet. Not even an owl made a sound. Hammerhead sniffled in the grasses and he heard the mules munching. He had run a rope through their hobbles, trailed it back to the wagon, looped it around the left front wheel.

He crawled out from under the wagon. Roberta squeezed his hand. He walked some distance from the wagon, keeping its boxy dark shape in view. He stopped, listening for the slightest sound. After a while, he heard Roberta crawl into her bed-clothes. She tossed and turned for several minutes and then was still. Lem listened to the sound of his breathing and then forced himself not to listen to it. He was not sleepy, but his senses seemed drawn up tight like fiddle strings, ready to pop if he turned the tuning keys one more twist.

He kept seeing the distorted features of the dead people, the severed limbs, the vacant eyes. He thought about the two men he had killed and he wondered if his actions had caused all of the others to die. What if he had not hunted the two braves? Would they have gone on, content to leave the travelers alone? Or were they waiting there for others of their tribe to show up so they could slaughter all of the whites? If he and Roberta had joined up with that bunch, they might be lying dead out there tonight just like them. What if he had agreed to lead them? He might be dead, too, and Roberta left all alone, never knowing what had happened to him.

A great emptiness filled Lemuel when he thought about these things. There were no hard and fast answers. The more he thought about it, he was sure he had done the right thing. Those red savages had meant to kill some white people and were sneaking up on the travelers when he had tracked them down. Maybe the two redskins he had killed were scouts sent out to the wilderness trail in advance of the main bunch. Maybe the Indians had planned all along to kill every white that came through their lands.

He tried not to think of the dead people lying along the trail, in the woods. He tried not to think of their last tragic moments. He tried not to hear the screams of the women and children.

But there was no solace in the bleak night, in the far cold stars that blinked so impassively and silent across the dark sky. In the ageless heavens, what did these lives matter? What did his own life matter?

His thoughts stunned him, left him with an immense sadness. There was no reason behind the deaths of the other travelers, yet he had seen reason when he had killed the two braves. Or had he? If he had not hunted them down . . .

Lem shook his head, struggling to dislodge the ifs that surged through his scrambled thoughts.

He tore off a stalk of grass, chewed it to the bitter root. He stopped looking up at the sky. The stars made him feel so small, so insignificant. The sky itself made him feel even emptier than before.

He waited for morning, praying that the light would wash away the images of the mutilated dead.

———•———

Roberta was sick again the next morning. Her vomiting jarred Lem awake. He had not meant to doze, but just before dawn, the exhaustion caught up with him. He jumped to his feet, ashamed. He walked over to the wagon. Roberta was doubled up, holding onto a tree. The sounds of her retching tore at him.

"What's the matter, Bobbie?" he asked.

"I'm sick."

"You been sick most ever' mornin'."

"And I missed my time of the month twice," she said.

"What's that mean?" he asked dumbly.

She stood up, wiped her mouth with a sun-browned arm. Her eyes were wet from exertion.

"It means I've got a baby growin' inside me. Don't you know anything?"

"A baby?"

"Yes. Your baby. My baby. Our baby. That's why I get sick. You are really a dunce, Lemuel. Didn't your ma ever tell you about babies?"

"I reckon not," he said, self-consciously. "Christ, what are we gonna do?"

"There you go, swearing blasphemous again. We're not going to do anything until the baby comes."

"When's that?"

"Oh, Lemuel," she cried, sweeping past him toward the wagon. "Can't you count?"

He finally figured it out after he got the mules hitched, Hammerhead saddled. By then, Roberta was in a pout and didn't want to talk about it anymore. He led off down the sloping trail, leaving the ridge where they had camped behind them. They forded the Clinch River, descended Walden's Ridge to Martin's Station in Powell Valley. The worst part of the Appalachians seemed to be behind them and they both breathed easier when they saw the settlement.

"That'd be Martin's Station," said Lem, holding up Hammerhead until Roberta could stop the wagon. "My, ain't it a sight?"

"I never saw anything so blessed to look at," said Roberta, the tension draining out of her at the sight of man-made structures. The settlement was dominated by a fort, or stockade, surrounded by stumps left when men had cleared the forest. It was small, by any standards, but it was the first human habitation they had seen in many days. There were a few log dwellings scattered over the clearing, and they saw travelers' tents and lean-tos pitched near the stockade's walls. They saw people walking about, peaceful as farmers at Sunday go-to-meeting.

"Let's go there, Lem. I can't hardly bear to sit here and look at it."

The trail widened into a road and they drove up to the stockade, eyes wide and bright as brass buttons. A half-dozen dogs, sure signs of civilization, bounded out to greet them. The pack followed them right up to the gates of the fort.

"Where you folks bound?" asked a man they encountered outside the stockade.

"Kentucky," said Lem.

"Well, you're most there already," he said. "Spit'n a holler away. Folks've been goin' through the gap yonder like bees to a honeycomb. Just got back from Lexington meself and Lord, it's a-growin' faster'n Philadelphy. Sam Parsons's the name. Got any goods to sell? Needin' any supplies? This be the last civilized settlement for a good long hunnert and twenny miles."

"Nope," said Lem. "We ain't got nothin' to sell. Nothin' we need."

"Lem, you goin' to tell him about those folks. . . ."

"Eh, what's that?" Parsons cocked his head. He was a short, scrawny man dressed in simple, homespun clothes. His wagon stood next to the gates of the stockade, its slat sides painted with the legend in red: PARSONS TRADE GOODS. Underneath, in smaller letters, the words BOUGHT & SOLD were scrawled in black paint.

Lem dismounted, slackened the cinch on Hammerhead's saddle. The horse heaved a deep sigh.

"We heard screamin' and hollerin' back up on the trail," said Lem. "A whole passel of folks was kilt, cut up by Indians. Warn't nothin' we could do."

"See 'em?"

"Who?"

"Them redskins. Did you get a gander at 'em?"

"No. They was gone." Lem didn't like Parsons's question. He didn't want to tell him about the two bucks he killed.

"Been a bunch of renegade Tuscaroras roamin' them woods. Ain't the fust time they caused a commotion. Thought they was all driv out. How many white folks they kill?"

Lem made an estimate. He sheepishly told Parsons that he did not try to bury any of the dead. Parsons seemed to understand.

"Likely as not, their bones will serve as warning to others comin' through the wilderness," said Parsons. "I'll speak some prayers fer 'em. Now, you got anything to sell or trade, son?"

"Nary," said Lem, anxious to get away from the settlement. He avoided making eye contact with Roberta. He knew she'd probably want to stay the night, where it was safe. "How's the trail ahead? Any Indians?"

"Well, now," said Parsons, stroking his chin, "they is and they ain't. Injuns don't know no better. They comes and they goes as they please."

"Any other folks goin' our way?" asked Roberta.

"I don't rightly know," said Parsons. "Just come in from the settlements myself. I kin ask. Passed a bunch what come through yestiddy. Musta been nigh onto twenny souls or so, not countin' niggers."

"Makes no never mind; we're going on," said Lem.

"Lemuel. Can't we stay the night, leastways?" Her voice held just the trace of a whine. "Rest up some."

Hawke squinted when he looked at her.

"I'd like to get on," he said firmly. "Mr. Parsons, can you point us the way?"

"Why, son, you jest go on toward Pinnacle Mountain yonder. Foller the trail up through the Cumberland Gap. You got some mountains beyond, but you'll go down and strike a ford at the Cumberland River. Easy goin' from there on, maybe, less'n you get rain."

"Thank you kindly," said Lem. He tightened Hammerhead's cinch, climbed back in the saddle. He beckoned for Roberta to follow. People emerged from the stockade and stared at them. Lem ignored their looks. The people behind the fort hardly gave them a second glance.

They camped that night at the base of Pinnacle Mountain.

"Beautiful, ain't it?" said Lem, after he finished pitching their lean-to. "That there's Cumberland Gap up yonder."

The dying sun rimmed the gap with gold, painted the clouds a salmon hue.

"I'll fix us some supper," said Roberta, still in her sulk. Lem listened to the clatter of pots and pans for the next several moments, finally shrugged and walked away and rubbed down the mules with grass just so he wouldn't have to think about her anger.

The next morning, before the sun was up and after Roberta finished with her toilet and being sick, they started the short ascent through a steep ravine leading to the summit of the pass. At the top, they gazed out over a Kentucky shrouded in morning mist. As the sun rose, they followed a tortuous mountain trail that strained every spoke on the wagon wheels, slowed them to a turtle's pace. The rough trail dropped them to a ford, well rutted with wagon tracks, at the Cumberland River. A dead pig lay on the far bank, crows picking at its carcass. That didn't stop Roberta from stopping on the eastern side to wash Lem's buckskins. He swam in the shallows downstream while she squatted at the bank, scrubbing the blood from his 'skins with lye soap. When they crossed the ford, the buckskins flapped from the wagon. Lem wore only a pair of homespun trousers until the flies got at him.

They followed the trail on a northwest course, meandering through gently rolling foothills rising on either side of them, reminding them of Virginia in the late afternoon. Beyond Flat Lick, they saw deer and turkey, heard the hens clucking on the ridges in the evening. Early one evening, Lem loaded his rifle with birdshot and brought down a gobbler that he had tracked atop one of the hills.

Two days later, the sky scudded over with black clouds at dawn. By noon, the Hawkes were in the midst of a blinding rainstorm, the trail awash, impassable. Streams flooded, became dangerous. Lem couldn't see twenty yards ahead, but when they came between two low hills, they were confronted with a raging stream that spooked the mules, made Hammerhead balk with fear.

"We got to turn back, find high ground," yelled Lem above the howl of wind, the slash of rain.

"Turn back where? Where are we?"

"God, I don't know, Bobbie. Just let's back up the wagon. That flood's rising fast."

It took Lem three hours to find a hill they could pull up with the wagon in a series of switchbacks on muddy terrain. Once, the wagon almost tipped over and Roberta screamed into the teeth of the wind, her hysteria full-blown. Lem drove the mules hard, made them stay on a safe line until the danger was past. When they reached a level, high above the roaring flood, Lem fell from his horse, exhausted. Roberta had to block the wheels and tie up the stock before she dared crawl under the wagon for shelter against the storm.

Lem dragged himself under the wagon. Roberta was shivering, chilled to the bone. Her teeth chattered so much he thought she was going to rattle apart.

Below them, the flood boiled between the hills, twisting and writhing like a huge serpent as it sought a path to the raging Cumberland River.

Lem put his arm around Roberta. She was soaked to the skin, shaking out of control.

"Damn, Bobbie, I'm sorry," he said.

"Make me w-w-warm, Lem," she pleaded. "God I'm so cold."

But he sat there, helpless, knowing there was nothing he could do.

The rain churned the open places on the hill to mud. Lightning razored the sky, speared the earth with jagged lancets of electricity. Thunder boomed in their ears, made them jump inside their skins. The wagon sagged under the weight of soaked clothing, foodstuffs. The sun went down and the wind never stopped for a breath. Lem finally climbed up into the wagon and began to throw things down to keep the bed from collapsing and crushing them. Water, he knew, was heavy; his pa had told him once that a gallon weighed eight pounds. He grabbed blankets and hung them over the sides to give them some shelter. But, there was no dry clothing. When he had finished all that he could do, he was shivering as bad as Roberta.

He clutched Roberta to him, holding her tightly, hoping he had some warmth to give her. He worried about Hammerhead and the mules, Goldie, the jenny, and Gideon, the jack, knew they were being battered by the storm without any safe place to go. The thunder had stopped, but there was no peace for them in

81

the ranting bluster of the wind and, although lightning no longer ripped electric scars in the sky, the rain speared the earth with silver lances sharp enough, it seemed, to break the skin.

The blankets helped to keep out the wind and most of the needling rain. But Lem and Roberta were sodden and trickles of water ran beneath the wagon. Their butts itched from the dampness and they could not lie down to sleep. In their discomfort, they clung to each other like half-drowned shipwreck victims washed up on a barren shore. Lem scooted toward one of the wheels on the high side of the hill and dragged Roberta with him. He leaned back against it and drew her to him. Her head fell on his shoulder and he closed his eyes, listening to the drum of rain on the wagon and the whip of wind against the blankets.

They dozed, despite their discomfort, occasionally sinking into fitful sleep only to awaken, startled, to find a new stiffness in a joint, a numbness in a foot or a toe, a cramp in a leg muscle. Lem dreamed of a warm fire and dry clothing. Roberta dreamed of a soft, dry bed, herself buried under thick warm comforters in a quiet breezeless room.

By morning, the storm relented, swept on past them with only an occasional rattle of rain in a wind gust, a tattoo on the wagon boards, a spatter against the soggy blankets like fine sand thrown against a windowpane.

Roberta whimpered in sleep, drawn under finally, by fatigue and some part of her mind that found shelter in dream. Lem lay awake, blind in the darkness, listening to the storm's tail lash feebly as its lumbering dragon cloud-breath passed to the south, losing strength as its thunderheads emptied and scattered, stripped of their plumpness and watery weight by the sheer force of its assault on the earth.

Rivulets of water still ran under the wagon, but they seemed harmless in the relative silence, feeble little streams that would peter out at the first furnace blast of sun. Lem heard only distant grumblings from the thunder, and the rain that fell now was so light he had to listen hard to hear it. The drip from the trees was stronger. A spoke from the wagon wheel had left a furrow of pain in his shoulder, but he didn't move. He knew that Roberta was asleep and she seemed so small and helpless in his arms he had not the heart to awaken her.

He dozed off again, shifted in his sleep. Sometime before dawn, he awoke again when he heard the scream of a woman. Jarred out of dream, it took Lem several seconds to remember where he was. Roberta scooted closer to him. He felt her breath on his neck. Her fingers dug into his arms. They both heard the terrified cries of children.

"What's that?" she whispered in the feeble half-light of dawn.

"Down on the flat," he said.

"I'm scared, Lem. Could be Indians."

"Sounds like just kids."

"I heard a woman."

"Me, too," he said. "But I don't hear it no more."

They listened, heard only the roaring of a distant stream. The silence stretched out from them, made them grow apprehensive. The rain had stopped, but the trees still dripped and water spattered on the ground in intermittent taps, off-key and without meter.

The dawn widened its crack and Lem tugged one of the blankets aside. Roberta slid away from him and he saw her sodden hair plastered against her face, the dark sockets of her eyes. She looked pathetic in her wet clothes, so childlike. He smiled, despite the ache in his shoulder, the cramps in his legs.

"You look like a drownded rat," he said. The blanket, weighted with water, slipped from the wagon, sogged to the ground.

"So do you," she retorted. "I have never in my life spent such a miserable night. I swear I thought the rain would never stop. Can you build a fire, Lem? I'm so cold my bones hurt. I fear I'l catch my death."

"I might find us some dry wood, cut us some tinder," he said, crawling out into the open. The sky was still overcast, but he no longer heard the rumble of thunder. He looked at his surroundings. They were on the slope of a round-topped, gently rolling hill, stippled with birch and maple, hazelwood, and other trees, grasses that had been flatted by the storm. The slope was not as steep as he had thought the night before and the grass had helped to keep the ground from turning to mud. They could make it back down if they were careful. He looked for fallen trees, something that might be dry inside. He made a circle around the perimeter of the summit. At a bare patch, he looked down and across to the other hills. He saw no sign of the trail, but he heard the faint roar of rushing water somewhere beyond his sight. He made a mental note to seek the stream out, see if the trail did not cross it at some point. He took his bearings, knew the general direction they must head.

Lem found some downed trees and dragged dead wood back to the wagon. Roberta was combing out her hair. She had clothes hanging from every conceivable low-hanging tree limb, and the wagon looked like a ragman's cart.

"I'll have to drive the wagon down this hill when we leave," he told her. "Be some brakin' to do."

"I'll walk," she said. "Bones are stiff."

He found the ax inside the wagon, began to tear at the wood with the blade, splintering off the driest chunks from the heart of the biggest log.

Lem started a fire with dry shavings, fashioned a drying rack from saplings that he stripped of leaves. The sun still lay behind banked clouds, but the morning brightened by the time some of their clothes were dry. Roberta was too sick to eat, but Lem ate dried turkey and a stale biscuit, washed it down with water.

When he was through, he packed everything up in the wagon, left his buckskins and one of Roberta's dresses laid out to dry in the air. He rubbed Hammerhead down, tightened the saddle cinch. Roberta led him down the hill while Lem took another course, careful to point the mules straight and ride the brake. As they traveled down the slope, he and Roberta both heard the sound of a hammer thunking nails into wood.

On the flat, Lem halted the wagon. Roberta climbed up, handed him the reins to Hammerhead.

"Do you know where we are?" she asked.

"No, but I got my bearings. We'll find the trail directly."

"What's that noise?"

"Somebody a-hammerin', I reckon. You just foller me, Bobbie. Maybe we'll find out what's a-goin' on."

"We should have stayed back there at Martin's Station," she said.

Lem said nothing, but mounted Hammerhead and rode out toward the sound of the carpenter's hammer.

After rounding a pair of low hills, Lem found the trail. It had been all but washed out by the storm, and he saw where the flash flood had unleashed its brief torrent during the night. Tree limbs, leaves, chunks of lumber marked its ravaging path. Along this floodline, he and Roberta came upon a couple working on a cart that looked as if it had been hammered together more than once. Broken pieces of lumber lay strewn nearby, and Lem saw drag marks in the mud that indicated the couple had lugged salvaged lumber for some distance. The odor of skunk hung in their nostrils, faintly pungent, faded, perhaps, in the scrub of rain and morning breeze.

"Mornin'," said Lem. "Looks like you had some trouble. Come far?"

"All the way from Winchester, Virginia," said the man.

"We're alluz breakin' down," said the woman. She had a high-pitched, squeaky, almost childlike voice. It was incongru-

ous in a woman so broad of bosom and stout of frame. Her face
was beautiful, despite her chubbiness. Roberta thought it cherubic and sweet.

"We're down to two wheels and a considerably shortened
bed, having started out with four wheels and a good ten foot of
wagon from Winchester," said Elmer Fancher. His corpulent
wife, Belinda, her face streaked with dirt, her dress soiled, put
her shoulder to the wheel as Fancher drove a wedge into a new,
makeshift spoke. Two children napped under a tree, rag dolls
clutched to their bosoms.

Lem dismounted to help, glad for the stretch. Roberta set the
brake and climbed down from the wagon, carrying a jar of sun
tea. She seemed relieved to see other human beings. She gave
Lem a begrudging look of gratitude.

"Give you a hand?" asked Lem.

"We pert near got it licked," said Elmer as he hammered the
shim tight against the spoke and wheel. "Lordy, I don't know if
this buggy will make it to Lexington. We've left so much in
sutler's gulches, the missus has her a list a yard long. Most of
what's gone, I built, so I reckon I can build 'em again for her.
Say, you'ns didn't see a little boy 'bout eight or nine wanderin'
about yester evenin' or earlier of a mornin' anywheres?"

"Sorry," said Roberta, puzzled.

Elmer stood up, extended a delicate, lean hand. He was
slender, in contrast to his wife's stout frame, billowing flab.

"I'm Elmer Fancher and this is the missus, Belinda."

"Would you like some tea?" asked Roberta, glancing over to
the tree. "My, you have a couple of nice children, I see. They
look all tuckered out."

Belinda grunted and glanced over at the children.

Roberta crinkled her nose. The skunk smell seemed to
emanate from beneath the tree where the children slept.

"Land, where's Martin?" Belinda screeched. "Elmer, you
seen Marty anywheres?"

Roberta wondered if that was the missing boy Fancher had asked her about.

Elmer tapped the wheel's spoke with the butt of the hammer. It seemed solid.

"He was with the young 'uns last I looked," he said. He spoke quietly in a thin, featureless voice. Although he couldn't have been more than twenty-five, he was losing his hair on top. Beneath the thinning dark locks, his bald pate glistened with sweat. He had a square, beard-shadowed jaw, fleshy lips, a slightly hooked nose, eyebrows that bristled like caterpillars over close-set, intense hazel eyes. He stood no more than five foot five, weighed no more than a hundred pounds. He turned to the Hawkes. "We done lost one young 'un somewhere back down at Flat Lick. Them two under the tree found 'em a pet skunk last night just before that flash flood struck us. We was right on your tracks until you turned off. A wonder you didn't hear us rattletrappin' ahind you'ns."

"You *lost* one of your children?" Roberta asked incredulously.

Belinda, oblivious to the conversation, waddled over to the tree, holding her nose with tweaking stubs of fingers. Her dress dragged on the ground and she stepped on it more than once with mud-caked boots. Her curls bounced in dark ringlets with every chunky step.

"Little Danny," said Elmer, without a trace of sadness. "He wandered off one day when we was all catching forty winks after comin' through the Gap. We looked for him high and low, stayed three days, hoping he'd come back to where we was. The missus cried her eyes out."

"You couldn't find him?" Roberta asked, in a daze. "And you just left him out there?"

"Well, we had to get on," said Fancher. "Danny, he was always confused about things. We found him ever' damned time until we got to Flat Lick. Danny took a fancy to salt, I reckon. We saw him a-settin' at a salt lick, pickin' at it and a-puttin' it on

his tongue. We hollered at him to catch up, but he never come
No tellin' where he went. The dog went with him and he neve
come back neither."

Lem stood there, transfixed, uncomfortable as a man standing
on a gallows' creaking trapdoor.

"You mean that little boy is still back there all alone? Hell, i
can't be more'n a day's ride back to Flat Lick."

"Well, he's got Skipper with him. Skipper's the beagle pu
what tagged along with us. Boy might be dead for all we know
We knew we wasn't going to find him. I mean we looked all ove
them hills and woods and hollered till we was hoarse. He jus
never come back. We didn't figger he'd turn up anytime soo
and what was we goin' to do? Couldn't wait on him forever."

"Jesus Christ," said Lem.

"Lemuel," said Roberta, her eyes in full flare with disbelie
Belinda woke up the two children.

"Where's Marty?" she squeaked.

"Aw, I don't know," cranked Earnest.

"Harriet, did you see your big brother?"

"No, Ma, I ain't seen him," said the little girl, rubbing he
eyes.

"Marty! Martin Fancher! You come on back here!"

There was no answer. Lem and Roberta stood there, struck
dumb by what appeared to be another tragedy in the making
Belinda Fancher began to climb a low hill, calling out her son'
name every few feet. Elmer looked at her once, then began t
gather up his tools.

"Want to make yourself some cash money?" he asked Lem.

"Huh?"

"I notice you'ns got a big wagon there. We got good
scattered from hell to scrapple and I got no room in thi
shrunk-up cart. My horses are tied about a half mile from her
where I gathered up all our trunks and goods. Flood caught u

during the storm and tumbled the wagon a good quarter mile or so before it struck a tree. Coulda lost the whole shebang. One thing. I got plenty of spare parts. We ought to make it to Lexington with this outfit." He tapped the single-axled cart and picked up a saw, threw it in the box with the hammer and other tools.

"How much you got to carry?" asked Lem.

"Oh, not much. I'll pay you five pounds when we get to Lexington."

"What about your son?" asked Roberta. The look she gave Lemuel was dark, with more than a trace of latent ferocity.

"Well, we ain't goin' back for him. He's either lost or dead or maybe he found his way somewheres. We rode back clear to Martin's Station. Saw you folks when you passed. We come along right after you'ns and passed you last night by no more'n a hair's thickness."

"I don't mean Danny," said Roberta. "The other one. Martin?"

They all heard Belinda calling Marty's name. She stood on the side of the hill, shading her eyes from the bleak sun, squealing in ever higher pitches.

"Oh, Marty's twelve years old. Danny was only eight or nine. I reckon Marty'll do some better."

"My God," said Roberta, not quite under her breath. Elmer picked up a wood chisel and a mallet, tossed them into the box. Harriet and Earnest began to tease each other. Earnest pulled on her single braid of hair and Harriet slapped him. Neither of them paid any attention to their mother.

"Ernie, stop it," whined Harriet. She jerked the braid out of her brother's hand.

"Don't you hit me no more," said Ernie.

Belinda disappeared from view. Her piercing voice carried, however. She was still screeching for Marty.

"Want to bring that wagon on down?" asked Elmer. "We just as well get to loading. We can pick up these tools when I bring back my horses and hook them up to the cart."

"What about your wife?" asked Lem. "Shouldn't we help her look for Martin?"

"Well, if your missus wants to help. We got to load my goods, bring them horses back here."

Lem looked at Roberta for help. She speared him with a look of pure puzzlement.

"I—I'll help Mrs. Fancher look for her boy," she said, after a moment. "You go on, Lem. We can do with the five pounds."

Lem tied Hammerhead to the cart, climbed up in the wagon. Elmer Fancher pulled himself up, sat next to Hawke.

"Giddap," said Lem, easing off the brake.

"Just foller that wash," said Fancher.

Salt from the licks had washed down the path of the flood, leaving traces white as lime. The mules kept stopping to lick at it. Lem and Elmer said nothing during these pauses, for Belinda's voice penetrated their thoughts. Elmer reached into his pocket, pulled out a twist of tobacco. He cut a piece off, handed it to Lem. Lem wedged it into his mouth, glad for something to take his mind off the skunk smell and that intolerable screechy voice of Belinda's.

"What's your business, Mr. Fancher?"

"Call me Elmer, Lemuel. Well, I do a lot of things, carpentry, hide tanning, tailoring, blacksmithing, a little tinkering."

"What you aim to do in Lexington?"

"Maybe a little of everything, Lem. Jack of all trades."

"I aim to lease me some farmland."

"A man of the soil. I wish you luck. They say Kentucky's got good land for farming."

"I just hope it's cheap," mused Hawke.

"Well, everything has its price, of course."

They no longer heard Belinda's screeching. Instead, they heard the croak of frogs along the wash. Soon, they heard the whicker of the horses. Gideon and Goldie perked up their ears, picked up their pace a little.

Lem heard the sound of rushing water, wondered about it.

"Well, there they be," said Fancher, as they rounded the base of a hill. "And there's Rockcastle River. Roarin' full, I'd say."

Two hundred yards from where the horses were tied, the wash ended up at the bank of a swollen river. Now Lem knew where the flash flood had gone. The choppy waters bobbed up tree limbs, logs, every kind of debris, carried the detritus along in its muddy race.

"You took a chance, leavin' your horses here," said Lem.

"Couldn't see anything in the dark. Looks like we got off the trail some. There's my goods, too. The Lord was watchin' over us, I reckon."

They loaded the trunks and wooden cartons into Lem's wagon, hitched the skittish horses to the back of the wagon. They kept eyeing the river, fighting their bits.

"They must have had quite a night," chuckled Fancher, as he climbed back into the wagon. "Glad to get my tools back. A man don't want to lose his tools."

"What about your boys?" asked Lem before he thought to hold his tongue.

"Sad, very sad," said Fancher, spitting out the dry husk of mangled tobacco. "God works in mysterious ways."

Lem snorted and cracked the reins. The mules pulled out in a wide turn. The wagon was considerably heavier now. He wondered what was in the trunks and boxes. No farming tools, he was sure. The trunk must have weighed two hundred pounds. He wondered if Belinda and Elmer had loaded it onto their wagon without using a block and tackle.

Fancher's horses whickered again as the mules began to trot

back the way they had come. The river purred in their wake, then the sound faded away as the sun climbed high enough to make the men pull their hat brims down to shade their eyes.

The two children stood next to the cart, naked as the day they were born. There was no sign of Belinda or Roberta. Hammerhead stood hipshot, shading them from the sun.

"Where's your ma?" asked Elmer as the wagon lurched to a stop. The children's faces were streaked with dark lines. They had been crying.

"That lady took her away," said Earnest, pointing.

The smell from the children was unmistakable.

"What did you kids do?" asked Fancher.

"Nothin'," said Harriet, a sullen scowl fixed on her face as if it had been painted there.

"Ma found our pet skunk," gloated Earnest, a mischievous gleam in his eye.

"What?" Fancher bolted down from the wagon. The children cringed as he came close, but he went right past them, began to search through the cart. "You kids stink to high heaven. What'd she do with your clothes?"

"That lady took them," said Earnest.

"She stole them," said Harriet, crinkling up her face.

"Where's that skunk?" asked Fancher, rummaging through a valise full of loose clothing.

"That lady run it off," said Earnest. "It chased Ma all the way here. You should have heard her scream."

Lem sat there, his nostrils full of skunk smell. It seemed he was watching some kind of strange dream unfolding in broad daylight. He looked around, wondered where Roberta had taken Belinda Fancher.

"Earnest, you take your sister over by that hickory tree and put some clothes on her. You get some pants on. I'll fetch your ma."

"Yonder she comes," said Earnest.

Belinda was wrapped in a blanket, her hair dripping water. Roberta led her through the brush, an arm around her shoulder. Elmer tossed some clothes to Earnest. Neither of the children made a move to leave. They stared at the two women in wide-eyed fascination.

"I washed her off in a little creek back there," said Roberta. "I don't think she can ever wear that dress again."

Lem climbed down from the wagon, but he kept his distance from the Fancher woman and her children. There was so much skunk smell in the air, his nostrils were burning.

"You get squirted?" Elmer asked his wife, as if he didn't know.

"Oh, I could skin those kids alive," said Belinda, fixing them with a murderous gaze.

"When you get finished, help me load up the cart. We got to get on, woman."

"I wish I knew where Marty had gone to," said Belinda. But she began gathering up the bedding and clothing. She dragged more trunks from a grove of trees. Soon, the cart was full. The children helped some, but only after their mother took a willow switch to them. Lem tried to help, but Fancher had his own ideas about loading and lashing down, so he finally retreated to Roberta's side.

Fancher hooked up his two horses to the little cart. It seemed a sound carrier. He had even built a little seat on the back for the children. The seat in front rode high on sturdy iron braces that were curved to take the shock from the road.

"You get to Lexington, ask for us," said Fancher. "I'll give you five pounds when you unload my goods."

"Good-by to you'ns," said Belinda. "If you run into that scalawag Marty, you tell him he'd better run and catch up." Belinda choked back a sob as the cart lurched forward. The Hawkes stood there watching the Fanchers as they wheeled back up the main trail. The two children waved for a long time, then

Earnest began pulling on Harriet's hair again just before the cart disappeared from sight.

"Well, Lemuel, I just don't know what to make of those people," said Roberta, heaving a sigh.

"Me neither," he said. "Reckon we ought to look for them two boys?"

"Where? Little Danny probably got washed away in the flood last night. If he was still alive. They haven't seen him in at least four days, maybe longer. That strange woman screamed for Marty. If he was anywhere around he would surely hear her."

"I reckon so," he said. He thought about calling out Marty's name himself, but it was so quiet now he felt awkward about it.

"It's so sad," said Roberta wistfully. "I feel sorry for that woman."

"Looks like they got used to losin' kids," said Lem.

Roberta gave him a funny look. He cleared his throat, caught up Hammerhead. By the time he was mounted, Roberta had the mule team turned and heading back to the trail.

Lem looked back over his shoulder several times as he rode behind the wagon.

He saw no sign of a young boy wandering lost in the wilderness of Kentucky.

9

The trail meandered, took a wide cut to the northeast, and then the Hawkes reached Hazel Patch, a flat, grassy plain at the foothills of the Cumberland Mountains. It had taken them almost five days to go that far, even though the trail was not that difficult. All along the way, they saw signs of others' passing, the detritus of other families left behind to blow in the wind, rot in the sun and rain. They saw the skeletons of furniture broken in transit and tossed beside the trail, articles of clothing that had worn out or had been torn beyond repair or caring, worn-out pots and pans, empty sacks, the remains of campfires, a crumpled boot, slats from a keg, parts of wagons. The junk littered the deeply rutted trail, the castoff parts from faceless nomads. It was depressing to Roberta, who felt as if she had been cast out of Eden, shamefully driven from home into the terrifying wilderness. She said nothing to her husband, but he felt the vibrations of her suppressed hostility at the end of each long day. As they drew farther away from their abandoned home, she kept looking back over her shoulder like Lot's wife, and every time she did, she stiffened on the seat of the wagon and she tugged hopelessly on the reins as if to halt their journey before it was too late.

But it was more than homesickness that tugged at her, she knew. A growing fear for her unborn child began to grow in her. And this, she knew, came from thinking about the two lost Fancher boys. She could not help her thoughts, could not keep the images of the children from turning hideous in her troubled mind.

Lem called a halt when the sun lay just above the western horizon, a disc of hammered gold, frozen there for a long moment.

"Bobbie," he said, "we ain't ever gonna get up to Lexington you keep jerkin' on them reins. You've plumb wore out them mules' mouths a-tuggin' on them bits."

"Lemuel Hawke, you just shut your flappin' mouth," she snapped. Her shoulder blades felt like wooden stakes jabbing into her back. Her legs quivered from fatigue. She had dawdled, she knew, because she couldn't bear to think of those two lost boys. Something in her heart told her that one or the other one might still be alive, crying his eyes out, looking for his parents. As for the Fanchers, she was sorry she had made Lem take their goods on the wagon. She thought they were cruel to just go on about their business knowing their sons were all alone, lost out in the wilds. She couldn't imagine anyone going off like that and leaving their flesh and blood behind.

Roberta set the brake, looked at the hills they had crossed. They shimmered golden in the sun, blazed with a green fire bright as emeralds. She was sweaty under her loose dress, her hands clammy from perspiration.

Lem stripped Hammerhead, hobbled him in grass, tended to the mules. Roberta laid out the camp, gathered stones for a fire ring. There were signs that others had camped there, but she liked to make her own place. Lem dug her a pit and searched for firewood as the sun crawled down the sky, stretched their shadows long and thin across the sward.

"What do you want for supper?" she asked, when Lem finished chopping kindling for the fire.

"You ain't goin' to keep lookin' under every damned bush and behind every damned tree for them boys, are you?"

A pair of red squirrels scampered past the wagon, quill-like hairs twitching on their nervous tails. High in a scaly-bark hickory tree, another squirrel barked a throaty invective.

"Lem, I got bad feelings about leavin' that place without lookin' for the Fancher boy. He could be lookin' for his folks."

"Well, you've wasted enough time," he said, setting the kindling in the center of the hole he had dug in the fire ring. "We'd a been to Lexington already if you hadn't dawdled every damned mile."

"Must you always curse?"

"When it's called for, hell yes."

"What are you really mad at, Lemuel?"

He stared at the crates that belonged to Fancher.

"I'd just like to carry my own baggage," he said.

"We need the five pounds," she said.

"Well, I need my freedom a whole danged lot more."

"You won't have to look at them much longer," she said.

"I done looked at 'em too much now. I see 'em in my sleep. Goddamn it."

"There you go again, Lemuel. Blaspheming the good Lord. He'll strike you down one day."

Hawke didn't say the next curse out loud. He picked up a chunk of dirt, bounced it off one of Fancher's crates.

Roberta went to the wagon, banged pots together in a deliberate attempt to vent her anger. She looked long and wistfully back down the trail as she slammed the pots down next to the fire ring. Lem flinched involuntarily as she tossed a ladle into the bigger iron pot. It rang like a horseshoe.

"Ham and beans," she said defiantly, as she whisked back to the wagon. "Fetch me some water."

"Ham and beans," echoed Lem. "You got any cornmeal left?"

"Maybe," she said, digging into the wooden box that held her condiments, flour, and meal. "You want corn cakes?"

"Naw, I was just exercisin' my gums, Bobbie."

"You don't have to be a smarty britches."

"Corn cakes would be fine. Keep them beans from swimmin' around in my belly."

"You ought to be grateful we have beans," she said.

"I am. I just don't like 'em swimmin' around in my stomach like water bugs."

"Lem, just stop flap-mouthin' about ever' little thing. You fray a body's nerves."

Lem set a piece of charred cloth on the ground, covered it with fine shavings. He took a small brass case from his possibles pouch, opened it. He struck flint against the curved face of the steel, showered sparks into the fine tinder. When the shavings caught, he leaned down, blew into them. They glowed a flickering orange. The edge of the cloth caught fire and he lifted the little bundle off the ground, set it against the cone of kindling. He blew on the tinder until it flared. When the kindling began to burn, he leaned back, grabbed some larger sticks and waited until the blaze was high before laying them on. Roberta shook beans into the big pot. They clattered like pebbles in a tin funnel.

The two squirrels scampered up a tree. Soon, all three of them were barking.

Lem looked up.

"That old bull sounds like he's got the croup," he said, but he knew that something was bothering the squirrel on the hickory branch.

"Probably doesn't like the fire," said Roberta.

"No, it ain't that."

Lem stood up, walked slowly over to where he had leaned his rifle against the wagon tongue. It wasn't the fire, he knew. It was more than that. Nor was it that they were interlopers into the fox squirrel's territory. The pair of scamperers had sensed what the old boy had been trying to warn them about. That's why they had treed.

Roberta lay out an oilcloth, retrieved her knives and a two-tined fork from one of the boxes in the wagon.

"Lem, what's the matter?" she asked.

"I don't know. Them squirrels are sure skittery."

Roberta looked around. Everything looked peaceful. There was no sign of danger.

"Bring that half a ham over when you get shut of lookin'," she said.

Lem gazed at the countryside. Far off, he heard other squirrels barking, but he didn't know if they were just responding to the ones nearby or whether they were spooked by something in the trees.

He waited several moments, then climbed up into the wagon. He found the half butt of ham in a cedar box, lugged it over to Roberta's oilcloth.

"Might be nothin'," he said aloud.

"What?" She unwrapped the cheesecloth from around the ham, sniffed at the meat. It was not spoiled.

"Them squirrels. Somethin's got 'em riled."

"Oh, Lem, you worry about nothin'. I still need you to fetch me some water. The keg in the back is nigh to full."

"I'll get it."

"Then, leave me be. You make me nervous with all your twitchin'."

"Yes ma'am," he said sarcastically.

Lem sat on a low hill, his rifle across his lap, surveying the surrounding country. Bees worked the patches of spring flowers in the wide meadow, birds flitted in the trees. The squirrels had gone silent. Wafted aromas of the beans and ham simmering in the pot floated to his nostrils. He smelled the heady scent of cornbread baking in the covered skillet. His stomach knotted into kinks of hunger, made low grumbling noises. The sun was setting over his back when he saw the slight movement, across the flat. It was such a slight ripple in the serene fabric of afternoon that he almost missed it.

But something had moved.

He forgot his hunger, leaned forward, his eyes narrowed to shut out the back light, focus on the movement he had seen. A squirrel barked in rapid staccato just above the place where he had seen a shadowy glimpse of an animal. He saw it again, and puzzled, grimaced. A fox? No, and not a rabbit, either.

Then, he saw its tail, saw the animal move along an invisible path at the edge of the meadow. The tail switched back and forth, almost making round circles in the air. The animal reversed its course, then reversed it again. A few yards closer, a cottontail broke from cover.

The beagle took up the chase, yelping in the high register of the tonic scale. The rabbit veered and the beagle's yelps grew higher in pitch. Lem stood up, thrilled to see the pup, hear its voice.

Roberta stood up, looked toward the sound of the beagle's cry.

"What's that?" she said.

"Might be that beagle pup Fancher told us about."

Lem called out.

"Skipper! Come here, Skipper. Here, Skipper!"

The beagle stopped in its tracks. Lem called to the dog again. Skipper began wagging its tail. The tail went round and round, scribing erratic circles with its black tip. The dog forgot about the rabbit, came waddling across the meadow. It seemed to smell the food cooking. Its tail wagged more furiously.

"Come on, Skipper," Lem said in a soothing voice as he arose from his seat. He walked toward the fire, talking low to the dog.

Roberta blew a vagrant hair away from her face, put her hands on her hips, turning them inside out.

"Seems to know his name," she said.

"Skippoo," said Lem, reverting to baby talk. "Skippoozers. Come on, boy. 'At's a boy."

The dog came right up to him as Lem stopped at Roberta's side. He reached down to pet it.

"Got a chunk of ham for this little feller?" he asked.

Roberta took a fork, raised the lid on the kettle, gouged out a chunk of ham. She blew on it, handed it to Lem when it was cool.

"Here you go boy," said Lem, kneeling down. He put the morsel in Skipper's mouth. The dog wolfed it down in a fraction of a second.

Lem rubbed the dog's back, kneaded him behind the ears. Skipper's tail continued to whirl in a circular motion. His brown eyes pleaded for more meat.

"Cut him another chunk," said Lem.

"Would you give him all of our food?" she asked.

"I want to keep him here. Might be that boy is close by."

"Boy? What boy?"

"The Fancher boy. Danny."

"Oh," she said, and forked a thick finger of ham from the butt, blew it cool before handing it to Lem.

Lem walked a little distance away from the fire and the dog followed him. He made the dog jump for the piece of ham. Skipper plopped down and swallowed twice. It didn't seem to Lem that he had chewed the meat at all.

"Where's Danny, Skipper?"

Skipper wagged his tail. He was brown and white and black, with soft floppy ears, a dust smudge on his nose, burrs in his dirty coat. Lem looked across the meadow.

"Danny!" he called. "Danny, come on. Have some supper."

There was no answer. Roberta looked all around, then at Lem.

"You're crazy," she said.

"This dog's been somewhere," he told her. "He's going somewhere. You think he followed our wagon tracks by himself?"

"I suppose he might have," she said, a trace of annoyance in her voice. "Maybe he smelled the Fanchers' wagon wheels."

"He's not no bloodhound," said Lem. He patted Skipper gently on the head. The dog wagged his whole body.

"Come on here, Danny!" Lem called. "You hungry?"

Lem saw movement again. The hackles on the back of his neck bristled. He strained to see into the long tree shadows that striped the far reaches of the meadow's tall grasses. At first he saw only a boy's head, then as the boy approached, he saw the upper part of his body. Then, he saw another head, and part of another boy. Lem held his breath, but his mind roared like a wind before a storm.

"Roberta, just don't make no quick moves to scare 'em off," Lem whispered.

"Whatever are you talking about?" she asked, but her eyes tracked the path of Lem's gaze. She stood there, rigid as her husband, as the two boys, one taller than the other, walked slowly toward them.

"It's them," said Lem, his voice low. "It's both of them Fancher boys."

Roberta gasped involuntarily.

The smaller boy was limping. The older boy helped him along, an arm around the younger one's shoulders.

"Martin Fancher," called Lem. "That you?"

"Who are you?" The boy's voice sounded thin and high-pitched, almost like a girl's.

"Why, I'm a friend of your ma's and pa's, son. I knowed you was lost. Come on, get yourself some vittles. Hungry?"

"I sure am," said the older boy.

The younger boy started to run toward them, but he stumbled and fell down. Martin helped his brother up. He had to carry him the last fifty yards.

Roberta dropped her utensils and rushed to take the smaller boy from his brother's arms.

Skipper cavorted like a double-jointed dog with a case of the fits.

"I'm Marty Fancher," said the older boy. "This here's my little brother, Danny. He's plumb tuckered. We ain't had no food in three days."

Roberta snatched Danny away from Martin. The boy's shoes were worn through the soles. The bottoms of his feet were blistered, black from dirt. His clothes were in tatters. His dark shock of hair was matted with dust and sand. His face was burned to a deep burgundy by the sun. Martin did not look much better. He, too, was dirty, and his shoes were rattling on his feet, the bottoms flayed to ribbons. He stepped gingerly over to Lem, looked up at him.

"Where you been, boy?"

"I—I went lookin' for Danny. He was plumb lost and scared. I took a bait of food with me, but he et it all up."

"You didn't save none for yourself?"

"No, suh, I give it all to little Danny there."

Lem smiled.

"Well, you done good, boy." He patted Martin on the top of the head. His hair was as hard as a saddle. "You set down and we'll put some pork and beans in you. Nice dog you got."

"Yes suh, Skipper he's a mighty good dog. He's a beagle pup with a good nose."

Lem laughed.

Marty was bright-eyed, dark-haired, chubby as a turnip, like his mother. He, too, had been sunned brown, but he seemed in much better shape than Danny.

Roberta washed the bottoms of Danny's feet, took off his shredded shoes. His legs were a mass of sores, insect bites, and red streaks. They looked as if they had been lashed with switches.

"Poor boy," she said. "He must be scared pure to death. Leavin' him alone out there like that."

"Bobbie, don't you say nothin' now. Just clean him up and put some vittles in him."

"But I—yes, poor thing. We'll take good care of you, Danny. Lem, he's thin as a rail."

Danny looked at her with dull brown eyes. He smiled weakly.

"That feels good," he said, in a soft voice. "My feet's pow'rful sore, I reckon."

"Why of course they are," soothed Roberta. "We'll get you all cleaned up after you've taken some food into your little stomach."

"Where'd you find your brother?" Lem asked Martin.

"Way yonder. He was a-follerin' the wagon tracks and Skipper, he barked when he saw me. Danny was scared, all right. He cried like a little baby when he seed me."

"I expect he did," said Lem. "Come on, that ham's got to be cooked. Beans might be a little hard yet."

"I don't much care how hard they are," said Martin, with a slow grin. "I'd as soon eat 'em raw."

Roberta fed Danny. Martin wolfed down his food, would have eaten more but Lem restrained him.

"Let your stomach swell back," he told the boy. "Then you can eat all you want."

Roberta made a bed for the two boys under the wagon. Lem pitched their lean-to on one side. Skipper crawled in with the boys, snuggled up to Danny. The youngsters were asleep in five minutes.

"It's a miracle," said Roberta, when she lay down next to Lem.

"That Martin's a mighty fine boy, all right. Takin' care of his brother like that."

"I'm going to give that Fancher woman a piece of my mind."

"Give her the whole thing," said Lem wearily. "And some of mine to boot."

———·———

A week later the Hawkes pulled into the town of Lexington, five hundred miles from their former home in Culpeper County, Virginia. For half a day, right after they passed Boiling Spring Station on Dick's River, they had followed a caravan of wagons bearing fresh-cut timber from the highlands. Lem had fretted at the slowness, but had been unable to pull out and pass the wagons because recent rains had made the ground soft. Through Harrodsburg and McAfee's Station, they followed the slow-moving wagons as if bound to them by gravity.

"Damn," he said. "A man can't go where he wants."

"Lem, it'll only be for a little ways. Can't you have some patience?"

"Oh, I got all the patience in the world when it's mine to spend. Not when it's forced on me like them damned crates of Fancher's."

"You're still frettin' about that."

"Hell, we got some of his kids now. Next thing you know, they'll be wantin' us to take them other two in, too."

He felt strapped in, trapped. The wagons lumbered along like turtles and he might as well have been tethered to them. The only times he'd enjoyed on the trail were when he was making his own way, looking at the country without seeing a whole lot of people cluttering it up. The boys seemed to pay no attention to the land they passed and it galled him. If he ever had a son, he'd by God teach him to use his eyes and ears and not be so damned caught up in foolishness. Roberta fawned over them like a mother hen and he didn't like that much either. At night they couldn't do anything and she seemed to thrive on continence. Didn't bother her none at all. Well, when he got his own place, all that was going to change. She'd not have Fancher kids underfoot nor neighbors wearing out their welcome. Her and them boys. He stared at the back of the timber wagon and grated his teeth on the grit in his mouth.

Roberta had taken possession of the boys, had mended their clothes, sewed harness leather to their shoes to make soles. After two days they were calling her "Aunt Berta."

"Aunt Berta, look, look," cried Danny as they glimpsed the town sprawled across the middle of the plain.

"Why there must be hundreds of homes here," said Roberta, "and it's so flat you can nigh see 'em all."

A multilayered pall of smoke hung over the plain, streaks of gray, and black wisps like dusty cobwebs. Plowed fields, some of them greening up, bordered small cabins well away from the town, and people had planted young trees near their homes that would bring shade to porches they would someday build. The scents of country and town mingled in a clash of zephyrs that scattered the lingering dust from the wagons. Lem smelled the change in the air. They'd be among people again and he bristled at the thought of it. Necessary, he knew, but he wished he could get him a place and just tend to farming, do some private hunting and fishing.

They drove for the center of town, asking directions as they went. They passed shops of every kind, heard cries of "welcome, pilgrim," and people waved to them, laughed at Skipper who barked at every dog, cat, chicken, hog and goat he saw.

Buggies and wagons, carts and sulkies streamed between the crowded courthouse square and the myriad shops on every street. People stood at open stalls, bartering, selling their wares. There were shoemakers and farriers, barrel smiths and whiskey drummers, tinsmiths and brewers, taverns and dry goods stores, greengrocers and butchers all plying their trades amid the mingled smells and sounds of a teeming, growing city.

Lem halted his wagon in front of the courthouse, for he and the boys had been riding with Roberta, pulling Hammerhead behind, as she sewed and fussed over their clothes.

"I'll see can I find the boys' folks," he said, setting the brake, wrapping the reins around it.

"It might take a year with all these people," said Roberta. "Lord, I've never seen so much bustle."

She looked longingly at the women in their poke bonnets, their crinoline dresses with high bodices and small frilled collars. The men dressed in a variety of clothing, from buckskins to frock coats; most of them wore hats, of every style and description.

"You boys stay right close to the wagon. I'll see can I fetch your pa."

"We want to go with you, Uncle Lemuel."

"Stay with Aunt Berta; mind her well. And, I ain't your damned uncle."

"Lem, there's no call to be mean to these poor children. They ain't done you no harm."

"I'll be glad to be shut of them," he said, and stalked off. He knew he was nervous. People made him so. And he'd never seen so many people, all strangers, at one place. He almost wished he had his rifle in hand so that he could make him a wide path through them.

Lem left the three in the wagon, wandered across the open spaces, dodging small barrows and handcarts pushed by industrious lads wearing linsey-woolsey shirts and little billed caps, knickers and long stockings. Chickens squawked as they were hauled to market in open slat-boarded crates; hogs grunted and squealed, goats bleated. The air smelled of fresh-cut lumber, cooked tripe and animal dung, of boiled turnip greens and corned beef, summer sweat and rain-soaked straw. The busy world of commerce teemed about him, so many people doing so many things, he felt as alien in their midst as they might have felt in his deep woods back in Virginia.

He saw the cart before he saw Fancher. It stood in the shade of a large stall with a striped canvas top near one of the side streets. The cart was empty when Lem looked inside and no sign of Fancher. The people manning the stall were selling cooking utensils, linens, bedding, even crudely fashioned wooden furniture. The women wore bonnets that hid their faces and the men were all young, mere boys, who stacked and arranged the goods at instructions from the almost faceless women. One old woman poured coins into a box and he saw her pull a bundle of pound notes from a pocket and deposit them with the metal shillings and pence. She slammed the box shut and hovered over it like a hen guarding eggs.

Lem's chest got tight when he looked at the people walking everywhere with no seeming purpose. None seemed to pay him any mind and he felt lost, all alone, even with all the people about. A sense of inane and inexplicable loneliness assailed him.

He looked around in panic for Fancher. He thought of calling out for him or asking after his whereabouts, but he was stricken with a kind of nameless fear that he had never experienced before. The ground seemed to quaver under him and he felt as if he must run as fast and as far as he could to catch his breath. He felt a suffocation that was strange to him. He felt that if he was not careful, the people would all move toward him and shut him off from light and air.

"Ah, there you be, Lemuel Hawke," said a voice. Lem jumped, literally, and was ashamed of his sudden fright.

"Fancher," said Lem as he caught sight of the man approaching him from a shadowed road between a pair of log buildings. "Been lookin' for you."

"You brung my crates?"

"Yonder. Brung you som'pin else, too."

"Eh? What's that?"

"Foller me," said Hawke.

"Hold on, Hawke. I got some news for you."

Lem stopped in his tracks. He looked at Fancher.

"What you got?"

"Why you wanted some farm land, didn't you?"

"So I do."

"You see a man named Horatio Bickham. South of Lexington. You'll see a road going to Frankfort. About two mile west, is where you'll find Bickham. He'll sell you good land, seven shillings the acre. Just tell him you're the man what Elmer Fancher told him about. My woman's working for him already, here in town, and his daughter's mindin' the childrens. Horatio Bickham. Fine man, Hawke. Fine man."

"Why, much obliged, Mr. Fancher."

"Call me Elmer, Hawke. We're going to be jolly friends, you and me. Now, let's get to that wagon of your'n. I'll fetch my cart."

Fancher bobbed back to his cart, bounced up onto the seat. He freed up the reins, clucked to the pair of horses. Lem's heart soared with the news of farm land. But the price was much too high for Lem's purse. Perhaps he could talk Horatio Bickham into leasing him a few acres until he made his crop.

The cart rattled along behind Lemuel. When he got to his own wagon, neither Roberta nor the boys were there. His heart felt clogged with heaviness.

Fancher pulled up alongside, hauled back on the wheel brake. He clambered onto the cart, stood ready.

"Now, if you'll help me with my goods, I'll pay you the five pounds I promised, Hawke. A goodly sum, mind you, but my tools be worth many times that."

"I wonder where my wife's gone to," said Lem.

"Be quick about it, son. I've much to do."

Lem nodded dumbly, climbed up into his wagon. He looked around for Roberta, finally saw her at the entrance to one of the shops. She carried a new dress over her arm. There was no sign of the boys.

"Bobbie!" he called.

Roberta looked up at him. She was beaming. She scurried towards him, radiant. She held the dress close to her. It was dyed with pink stripes and had a white collar. He saw that she had a matching bonnet dangling from one hand.

"Oh, Lem," she exclaimed, "look at this. Isn't it pretty. I just couldn't help myself. It was only two shillings. A bargain."

"Two shillings!" he exclaimed.

Her face darkened.

"Why, I knew you'd find Mr. Fancher and be paid for your hauling."

"Where are the boys?" he asked tightly.

"I'll discuss that with Mr. Fancher," she said.

Fancher swayed to keep his balance in the shaky cart. He looked at Roberta in abject bewilderment, his face a blank bowl of paste.

"Boys? What boys?" he asked.

"Why your boys, Mr. Fancher," she said sweetly. "We found 'em. But first I want to discuss the price you must pay for their return."

Fancher scowled.

Lem went to his knees, gripped the side of his wagon. His eyes squinched to dark slits and his stomach swirled with a sudden sickness.

Elmer Fancher's eyes bulged from their sockets. A band of color rose from his neck and suffused his face with a pink stain. His shirt swelled under an apoplectic strain.

"Are you holding my boys for ransom, Mrs. Hawke?" he asked, his voice a phlegmatic rasp.

"You offered to pay my husband five pounds for carrying those crates," she said. "I thought you might be willing to pay for hauling your sons all that way practically from Hazel Patch. I'd think the boys would be worth a lot more than your personal goods."

"Mrs. Hawke, this ain't hardly toler'ble," spluttered Fancher. "This is . . . why, you're some such, no better'n a damned brigand. You fetch my sons to me right quick, hear?"

"What are they worth to you, Mr. Fancher?" she asked, her tone hard and flat as a sterling coin and just as cold. "If you're a-payin' Lemuel five pounds for those crates, why I would think

111

Martin would be worth fifteen and little Daniel at least ten pounds."

"Bobbie," interjected Lemuel, "what are you doin'? Those boys ain't for barter. We found 'em, we brung 'em here. Now fetch 'em for Mr. Fancher here."

"When he's made me an offer," she said, her gaze fixed on Fancher the way a snake watches a cornered mouse. "We did you a service, Mr. Fancher. We expect payment in kind."

"If this don't beat all," said Fancher.

"I'll talk to her, Mr. Fancher," said Lem, bounding down from the wagon.

Roberta backed away when Lem approached her. He grabbed her upper arms, held her tight in his grip.

"Don't touch me," she muttered under her breath.

"Have you gone daft, woman? You fetch them boys to their pa right quick or I'll lay a leather strop to your behind."

"You wouldn't dare!"

"Bobbie, do what I say," he said through gritted teeth, "or I'll put you over my knees right here and now."

His grip tightened on her shoulders. He shook her once, hard enough to jar her.

"Damn you," she said and her eyes narrowed. She stiffened as if in shock.

"I mean it," he said. "You get them boys now, woman."

Roberta paled. Lemuel had never talked to her in this way nor had she ever felt his strength used against her. His fingers dug into the soft flesh of her upper arms, burned furrows of pain clear to the bone.

"Let loose of me. I—I'll get the boys." People had begun to gather around. Roberta looked at them, panic flaring in her eyes.

An old woman glared at her accusingly. A man in a leather apron frowned at her. Children crowded forward and stared at her so hard that she cringed.

"You better," said Lem, releasing his wife. Roberta dashed away, disappeared between two buildings.

"Maybe you better go after her," said Fancher.

"She'll be back," Lem said defiantly, but he wasn't so sure. "I'll load them crates for you."

He climbed back up into his wagon, wrestled the heavy crates into Fancher's cart. Fancher reached into his pocket, pulled out a crumpled five-pound note.

"You'll get this soon's I get my boys back," said Fancher.

"Fair enough," said Lem. "I'm real sorry about this, Mr. Fancher. I don't know what got into Roberta."

"I wouldn't let no woman shame me like that," said Fancher, sitting atop one of his boxes. He folded the five-pound note, unfolded it, folded it again.

Lem's mouth went dry. He turned away from Fancher, sick to his stomach. He needed the money, but Fancher was right about Roberta. She had shamed him. She had done it deliberate and open. Lord, no wonder she had fussed over them boys. She had a scheme all set up to get her some money for bringing them to Fancher. It made him sick inside. It made him too sick to look at what she was doing to him.

A few moments later, Skipper ran from between the buildings. Fancher saw the dog, stood up in his cart. The crowd had dispersed, but there were still a few shop people looking their way. When Roberta and the boys appeared, Fancher waved his arms.

"Pa, Pa!" squawked little Danny.

Marty broke away from Roberta, who had his hand in hers. He lifted Danny up in his arms and ran to the cart. The beagle danced on his hind legs when Fancher lifted Danny up into the cart with him. Marty threw the dog inside the cart and scrambled up over the side.

"Danny, God, your ma will faint when she sees you. Marty, oh Marty, where did you go?"

The boys hugged their father. Fancher set Danny down and reached across the space between the cart and Lem's wagon. He handed Hawke the five-pound note.

"I'm mighty obliged you found my boys," said Fancher. "I thank you kindly."

"Twarn't nothin'," said Lem, taking the note. "Good-by, boys."

"Good-by, Uncle Lem," said Danny.

"Good-by," said Marty.

"Come on boys, let's be gettin' to our new home," said Fancher. He looked at Roberta coldly as he climbed onto the seat of his cart. Danny sat beside his father. Marty stayed in back. He did not wave to Roberta as the cart rumbled away.

Lem watched them go, sighed deeply, and climbed down from his wagon. Roberta stood a few yards away, biting her lip as she watched the wagon thread its way past the Clark Courthouse, turn onto a road leading south.

"You take that dress to where you got it," Lem said to Roberta. "See can you get our money back."

"I won't," she said.

"You better, or I will," he said. "We can't spare a shilling on such foolishness."

"Foolishness? I buy myself a dress to wear so that I'll look nice for you. You been tellin' me about a new life in Kentucky and now we're here and still poor. You got five pounds from Mr. Fancher and begrudge me a few shillings. Here, take the dress back yourself. I won't never ask another thing from you, Lemuel Hawke. You're stingy, mean, cruel, and I don't know what all. I hate you. I hate you for draggin' me all this way so's we can live poor as churchmice and get in debt all over again. Where will it end? Where will we run to next? You got no gumption. We could have got somethin' with that money I asked Mr. Fancher to pay us. We did him a favor and he owed us. Oh, you blind, dumb no-account. Foolishness? You're the fool, Lemuel. You're the stupid fool."

She threw the new dress and bonnet at Lem. She opened her small cloth satchel and took the money purse out, threw that at him too. The purse struck him in the chest, then fell to the ground. People stared at him as if suddenly discovering he had leprosy.

"There," she said, "you might as well have it all. All of our miserable savings."

Roberta stormed past him, climbed up onto the wagon seat. She sat there, stiff as a post, then crumpled over as the tears boiled up in her eyes.

"You beast," said a woman, scowling at him a long moment before she jerked her child away.

He picked the purse out of the dirt, stuck it in his waistband. Ignoring the woman, he entered the store with the dress and bonnet. A woman glared at him from behind the counter.

"I've a shilling for you," she said. "That's all I'll pay for used goods. It's more than fair for the likes of you."

"Ma'am, this dress ain't been wore."

"One shilling. Take it or leave it."

Lem slammed the clothes down on the board counter, picked up the single shilling, made a fist over it.

He stalked from the store without a word. Whispers rose up behind him like mosquitoes from a stagnant bog.

Lem mounted the wagon, sat next to Roberta. He sighed heavily as he unwrapped the reins, released the brake.

"Well, did you get your money back?" she snapped.

"One shilling is all."

"Ha. Cost you a shilling, did it? You miser."

"Bobbie, if you say another word, I'll take you across my knee like the brat you are."

"Right here? In front of everybody?"

"Right here, in front of God and everybody," he said.

He flapped the reins, made them ripple across the mules' backs. They moved. Hammerhead snorted behind them as they pulled across the commons. Lem found the road leading to Frankfort on the west, stopped at a roadside inn. He noticed an unplowed field beyond the inn, grass for grazing, plenty of open sky. The inn was a ramshackle affair, unpainted, slapped together with crooked boards, logs, scrap lumber. The sign out front read: ROOMS AND MEALS. There was a stable, a stock pen that bordered a grazing pasture, pigsty full of fat Hampshire reds, a corncrib. A row of haymows bordered one edge of a fallow field. A boy out back was chopping kindling. Four cows grazed in a far pasture that was fenced with split rails.

"Why are we stopping here?" asked Roberta. "I thought we'd stay in town where I could bathe and see some of the sights."

"I aim to see can we camp in that field yonder."

Roberta slumped, shook her head wearily.

"I want to sleep in a real bed," she said.

"We got to watch every farthing for a time."

Lem sprang from the wagon, strode to the inn. Mud clung to his moccasins. He knocked on the door. A stooped-over man stepped outside. He was bald except for thatches of tangled white hair that clung to the sides like snow-covered moss. He looked at Lem, beyond to the wagon.

"Reckon you got the Kentucky fever, son. You want bed and board?"

"Wondered could we camp in that field back there. For the night. I'll be looking for land I can rent from a man named Bickham."

"Horatio Bickham? Lives about seven miles down yonder road. He might sell you some land. Don't know if he rents. You want to stay here? Two shillings the night. Either in the bed or in the field."

"I could chop wood. Do some chores for you."

"I got a boy what does all that."

Lem thought of the shilling he had gotten back on the dress and bonnet. He looked back at Roberta. She was watching him intently.

"Anyplace we might camp?"

"Son, I'm in business. This is all private land hereabouts. Cost money to clear it. We all got taxes to pay."

"Two shillings you say?"

"That's the cheapest you'll get anywheres."

"All right."

"Pull your wagon out back. They's a door back there. First room on your right. Pay in advance."

Lem pulled out the two shillings in his pocket, placed them in the man's hand.

"Supper's at dark, breakfast at sunup. Put your stock up in that pen out there. Feed's a shilling extra."

"They can graze," said Lem. "I'll hobble 'em for the night."

"Still a shilling."

Lem pulled the purse from his waistband, fished in it for the right coin. He put another shilling in the man's open palm.

"A pleasure to do business with you," said the man. "Well's out back, too."

"It's a damn wonder you don't charge for that too."

"Thinkin' on it."

Lem held his tongue. He was raised to show respect for his elders, but the old man tried his patience. So far all he'd found in Kentucky was a hole in his money pouch. Not even a full day in Lexington and he was already short four shillings. At this rate, they wouldn't be able to rent enough land to support them, much less buy seed and food to put on the table.

The door slammed shut. Lem walked back to the wagon.

"You got yourself a bed," he told Roberta.

She glared at him in tight-lipped silence.

———·———

The Hawkes spoke little during supper. The innkeeper introduced his wife, Katrina, and their son, Wolfgang. He said his name was Adolph Werner, but he pronounced his last name with a V sound.

Katrina was a dour woman, round as a beer keg. Wolfgang seemed a quiet, brooding youth, respectful of his parents. He had flaxen blond hair, a small, thin mouth like his father's. All of the family had blue eyes, but Adolph's were dark, his wife's lighter and Wolfgang's lightest of all.

They spoke with a thick Germanic accent, shoveled the pork and potatoes into their mouths as if they were eating at gunpoint. Lem watched them furtively, but Roberta stared at her plate, picked at her food.

"You not hungry?" Katrina asked Roberta.

"Huh? Oh, I don't feel well."

"But you must eat, child. The baby. You must think of your baby."

"Oh, I didn't know you could tell," said Roberta.

"I can tell. We don't have no more babies. Little Wolfgang, he tore me all up."

Roberta blushed. Wolfgang stared at Roberta with his cold, pale eyes.

"Eat," said Adolph to his wife and son, as he took another helping of boiled turnips.

Lem got up from the table.

"Thank you for the food," he said. "I'll see to our stock, Bobbie."

Roberta didn't answer. She picked up a small piece of roast pork, chewed it daintily. There was no more talk at the table. The back door slammed shut and there was only the clank of eating utensils on metal plates. She excused herself and walked to their rented room without saying good night to the Werners.

The room was dreary even after she lit the small lantern hanging from an overhead beam. The wick smoked and black-

ned the glass chimney until she turned it down. She looked at
he homely bed with its lumpy mattress, its simple gray coverlet.
There was a small chest of drawers with a pitcher atop it. A
hamber pot stuck out from under the iron bed. She shoved it
ack under with the toe of her boot. The sound, like a knife
craping bone, grated in her ears.

She opened the trunk Lem had brought inside. She rifled
nrough her clothes until she got to bottom, to the new things
he had made for herself. She touched the material and felt the
itter ache in her throat as her eyes stung with unbidden tears.

She thought of the pretty dress she had bought that was now
ack on the display rack. She looked at the dreary room and sank
nto a rising sea of self-pity. She patted the clothes back down
nd closed the trunk. She took a kerchief from her valise and
abbed at her eyes. Lem would never know what he had done to
er today. She would never tell him how much it had hurt to
ave him take the dress back.

Roberta removed her nightgown from the valise. She had been
aving it for Kentucky. It was made of soft spun cotton and had
een dyed a pale pink. She had sewed little satin ribbons into the
ollar and onto the sleeves. The ribbons were blue and she liked
he feel of them between her fingers. She undressed, put on the
own and brushed her hair.

Lem came in after a while and she pretended to be asleep.

"Bobbie," he said. "You awake?"

She didn't answer.

She listened to him undress, heard him blow out the lamp.
The bed creaked under his weight. He moved close to her, found
er hand. She stiffened.

He kissed her on the cheek. His hand sought her breast. She
urned away from him.

"Bobbie," he whispered. "I want you."

"No," she said.

"What's the matter?"

"You're cruel," she said. "I hate you."

"Don't say that," he said. She pulled the covers up over h
head and thrust his hand away from her breast. She heard hi
grumble for a moment, then turn over on his side, his back
hers.

She lay there for a long time, gloating in the dark.

"I guess I hate you too, Roberta," he said, and his voi
surprised her. She had thought he was asleep. "I guess I start
hating you when you tried to ransom them kids to Fancher. A
now you're using your body like it was a weapon. I won't ha
no woman treat me like this."

Roberta fought for words to say, but her heart was poundi
and the fear in her heart rose up so big it smothered her. She l
there, fighting down the trembling, hoping Lem wouldn't noti
that she was shaking.

Soon, she heard him snoring and she stopped quivering fo
moment. She felt a sudden impulse to reach over and touch hi
draw him close to her, but the gulf between them was too gre
Their first big battle was over. She had fought him and won. S
had kept him from entering her body. That was a victor
Surely, it was. When he came to her and apologized, maybe the
she would allow him to exercise his husband's rights. When
someday brought her the dress she wanted, then and only the
would she allow him to share her body as well as her bed. T
quivering began again and she didn't know why. It was as
something small had broken loose inside her and was slitheri
around like a worm. As if something inside had broken open a
was bleeding very slowly.

She couldn't sleep for the rest of the night. Her decision, t
decision to deny Lemuel his marital rights, was like a scratc
woolen coat against her soft, delicate skin.

That something that was loose inside her, that little worm th
was making her bleed, began to grow in her mind until sh
thought she knew what it was. She hated Lemuel, hated him f

reasons she couldn't even say out loud because they were so little and hard and darted around so fast, making her bleed in secret because she couldn't see any wound, couldn't feel any real pain. A tapeworm devouring her innards. A parasite so small it could not be seen nor felt except in her mind. But it was hate, she was sure of that. And the wormy hate began to fester inside her like a cancer.

She touched her swollen belly and sighed. The baby would be still another weapon she could use against Lemuel Hawke.

11

Lem struck a deal with Horatio Bickham, the ambitious and miserly owner of considerable property in Woodford County. Hawke moved Roberta into a wood and stone shack built by Bickham's slaves on 80 acres of land, penned up his stock, bought seed and rolled up his shirt-sleeves. For a few shillings and a portion of each crop, the land belonged to Lem. The contract had to be renewed every year. Lem was required to clear so many acres of woodland on other property owned by Bickham. He had to provide the landowner with three cords of firewood each fall.

The work was backbreaking. Lem had to turn the fields with a crude, homemade wooden plow, harrow it with brush, harvest the crops by hand. Roberta was unable to help since she was growing heavy with child and had her hands full just doing the chores morning and night, tending to their little garden where they grew beans, corn, squash, melons, cabbage, lettuce, tomatoes and cucumbers for their own table. The distance between them had grown since that night at the inn, but they were civil to one another.

Lem finished plowing, planted small crops of corn, hemp and tobacco, knowing he'd have to tend and harvest the crops himself that first year. He planted ten acres in alfalfa, wondering how he'd ever get it mowed and stacked without help. But, the hay would feed his horses through the winter, and he hoped to have a milk cow following the sale of his tobacco crop.

Lem put his energy into his work. Roberta spoke to him when he came in from the fields at night, but when he tried to touch her, she took his hand and pushed it away.

"A man has needs," he told her, more than once.

"It hurts with the baby," she said.

So Lemuel lived with his rage and quelled his desire. Roberta continued to swell until she walked with a backward tilt and let out her thin dresses so that she could breathe. Some of the dresses rode high on her belly so that the hems were above her knees.

She did not glow like most pregnant women he had seen. Her face grew ruddy from the sun, but when Lem looked at her she seemed to be in perpetual shadow. She combed and brushed her hair at night, endlessly stroking her locks until they shone. She patched his clothes and darned his socks, cooked his meals, but she gave him none of herself. Her body was locked away from him, like her mind.

In October, he heard Roberta scream. He raced across the field to find her in agony.

"Get Mrs. Bickham," she said tightly. "Quick."

"What's the matter? What's wrong?"

"It's the baby. Hurry." She clenched her teeth and he saw that her face was drenched in sweat, her hands balled up tightly into fists as she leaned against the doorjamb, propping herself up to keep from falling.

"I'll be right back," he said. "Hold on."

He rode Hammerhead bareback at a gallop the five miles to the Bickham place.

Nancy Bickham heard him yelling for a quarter mile. She stood up from the butter churn, went to the window. She was a thin, hawk-faced woman with sunny copper hair and hazel eyes, piercing as needles.

"Mrs. Bickham, you got to come quick. My wife's having the labor pains."

"Lands," said Nancy Bickham through the window, "you get back there and put some water to boiling. I'll be there directly."

"God, hurry," said Lem, wheeling Hammerhead in a tight circle.

"I'll be there within the hour. You put that poor woman to bed and tell her to hold on."

An hour later, Horatio Bickham drove his sulky into the shadow of an oak tree bright with autumn leaves. Nancy Bickham, wearing a loose shift of striped calico, carried a satchel and an armful of towels as she trotted up to the shack on long, lean legs.

Roberta lay on the bed, drenched in sweat, her body flexing in agonizing spasms. Lem stood like a stick at the foot of the bed, his face blank as clay.

A pot of water boiled on the wood stove. Clouds of steam floated toward the sod ceiling.

Nancy took one look at Roberta and gasped.

"Land, the baby's coming now. Mr. Hawke, you go on outside. Now."

Confused, Lem seemed rooted to the floor. Nancy had to give him a shove to get him started. Before he was out the door, Mrs. Bickham had begun to strip Roberta's clothes from her. Before he reached the oak tree, where Horatio waited in the sulky, Roberta screamed. Lem hesitated, started to go back to the shack.

"Son, you come on over here. You'll just be in the way in

there. Mrs. Bickham knows what to do. We've got three daughters and three sons of our own."

Bickham climbed down from the sulky, took a pipe from his pocket, filled it from a leather tobacco pouch. He wore a shirt of fustian, trousers of gray wool, a felt slouch hat, boots made of ox-hide. He was a broad-shouldered man, at five foot six two inches shorter than his wife. His brushy face was florid from good living, bronzed lightly by the sun. His slightly bulbous nose was spider-tracked with blue veins and mottled with small red splotches. His belly hung a quarter inch over his wide belt. He stuck the pipe between pudgy lips and held a magnifying glass above the bowl to catch the rays of the sun.

"Got your pipe with you, Hawke?"

"Nope." Lem kept looking over at the shack. "I reckon I'd be too nervous to smoke right now."

Bickham directed a shaft of sunlight into the midst of the tobacco. In seconds, a thin tendril of smoke curled up out of the bowl. Bickham sucked air through the pipe until the tobacco caught. He inhaled deeply.

"It's women's business now, Hawke. Nancy will tend to your wife and newborn."

"Yes sir."

"You'll have to work harder now, Hawke. Children are a responsibility. I have six of them. Fine children. You should think about your wife, too. She'll need some help. You might want to think about buying a slave, maybe a man and wife. A Nigra woman can help with the household chores. A strong Nigra man could help you with the fieldwork. You'll have to plant bigger crops next year."

"I don't rightly think I could afford to keep slaves just now," said Lem.

"Well, you think about it, son. This is good land, but until you have grown children to work it with you, it'll sap you. Nigras are cheaper to keep than children, in the long run."

"Yes sir," said Lem, respectfully.

Fifteen minutes later, the two men heard a squawl. Lem started to bolt toward the shack, but Bickham restrained him. Then, it was quiet for a long time before Nancy appeared at the door of the cabin. She beckoned toward the two men.

"It's a boy," she told Lem, who burst past her into the shack.

Roberta's eyes fluttered. The baby lay next to her, swaddled in a tiny blanket. His face was squinched up, flushed a dark red. A shock of black hair adorned his pate. He waggled tiny fists in the air, moved his mouth as he drew air into his lungs.

Bickham slapped Lem on the back.

"By God, a son!" he exclaimed.

"Thank you, Mrs. Bickham," said Lem. "I'm going to call him Morgan after a friend of mine back in Virginia."

"That's a fine name," said Nancy.

Roberta opened her eyes for a moment, glared at Lem. The baby squawled again. Roberta turned over, her back to little Morgan Hawke.

"She'll be all right," said Nancy Bickham nervously. She picked up the baby, held it to her breast. "It's the shock."

Lem looked at the child, then at his wife.

"I reckon so," he said.

Horatio coughed.

"You need anything, you come by," he told Lem. "Come on, Nancy. It's time we let these folks to themselves."

Nancy put the baby back down on the bed, next to Roberta.

"Here, Mrs. Hawke. Your new son. You'll need to nurse him soon."

"Go away," said Roberta. Lem's face reddened and he hung his head in shame. The Bickhams left and it was quiet in the cabin for a long time.

"You ought to have been more polite," Lem said to Roberta.

"What a terrible name for a child," she said.

"It's a good strong name, Bobbie."

"It's a poor name, Lem. As poor as you're bound to be all your life."

Her words stung him. They bored so deep he knew he would never forget them.

———·———

· Morgan Hawke was a bright, playful baby. He had dark brown hair, brown eyes, rubbery features that soon became shaped into composites of Roberta and Lemuel. If anything, he favored Lem the most, which pleased the boy's father. Roberta nursed the tyke through the winter, but she refused to call him Morgan. Instead, she gave him a middle name, Llewellyn, after her father's name, and she called him Lew, which irritated Lem.

"You'll confuse the boy," he told her.

"Lew is a prettier name than Morgan. Why would you name your son after a dirty, filthy, ne'er-do-well like Silas?"

"Silas was a good man. He taught me a lot. Like I aim to teach young Morgan."

"Well, if you have your way, Lew will never amount to much. Look at you."

"We're doing just fine. I'll be able to pay my taxes next year."

"Pshaw. Look at this hovel we live in. Our place in Virginia was nicer than this."

"I'll build another room on in the spring, put a porch out front."

"It'll still be a shack," she said.

Her milk dried up when baby Morgan was five months old. Roberta seemed to lose interest in her son when he stopped suckling at her breast. The winter seemed long to Lem, but he hunted the canebrakes and roamed the forests of maple, walnut, sycamore and oak, brought home deer and turkey for the larder. He sold venison in town, added a few shillings to his meager savings. He had sold the tobacco and hemp, some of the corn following the harvest, put the money aside.

The hunting did not take away his desire for a wife, nor the fishing on cold winter streams. One evening, early in March, when there had been sun for days and little snow on the ground, he came home and hung his rifle over the door, his possibles pouch and powder horns on the wall underneath where he had set hard deer antler tips in knife-carved holes and glued them there for hooks. Supper simmered on the stove; Morgan played on the floor with a ball made of buckskin sewed around scraps of cloth. Roberta was lacing grosgrain to the front of a bodice she had made of coarse linen. She sat by the fire in a rocker he had made from a lightning-struck walnut that had aged for three years in the sun at the edge of cleared land.

"Put the boy in his crib," Lem told Roberta.

"Let him play," she said. "He ain't botherin' me none."

"Do what I done told you," he said sternly.

She looked at him, her face splashed with firelight.

"You better set down and put some of those vittles I fixed in your belly," she said.

"You can have it hard or easy," he said, grabbing Morgan up and carrying him to the dark corner of the room where his crib stood in the shadow. The boy made sounds in his throat. Lem put him in the crib.

"Don't you start up," said Roberta.

"I aim to take my pleasure of you," he said.

She set the bodice aside, stiffened in the chair. Morgan cooed in his crib, filling up the silence between them. Lem strode over to her, stood above her. He had filled out; his muscles had hardened at the plow and the stump.

"You leave me be," she said.

Lem slipped a hand under her armpit, lifted her from the chair. He looked deep into her nut-brown eyes, stroked the fine brown hair that took on sheen from the dancing fire and remembered other times when she wanted him as much as he wanted her.

She jerked away from him, but he grabbed her, drew her close. "I'll say please, first," he said. "Let it be like it was."

"It can't never be like it was," she said and her nostrils flared with anger.

"Then, by God, it'll be like it's got to be."

He lifted her up in his arms and started to carry her to their bed in the corner of the room opposite the place where Morgan slept. Roberta began to kick and pummel his head and shoulders with her fists.

"Put me down," she said.

He threw her onto the bed. The wooden slats took up the shock of her sudden weight and the sound they made was like groaning. Lem blew out the lamps until there was only the firelight throwing shadows around the room. He slipped his galluses from his shoulders and the ribands hung from his waist like military gun-slings.

Roberta tried to get up from the bed, but he blocked her way, pushed her back down.

"You're cruel," she said.

"You don't know what cruel is," he said, thinking of how he had wanted her all these months and how coldly she had treated him.

"You're no better than a savage."

"If you don't get out of them clothes, Bobbie, you're going to be sewin' well into summer."

"Damn you," she said.

Lem stripped to his skin and went after her. She struggled, trying to fight him off. Little Morgan saw the shadowy figures from his crib, heard his mother scream. He began to cry. The noise of the shaking bed scared him. He whimpered for a long time before he dropped off to sleep, alone and untended.

Lem added a room onto the shack in the spring, as he had promised. Late in the summer, he built a porch onto the front of the shack. He hired one of Horatio's sons to help him during the harvest and still earned enough to pay his taxes, set money aside. For Morgan's first birthday, on October 7, 1794, he gave the boy a beagle puppy that he had gotten from Bickham in trade. Lem named the puppy Friar Tuck. Morgan called him Tut. At Christmas, he gave Roberta enough money to buy herself a dress. He made a wooden rifle for Morgan, sewed him his first pair of moccasins.

As Kentucky grew, so did little Morgan. Roberta began to spend more and more time in Lexington, since she had begun working in a print shop during the winters. Although she didn't tell Lem, she ran into Barry O'Neil in town one day when Morgan was five years old.

Barry was dressed like a gentleman in a striped waistcoat, top hat, shiny boots. Roberta, wearing an inexpensive summer frock, tried to avoid him.

"Roberta," he called. "I've been looking all over for you." He tipped his fine beaver hat and the sun flared in his red hair for a moment.

"Me?"

"Why, yes. I knew you had come to Lexington. I've hoped to see you every day."

"Barry, I—I must get to work."

He stood close to her, blocking her way. He smiled at her. His eyes scoured her, brought a rosy blush to her cheeks.

"Where do you work?"

"Kroger's printing."

"Why, that's right on my way. I'll walk with you. I'm a hatter. My office and plant is just over on Fourth and Main. Kroger's is in the next block."

"I know." She had passed B & J Hatters almost every day since they had opened a year before. She saw it on her noon walks to the dress shops on Broadway. She had never associated it with Barry O'Neil. "Do you own the establishment?" she asked, trying to appear sophisticated.

"With my uncle John. Oh, it's a fine business. There are only five or six hatters here, but we're the biggest. We make beautiful and fashionable hats of wool and fine felt hats of raccoon, beaver and muskrat. We buy only the highest quality furs."

"I've seen your hats," she said. "They are truly most fashionable. The one you're wearing now is most attractive. It looks elegant." She looked at his moustache. It was neatly trimmed, made his lips more sensual than she remembered.

He laughed, and took her arm as they crossed the bridge over the little spring-fed stream that coursed through the city. The dreary tanyards bordered both sides and beyond them, Lexington's industries thrived, the powder mills, print shops, potteries, ropewalks, breweries, ironworks. People bustled past them, smiled at them both. Some nodded to Barry and spoke his name, calling him "Mr. O'Neil." Roberta was impressed.

"What do you do for Bill Kroger?" he asked.

"Everything. I file the type and the furniture, help set type in the chases. I'm learning to do the books."

"Ah, then you might be interested in a proposition I have for you."

"For me?"

"Yes. I need someone to help with our accounts. You would be perfect."

"Oh, I'm not very good at figures yet. Really I'm not."

"Well, I have a lady who will teach you. Think about it. I'll pay you more than Kroger does. Besides, it will give us a chance to see more of each other. Lexington is growing. Kentucky is an important state. You should be a part of it. I think you would look wonderful wearing some of our hats when buyers come to call."

"Me? A model? It could only be for the winter. I must work on the farm in spring and summer."

"We'll see. Kroger is a slaver at heart. I'll bet he doesn't invite you to tea in the afternoons."

"Well, no."

"There, you see. We always have tea in the afternoons, talk about new fashions, look at hat designs, talk to artists. Important people stop by to chat. Dressmakers show us their latest goods. Some of our ladies even try them on and they can buy them at a discount."

"It sounds wonderful," she said, thinking of the few dresses she owned. She had made them herself and they were all a step or two behind what she saw in the shops.

Barry squeezed her arm and she felt a tingling shock ripple through her flesh.

"Why don't you come by tomorrow 'bout noon? I'll buy you lunch and show you around."

"Why, that would be fine," she said, surprised at her own boldness.

They reached the offices and plant of B & J Hatters. The name stood out in large letters on the outside of the brick building, one of the few in Lexington.

"I've missed you," said Barry, as he stood at the entrance. "Did you think about me?"

"A little," she admitted. But, it was more than a little. She had often wondered what would have happened had she let Barry partake of her favors that last time they saw each other. It was wicked of her to think such things, but she couldn't help herself.

He doffed his hat.

"See you tomorrow," he said.

"Yes," she said. "Tomorrow."

She skipped lightly down the street. She hesitated before entering the shop that bore the legend: KROGER'S PRINTING. Her heart thrummed with excitement. She clutched her purse to her breast, took a deep breath to clear her mind, compose herself.

Suddenly, she didn't want to enter the print shop. Not now, not ever again.

She looked down the block toward the hattery. She wondered if she could wait until tomorrow.

Roberta had already made up her mind what she was going to do. She was going to live the life she wanted.

Before the farm life crushed her; before Lem stripped away her last shred of dignity and hope. Lem didn't care about her suffering, about living poor. He didn't long for better things as she did. He offered her no hope for a better life. That's what she needed. Hope.

Barry O'Neil could give it to her.

12

During those winter days, when Roberta was working in town, Lem took care of the raising of their boy, Morgan. Sometimes Bickham's slave, Calvin Moon, would come by, bringing some of the slave children to play with young Morgan. Sometimes Lem would take him over to the Bickhams' where he could play with the older children. The boy was always ready to come home, but he said he liked Mrs. Bickham. Horatio, he told his father, scared him.

In Morgan's seventh year, Lem made a little rifle for him. Roberta was working for Barry O'Neil at the hattery, had been there for two years. Lem thought she was still working for Kroger because she hadn't told him about Barry. She kept the extra money for herself, bought dresses which she kept at a friend's, another woman who worked in the hattery, Ernestine Gerson. Ernestine was the head bookkeeper and had taught Roberta how to keep the ledgers, where to file receipts, bills of lading, orders, employee records.

Lem found an old .36 caliber rifle barrel in a heap of scrap at the edge of Bickham's land one day. The stock had rotted away, but the lock was still intact, a small German mechanism that could be cleaned up, oiled, made to work. Both the rifle and lock were rusted, but he soaked them in hot grease, bear oil, to make them shine. He carved a new stock from walnut, sawed off part of the long barrel and set it in the rough hollow of the stock for measure. Morgan watched the whole process, compared it to his father's long rifle.

"Papa's goin' to make you a rifle just like his'n," Lem told him.

"Can I shoot it?"

"For certain."

"I'll make you a possibles pouch, too, and powder horns. We'll find us some good flints."

"I want to go huntin' with you, Pa."

"We'll do it," said Lem. "You'll be a reg'lar Kings Mountain boy when we get finished."

The boy doted on his father. Morgan followed Lem everywhere, especially during the winter when Roberta spent long hours in town. There were times when she said she had to work late and would not come home for supper. At such times, Lem fed Morgan and they worked on the rifle until their eyes drooped with tiredness. Often, Roberta would return home to find Lem and their son asleep on the floor in front of the fire, the cabin smelling of bear oil, sweat and burned meat.

"I don't want to be a King's Mountain boy," said Morgan. "I want to be your boy."

"Them was fightin' men, son. Happened about the time I was born. My pa, he was there."

"What happened to him?"

"Your grandpap? Why, nothin' son, I don't reckon." Lem frowned, pulled in a deep breath. "You ask too many questions for a little feller."

The truth was that Lem didn't know what had happened to his

father. One day he just disappeared. But it was after his ma had
been seeing a man Lem knew only as one of his uncles. After his
pa left, the uncle, a man named Cletus McEllerby, moved in and
slept in his ma's bed. Now, he knew that Cletus was no kin, but
he never had figured out why his pa had run off like that without
saying good-by.

In Lem's hands, the file and the rasp were sculptor's tools,
capable of great artistry. The rifle he fashioned for Morgan was
not fancy, but he took off all the metal burrs, burnished the iron
down past the rust, worked the stock delicately with emory
cloth he had made himself of grit and linen. At a table set in the
center of the room, in front of the hearth, he polished and
carved, hammered in a tenon that made the short barrel fit snug
in the stock. He made a new front blade sight, a fancy buckhorn
for the rear. He oiled the lock until it worked smooth and
quietly. The spring was tight enough to set sparks off quartz.

One morning, before noon, Lem sat again at the table, wiped
the rifle down, held it to his shoulder, sighted down its 19-inch
barrel.

Morgan, who had been going through his father's possibles
pouch, one of his favorite pastimes, looked up. Lem held the
finished rifle out to him.

"Pa! Is it really finished?"

"It's your'n, Morgan. We'll load her up with maybe twenty
grains of powder, see can you shoot true enough to pop the eye
out of a squirrel."

Morgan took the rifle in his hands. He held it with a kind of
reverence, looking at the polished walnut stock that gleamed
from butt to an inch below the muzzle.

"It's even got a ramrod," said the boy, grinning.

"Be careful, it ain't the best. Mighty small caliber, so the rod's
thin as any I ever saw."

Morgan held the rifle to his shoulder. It felt light in his hands.

He sighed with pleasure as he swung the barrel toward the door, then back to the stove, squinching his left eye shut.

"It's real beautiful," said Morgan. "But you ain't put no flint on it yet."

"Give me back the rifle and we'll set you in a flint. I got me some of Brandon's best from England I been saving."

Lem walked over to the bed, slid out a small box. He took it over to the table where he had been working. Morgan's eyes grew wide as Lem opened the box. It contained more than two dozen flints, all chipped square, but of different sizes.

"My own flint," breathed Morgan.

"See you set it right in the cock," said his father. "You put the flat side either up'ards or down'ards. Depends on how big it is and what its shape is. You want to set it just so."

Lem twisted the screw on the cock, the arm that held the flint, opening the jaws.

"Fetch me a small piece of leather. Might be a piece in my possibles bag, son."

Morgan gathered up his father's tools and such, put them back in the pouch. He brought the pouch over to the table. Morgan felt around inside, retrieved a small patch of leather. Lem took his knife and cut a square piece just big enough to cushion the flint. He folded the leather over the flint, leaving the striking edge exposed.

"There," he said to Morgan. "We just push this outfit in the jaws of the cock, screw her down a bit and check to see it hits the frizzen just so."

Lem let the cock down gently and hunched over. He and Morgan peered at the place where the flint touched the frizzen.

"Every part of that flint's got to scare sparks off that frizzen plate," said Lem.

"Whole thing's got to touch," said Morgan seriously.

Lem smiled.

"You pay partic'lar attention after each shot to see it stays square and strikes true."

"I will, sir," said Morgan, an obedient tone in his voice.

Lem jiggled the flint until it was perfectly set, then screwed the jaws down tight on the leather.

"There," he said to himself. "Morg, get Tut and let's go see can he scare us up a rabbit."

"Yes, Pa," said Morgan, taking the proffered rifle.

Lem stood up, wiped oily hands on his woolen trousers. He grabbed his wool-lined buckskin jacket off a peg, picked up his rifle, horns, the possibles pouch off the table.

"Come along, son," he said. "Let's make that rifle talk."

Morgan beamed. He grabbed his little coat from his bed, wrestled into it. He set a coonskin cap on his head, stuffed mittens in his pocket. He shouldered the new rifle like a soldier, marched outside behind his father.

There was snow on the ground; the sky was overcast. Their breaths made steam in the frosty air. Lem looked at the sky, the tendrils of smoke rising from the sugar camps in the hills. Bickham had the only sugar house around and he forbade Lem from tapping the maples in the gaunt forests that surrounded his rented land. But, he could buy a white loaf from his landlord at low cost and Lem supposed that was good of the man. Roberta and Morgan could not live without sugar.

"More snow comin'. Your ma may not get back from town tonight, less'n she leaves pretty quick." Sometimes Roberta stayed over when it snowed heavily. From the look of the sky, she might not be home for several days unless she rode in pretty quick. Lem had bought her a gentle bay mare, which he called Rose. Roberta rode the mare back and forth to town, stabled the horse when she had to spend the night at her girlfriend's. Lem didn't know the woman, just her first name, Ernestine. Roberta said she worked for Kroger and was a widow, lived alone.

"I don't care," said Morgan, interrupting Lem's thoughts. "I just want to shoot this beautiful rifle."

Lem knew how Morgan felt. He remembered his first rifle. It was so heavy he could barely lift it, but there was power in the holding of it. There was even more power in the buck and roar of it when he had touched it off for the first time.

Morgan called the dog.

"Here, Tut. Come here, Tut."

The beagle rounded a corner of the house, snow flying from his paws, ears flattened against his neck.

"Well, he's about ready," said Lem.

"Pa, that hound's plumb ready," said Morgan, stretching himself to be tall next to his father.

"Let's set us some kindling wood to shoot at," said Lem. "See can we find us a place to stick 'em. Grab a bunch of them little ones off the pile." Lem pointed to the stack of kindling next to the woodpile. Morgan scurried off, Tut hard on his heels, to grab several pieces of kindling.

Lem picked up several three-foot, unsplit logs, carried them in back of the cabin. He made a square, cabinlike structure two feet high. He began to pile snow inside. Morgan saw what he was doing and joined in. They heaped snow up and then Lem started poking kindling sticks in the snow at three-inch intervals.

"Those be our targets?" asked Morgan.

"Yep. We're going to start you off at twenty yards."

Lem walked off twenty yards, Morgan tagging along in his tracks. Tut, the beagle, scratched a bed for himself, digging through the snow until he struck solid ground. He kept busy at that, widening it, until it was big enough for him to plop down and make it warm.

Lem cradled his rifle and pulled the peg out of the primer horn with his teeth. He sprinkled powder in the pan, blew on it to get rid of the excess. Morgan handed his rifle to his father.

"Do mine," he said.

"We got to get you a horn, boy."

"Yes sir. I got to get me a horn. Two of 'em like you got."

"You need a heap of things, Morgan. There's one thing you ain't asked me about. It's real important."

Morgan cocked a squinched eye and looked at his father, then at the new rifle. A puzzled expression etched furrows in the boy's forehead, knitted his brows. Then, his face softened and he cried out.

"Lead ball!" he shrieked. "I don't have no ball to shoot."

Lem grinned, dug into a pocket of his coat. He pulled out a handful of .035 balls.

"I cast these when you was asleep," he told his son. "Got you a mold, too, at the smith's. And you can use my patches 'til you cut some for yourself. Let's load you up. You watch what I do and do it that way ever' time."

Lem showed the boy how to measure the powder. He put a ball in the center of Morgan's palm, poured powder from his big cowhorn on top of the ball. When enough grains had trickled to cover part of the ball, he took the ball away.

"Pour that down your barrel, son. Don't spill any."

Morgan set his rifle butt in the snow, made a funnel of his hand. He poured the powder down the barrel. Some of the powder stuck to his palm. He rubbed it off on the muzzle.

"Now, pick up your piece and whack it a few times just above the lock to shake that powder down all the way."

Morgan did that.

"Now for patch and ball," said Lem.

Lem laid a strip of greased patching across the muzzle of Morgan's rifle. He placed the ball on the cloth, poked it down inside the barrel until it was flush with the muzzle. He took a patch knife from his belt and cut off the excess material. He rammed ball and pouch six inches down the barrel with a short starter. Then he took the ramrod and seated the ball.

"I can do that," said Morgan.

"Here, take my little horn and prime your pan. Point the barrel toward the ground and away from you. Once you've put powder in the pan, you've got yourself a dangerous weapon."

Lem watched as Morgan poured fine powder into the pan. He poured too much.

"Now, blow gently on it. You've got so much powder in there you'll burn your face off when that flint strikes sparks. You want just enough to cover the bottom of the pan."

Morgan blew away the excess powder.

"Now, take aim at that stick farthest to the left," said Lem. "When you're 'most ready, pull back the cock until she clicks. Make sure the frizzen is down. Hold the rifle snug to your shoulder and catch you a little breath and hold it. When you've got your barrel steady, you squeeze the trigger. Real smooth and easy."

"I'm ready, Pa."

"Go on then and make some thunder."

The boy stepped up to the imaginary firing line and faced the target as he had seen his father do many times. He set the cock back full and shouldered the small rifle. Lem watched him, saying not a word. He noticed how the boy lined up his sights on the target, held steady. He saw Morgan take a shallow breath, hold it in without strain.

Morgan squeezed the trigger. Fire and smoke belched from the muzzle of the .36 caliber. Lem's eyes tracked to the target. The stick snapped in two.

"I got it, Pa," said Morgan. "Looky yonder."

"I see it, son," said Lem. He touched the boy's shoulder, gave it a gentle squeeze. "You're a right smart shot, less'n it was just luck."

"Warn't no luck to it," said Morgan. "I saw that stick and I held on it real steady."

"Umm, you did that." His father hoisted his rifle, pulled back the cock until the sear engaged. He aimed for the second stick from the left, but it was all one flowing motion. Cocking, aiming, firing. The stick broke in half. White smoke blew back on the boy and his father. The shot echoed in the snowy hills, then faded into nothingness.

"Good shot," said Morgan, his voice thin as a girl's. His breath mingled its vapors with the smoke.

"Maybe you got the gift," said Lem. "Maybe you've got the hawk-eye. Let's reload and see can we scare up a hare or two before noon."

"A rabbit? Oh, Pa, I can't wait."

Tut whined.

Man and boy reloaded their rifles. This time, Morgan did it all himself. Lem watched him carefully. The boy made no mistakes. He would, Lem knew, but for now, he was mighty careful.

They started out for the woods. Tut ranged back and forth in front of them, crossing and recrossing the rabbit and bird tracks that threaded the open pasture. Soon, he gave throat to his hunting cry and dashed off on a fresh spoor trail. The dog disappeared in the woods. His high-pitched yelps carried on the clear winter air.

"Tut's got him a rabbit trail," said Morgan.

"If he's good, he'll run the game our way. You be set, son. You see the rabbit, you start your aim behind it. Swing your rifle on the same line, squeeze off a shot just as the muzzle blocks out the rabbit. Foller on through as if you ain't shot yet."

"I been practicin' that with my wooden gun, Pa."

Lem swelled up with pride. The boy could barely straggle along through the snow. His trousers were wet to the knees, yet he was game, game as any boy might be. It was plumb cold and there wasn't a trace of a shiver in the boy.

Tut's yelps unraveled like ribbons to a higher pitch. They faded only to grow loud and piercing again. Lem and Morgan drew closer to the edge of the forested hill where Tut had begun tracking the rabbit. Lem put out a hand as Morgan caught up with him.

"We'll wait him out," said his father.

Morgan nodded, his dark eyes glittering. He gripped the rifle with mittened hands, a thumb on the dog cock of his rifle. The beagle's yapping grew more excited. Then, the rabbit broke from cover, angled out of the woods on a line that would bisect the open field.

"Take him," said Lem.

Morgan thumbed back the cock. He shouldered the rifle. He aimed at the running rabbit. The snowshoe hare bounded in erratic patterns, zigzagging away from the two hunters. Morgan fired and the rabbit changed course. A puff of snow erupted several yards behind the animal. Tut broke from the woods, short stubby legs flying, in full cry.

Lem shouldered his rifle, tracked the darting rabbit, squeezed off a shot.

"Just like on a string," he said aloud as the rabbit jerked up short, flew straight up in the air, then fell to the snow in a furry heap.

"You got him!" screamed Morgan. The boy raced toward the downed rabbit. Lem laughed and slogged after him.

Tut reached the rabbit first. It was still kicking. The beagle bellered as if it had been cuffed, circled the twitching hare as if he had gone mad.

Morgan snatched the rabbit by the hind legs, held him proudly aloft.

"You was way behind him," said his father.

"I know."

"Know what you done wrong?"

"I think I stopped swinging the rifle barrel."

"Likely," said Lem. "You'll do better next time."

"Well, you sure got him, Pa. He's a big 'un too."

"Want to gut him out?"

"Do I?"

"Take my knife. Get his entrails. You can skin him back home."

"Can I have his fur, Pa?"

"You got to tan it yourself."

"Oh, I will, I will," said the boy, excited.

"Think about this one next time you shoot. Think about how hungry you could get and have only one ball. You might depend on a rabbit's meat for your supper one day."

"We got plenty of meat, Pa."

Lem frowned. He handed Morgan his knife, butt first. The boy took it eagerly.

"Might come a time when a rabbit's all you got. You miss him and use up all your powder and ball it would sure do powerful bad things to your disposition."

"I won't miss next time, Pa. I promise cross my heart."

Lem laughed. The boy made a mess of gutting out the rabbit until his father showed him how to make a clean gut.

"Don't saw at it. Keep your knife sharp and slit your game from asshole to rib cage."

Morgan made a sound raspy with disgust.

"Reach in and pull out the guts, just strip 'em out. If you was really hungry, you'd clean them entrails and fry 'em. Save the gizzard and the heart."

The boy watched his father deftly remove the entrails, slice through the windpipe, crack the anal cavity open. Lem washed the insides with snow. He stuck the rabbit inside his shirt at the back. It made a bulge along the small of his back.

They heard a sound.

"Listen," said Lem.

"Them's sleigh bells, Pa."

"Right enough. Somebody's a-comin'."

"Might be Calvin. Or Mrs. Bickham, maybe."

They knew the sleighs by the sounds of their bells. Th

woodcutter's used the heavier, clanking bells. The Bickham
sleigh used the smaller, higher-pitched bells. Lem and Morgan
started walking toward the road that bordered the field. Lem's
leased property stood west of Bickham's, well off the main road
to Lexington.

"Wonder why somebody'd be comin' here," said Lem. He and
Morgan had only seen the Bickham sleigh on the main roads.

"I don't know, Pa."

As they crossed the open field, the sleigh came into view
where the hedgerow and the forest parted and the road came
through. It was drawn by a single dray horse wearing blinders.

"Can you see who it is?" Lem asked his son.

"Calvin, I think. Only one person near as I can figger."

The boy was beginning to sound like him, Lem thought.

"Sure enough."

Lem waved. The sleigh veered from its course and headed
straight for them, across the snowy field. The snow was wet
enough to pack. The sleigh left parallel tracks in its wake. The
bells crackled like crystal, making sweet music. Tut started
barking.

"Shut your gob," said Lem.

"Shut up," said Morgan and the dog crept away, its tail
drooping.

The sleigh pulled up a few yards from the man and the boy, its
runners hissing underneath the sound of bells.

"Whoa, Ben," said the driver, Calvin Moon. The horse
slowed to a stop.

"Calvin," said Lem.

"Mista Lem, Mizriz Bickham says to come quick."

"Something the matter?"

"It's your Mizriz. She come to the house and done fainted I
'pose. Mizriz Bickham says to take you there in the sled."

"Go on back home, Morgan," said Lem.

"But, Pa—"

"Don't you argue with me, boy. You take this rabbit and Tut and get on home. I'll be back directly."

Lem took the rabbit out of his shirt, handed it to Morgan. The boy looked as if he was going to cry. He took the rabbit by the hind legs.

"You got you a nice hare, Mista Lem," said Calvin.

"Pa," said Morgan.

Lem climbed up on the seat next to Calvin. He did not look at his son, but nudged the slave in the side.

Calvin slapped the reins against Ben's rump. The horse took up the slack in the traces. The sleigh began to move. The horse turned in a wide circle, headed back the way it had come. Soon the new tracks blended into the old.

"What's the matter with my wife?" asked Lem when they were out of earshot of the boy.

"She pretty sick, Mista Lem. Her face all pale and white like a ghost and she having trouble breathing. Mista Horatio, he done gone hisself for the doctor."

Lem said nothing. He looked back and saw Morgan still standing in the middle of the field. He looked so small and alone out there. Tut sat there on his haunches like an andiron, next to the boy. The sleigh bells jangled mindlessly and a few flakes of snow began to fall. Calvin Moon took the buggy whip and snapped it over the rump of the horse. The sleigh picked up speed, the runners gliding over the packed snow of the road, the brassy tintinnabulation of the bells settling into a steady, frantic annoying monotony.

Lem handed his coat to the black woman. A little black boy dusted the snow from Hawke's trousers and moccasins. The woman shook out his coat.

"You can go inside now," she said. "Mizriz Bickham, she's with the doctuh."

"I'll show you where they is," said the little boy.

Lem felt strange entering the Bickham house. He had never been inside before. Calvin had stopped the sleigh by the back door. Lem followed the servant boy through the hallway and into a large kitchen with the biggest stove he had ever seen. Utensils hung from hoops attached to the ceiling. The house was two stories and looked bigger than a barn from the outside.

"This year's the parlor," said the boy. "I'll tell Mizriz Bickham you's here."

The boy disappeared. Lem looked around the room. The furniture was elegant, probably expensive. There was a Philadelphia Chippendale side chair made of gleaming mahogany with a matching hassock, a scroll-ended English couch, a cabriole armchair, a walnut desk and chair. The carpet felt soft and velvety to the soles of his moccasined feet. It was still light out, but the snow was falling faster and heavier now and the room was growing dark. He hoped Morgan had sense enough to bring more firewood in and to put logs on the fire.

Lem heard voices. One was Horatio Bickham's. Another belonged to a man he didn't know. He heard Nancy Bickham's soft voice underneath. He heard the Negro boy's high-pitched squeak, then footsteps broke the conversation, grew louder as they approached.

"Lemuel," said Nancy, entering the parlor. "I'm so glad Calvin found you. Come with me."

"What's the matter with Roberta?" asked Lem.

"The poor dear. She collapsed right at our doorstep. I don't think the fall hurt her. Calvin was right there."

"She fell?"

"From her horse. The doctor's here, talking to Horatio. We'll find out more from him."

Lem felt queasy. His stomach shrank and quivered. He and Mrs. Bickham entered the foyer of the house. Horatio Bickham stood at the foot of the stairs, listening to a short stub of a man wearing a wrinkled coat. His collar was soiled, unpressed, his shoes were unshined, muddy and damp from melted snow. He held a small leather satchel by its handle. The satchel was marred by wrinkles and minor rips and tears.

"Ah, here's the woman's husband now," said Bickham.

The man turned to look at Lem.

"Doctor Guenther, this is Lemuel Hawke," said Nancy.

"Your wife had a spell. I gave her some powders. You may take her home in a few moments."

"What's wrong with her?" asked Lem.

The doctor sniffled, wiped his nose with a handkerchief.

"She's going to have a baby," said Guenther. "In another two or three months, I'd say. I'd advise her to avoid the tippling houses until she's had her child." He turned to Bickham. "Horatio, I'll be going now."

"Thank you, Kurt," said Bickham. "I'll show you out."

"What a minute," said Lem. "My wife don't go to no tipplin' house. She's a temperate woman, same as me."

"Whatever you say, son," said the doctor.

Lem watched them walk to the door. Bickham stepped outside with the doctor.

"Do you want to go upstairs and see her?" asked Nancy.

"I don't understand," said Lem, dazed. "He said she was going to have a baby. And, what did he mean by sayin' Roberta's been intemperate."

"Perfectly natural. About the baby, I mean. And we did smell spirits on your wife's breath. The aroma was quite strong and unmistakable."

"Yes'm," said Lem. But he was puzzled about both matters. He had never known Roberta to take or want strong spirits. And he had not shared Roberta's bed in more than six months. The queasy feeling in his stomach did not go away. He fought down the sickness, swayed inwardly for balance on the pitching deck of his imagination.

———·———

Three months later, Roberta gave birth to a baby girl. She named it Chastity, which puzzled Lem more than a little. More startling than the child's name, however, was her shock of red hair. The girl was thin and sickly. She died six weeks later of strangling colic. It seemed to Lem that the infant had no will to live. She cried all the time and did not take to the milk of her mother's breast. Roberta acted restless and inattentive, seemed almost relieved when the baby turned blue during a choking spell and expired in Roberta's arms. Lem dug a grave on the corner of his leased property and made a small coffin out of maple. Morgan didn't understand what had happened to his baby sister. Lem tried to explain death to him, but he couldn't tell if Morgan understood. Roberta sank into a deep depression after Lem interred the child.

She took to her bed for a week. He and Morgan waited on her, fed her soup and broth, tried to cheer her up. A week later, she announced she was going back to work. She also told him that she was going to move into town.

"But this is your home," Lem said. Morgan was making a snowman out by Chastity's grave.

"No, Lem, it's your home. I can no longer bear to stay in this squalid hut."

"You're just walkin' out?"

"You can live in town, if you want. You'll never amount to anything staying here. There's jobs aplenty for a man with gumption, for a man who wants to better hisself."

"This is good land, good soil. In a few years, I ought to be able to buy it from Bickham."

"You couldn't meet his price," she said.

"Well, somewheres else, then."

"Lem, don't you understand? I don't want to be a farmer's wife. I want to wear fine clothes and be gentry. I want to improve my lot in life."

"Well, by God, you are a farmer's wife. You can't just walk off and leave Morg and me. Hell, what do you think I'm working for? It's for you, Bobbie. All of it's for you."

"Well, I don't want it. Not this. I want to have a life."

"Can't you just be patient?"

"I've tried that."

"Bobbie, there's somethin' else to it."

"Damn you, Lem. Isn't that enough for you?"

"How'd you get that baby? It warn't mine." As soon as he had said it, he was sorry. He had gone too far. It had just slipped out.

But, the thought had been buried in his mind, buried and rising up out of its grave every night to torment his sleep, to make him wake up angry every morning.

She slapped him, then, and he saw the rage in her eyes. He saw, too, the loathing she had for him, a look like none other he had ever seen. It cut through him, cut deep, and hurt like a knife driven into his heart. He stood there, not feeling the sting of the slap, but hurting so bad he wanted to die in his tracks.

"Don't you ever accuse me of anything like that again," she said, her gaze fixed on him so tight, her eyes flickering so dangerously, he stepped back. Her face was a bloodless mask, chalk white with rage. He wanted to protest, but his voice caught in his throat and the moment was gone as she wheeled away from him. He stood there, transfixed, as she packed her satchel, saddled up Rose and rode away without a word. Little Morgan saw her going, came running in from the field. He called to her, but she never spoke.

"Where's Mama goin'?" asked Morgan as he ran to his father, breathless.

"She's goin' to live in town for a while."

"She is?"

"You come on inside now, boy. We got to do some thinkin'."

"What about, Pa?"

But Lem couldn't answer him. Something had happened, but he didn't know how to explain it, neither to himself nor to his son. Roberta had gone crazy when the baby girl had died. That was the only thing that made any sense. Maybe it was just temporary. Maybe she would get over her anger in time. That was all he could hope for because she left him no room for anything else. He had never seen such a look of pure hatred in another human being's eyes. For a moment, he thought she meant to kill him, would have killed him in some way, if she could. That terrible look in her eyes still gave him the shivers.

Lem and the boy ate a quiet meal that evening. Morgan started to ask again where his mother was, but his father shook his head and there were tears in his eyes. Lem jumped at every sound. He kept hearing the sound of hoofbeats, a footfall on the snow, a faint tap against the door. He tried to shut out all the sounds by banging the plates and utensils when he was cleaning up after supper. He threw more logs on the fire. He turned the lamp in the front room up high and kept the curtains open so the light would shine out. He went out, late, and looked at the snow glistening in the moonlight and let the cold numb him, deaden his thoughts until they were like frozen wood and empty of all but a bitter, distant pain.

"Pa, you comin' to bed?"

Lem turned, saw the boy and Friar Tuck silhouetted in the doorway. Saffron light splashed on the snow outside.

"I'm a-comin'," said Lem, a catch in his throat as if he had swallowed sand.

His moccasins crunched on the snow. In the far woods, he heard the throaty crow of an owl and the faint ribbons of laughter from the sugar camp on the ridge. The beagle wagged its tail as he approached. Morgan shivered in his pajamas.

"It's cold outside," said Morgan. "Mighty cold, Pa."

Lem said nothing. It was cold inside, too.

———·———

It was another six months before Lem saw Roberta again. Spring came and he and Morgan did the planting, working long hard days from dark to dark, plowing, seeding, cutting poles for a corral he put together at odd moments, mending harness at night. He went on lone hunts for quail and woodcock in the canebrakes, called the turkey gobblers down off the hardwood ridges, shot a 10-point whitetail buck at the steaming pond one glistening morning in April. Morgan missed his mother and Lem promised him that he'd go looking for her when he could find a clear day. But, in truth, he dreaded seeing her again. He never wanted to see that look in her eyes again.

But in early summer, when the meadow larks called from the fence posts and crows ragged a sleepy barn owl in the hayloft, Lem decided it was time to talk to his wife. It was early June in 1807 when he summoned the courage to go into town. Morgan was thirteen, growing like a thistle, his hair down to his shoulders, his cowlick drooping like a leafed-out willow branch.

"I could cut your hair, boy," said Lem, "but we might hunt us up a barber in Lexington."

"Oh goody," said Morgan, his eyes bright as coppers in a stream.

"You be ready tomorrow, early," said his father. He said nothing about going to find Roberta.

The next day, shortly after dawn, with the chores all done, Lem saddled Hammerhead, tied the beagle, Friar Tuck, to a crossbrace on the new corral he had finished putting up a few weeks before. He set out pork scraps and bones to keep the dog happy, filled a wooden pail with water, tied it to a pole with rope so the dog wouldn't spill it. He donned his best linsey-woolsey shirt, cotton trousers, slicked up his moccasins, brushed his wool felt hat free of lint. He saw to it that Morgan was neat and his hair combed and greased enough to keep his cowlick from spiking up in the back of his head. Lem carried a few pounds and some loose shillings in a small possibles pouch he draped over his wide leather belt.

"Come on, boy, let's look up your ma," said Lem as he climbed into the saddle. He had thought about telling Morgan all night. No sense in fooling the boy. "Get you a haircut too, maybe."

Morgan's face lit up with excitement. He took his father's outstretched hand and flew up behind the cantle.

"Hold on," said Lem.

"I'm ready, Pa."

It took them an hour and a half to ride to Lexington for they didn't dawdle along the way. They waved to travelers, other farmers, Calvin Moon, Nancy Bickham, but they didn't stop to explain their mission. Lem kept looking at his fingernails. He had trimmed them down with his patch knife and dug most of the dirt out. Morgan held onto his belt as he bobbed up and down like a sack of potatoes on the back of the horse.

Quail piped in the fencerows and martins flickered like feathered darts as they scooped insects above the summer ponds. Morgan laughed at a funny scarecrow in one of the fields they passed.

"It looks like Calvin Moon," said Morgan.

"It sure does," agreed his father.

Lem was surprised at how Lexington had grown. Everywhere he looked, new buildings were going up and they all seemed to be made of brick. Men hammered and sawed; hod carriers hefted their loads, streamed like ants back and forth between brick piles and structures, groaning under their heavy loads. Morgan stared at the workmen in silent fascination.

"Where we goin', Pa?"

"Why, to where your ma works, son. To Kroger's printing establishment, I reckon. This is Tuesday and she ought to be hard at work."

"Where is it?"

"I don't rightly know," replied Lem, "but we'll find it."

"I never saw so many big buildings," said Morgan. Block after block of finished brick buildings clustered around the center of town. The streets were broad and hard-packed. The store fronts became a bewildering maze. Lem had never seen so many different shops and he struggled to sort them out. Finally, at the courthouse, he dismounted and asked a young man for directions.

"Where might I find Kroger's Printing Shop?"

"Why, they was over on Third and Broadway," said the youth. "On Third, yes sir. Since last year."

"Can you p'int me?"

"Yonder," said the boy, extending an arm. "You can't miss it. Center of the block. Biggest building there."

Carriages wheeled through the center of town; men and women scurried from every direction, all seemingly in a hurry with urgent business to transact. Men yelled at dray horses pulling wagons loaded with cotton and pottery and farm implements. Morgan's eyes widened. He had been to Lexington before, but never on such a busy day, and not for more than a year. Calvin usually brought out supplies on his regular runs into town. Since his mother had left home, his father had shown no interest in going into town. It had been lonesome with just the two of them. The work had made the time pass, but the nights were long. Often, Morgan wept into his pillow, holding back so his father wouldn't hear him, burying his face in the pillow until his eyes grew tired and the sadness left him hollow inside.

Somehow, Lem found his way to Kroger's. The sign over the large brick front said KROGER'S PRINTING COMPANY in huge letters painted black with yellow gold trim.

"Is that it, Pa?" asked Morgan when they pulled up to the hitching post sticking about two feet out of the ground.

"Looks sure enough like it."

He tied the reins to the hitch-ring. Morgan slid off Hammerhead's rump, landed squarely on both feet. He followed his father as Lem entered the shop.

Behind the long wooden counter, a man and a woman worked at facing desks, leafing through sheafs of papers, spindling some, putting others in square boxes. The girl wrote something in a ledger, then looked up.

"Good morning," she said. "May I help you?"

"I'm a-lookin' for my wife," said Lem.

The young man looked up then, regarded the pair at the counter. Morgan had to stand on tiptoes to look over it. The girl, in her early twenties, smiled indulgently and stood up. She walked to the counter, her summer dress flowing gracefully from her hips, hugging her thighs and waist. She had light sandy hair, blue eyes, dimples.

"Does she work here?"

"Yep. Her name's Roberta. Roberta Hawke."

The girl turned to the young man. Beyond the door, the presses made loud whispers.

"Anyone with that name work here, Stephen?"

"Used to," said Stephen, once again absorbed with the papers on his desk. He dipped a quill pen into a well, signed a document with an exaggerated flourish.

"I'm afraid she doesn't work here any longer," said the girl.

"Well, she surely does," said Lem. "Roberta Hawke. You got to be mistook."

Stephen looked up at Lem, shook his head.

"She hasn't worked here for six or seven years. She went to work over at B & J Hatters a long time ago."

"Where's that?" asked Lem.

"Fourth and Main. Right around the corner. Broadway's the next street over, and you go one block up."

"Thanks," said Lem.

"Ain't Ma here?" asked Morgan.

"No, she ain't," said his father.

The girl went back to her desk. Stephen looked across at her and winked.

"If that's Mrs. Hawke's husband, he is in for a surprise," he said.

"What do you mean?"

"She's taken up with Barry O'Neil. Scandalous, Marie, quite scandalous."

"Well, I hope that man's not the jealous type."

"If you hear screams, you let me know."

Stephen scrawled a note on a piece of foolscap. Marie tried to busy herself in the ledger, but her thoughts were on the little boy peering over the top of the counter.

———.———

Lem left Hammerhead hitched in front of Kroger's. He and Morgan walked over to Main, then up to Fourth. The large building stood out from the others because the wooden frame was being replaced with new brick.

The storefront had large doors that were open in clement weather to display the company's hats on shelves and staggered wooden racks with pegs. Small glass display cases featured other headwear on attractive wooden trees.

A young man approached Lem and Morgan as they entered the display room. He wore a high starched collar, drooping ribbon tie; was thin and vestless. His hair was coiled with foppish curls.

"Something for your head?" asked the clerk.

"No, I'm lookin' for Roberta Hawke."

"Miss Hawke is not in, sir. She just left a few moments ago."

"She works here then?"

"Yes, she's our top model. Mr. O'Neil's personal favorite."

"Mr. O'Neil?" Lem felt the back of his neck prickle.

"Yes, Mr. Barry O'Neil, one of the owners. I believe you'll find them at Worthington House in an hour or so." The clerk pulled a brass watch from his pocket. The watch was on a chain. He opened the lid elaborately, looked at the time. "They have a noon showing there and a tea, later this afternoon."

"What's 'at?" asked Lem, bewildered.

"Worthington House is one of our finest hotels and restaurants, sir. It's quite elegant and one must dress to dine there." The clerk looked haughtily at Hawke. "If it's about furs you wish to sell us, perhaps I could—"

"Nope, it ain't about that. Where is this Worthington place?"

"Worthington House is on First and Walnut. You can't miss it. Just go down to First and it's three blocks from Broadway."

"I'll find it," said Lem. "Where is she now?"

"Why, she and Mr. O'Neil went to meet someone, another model, I believe."

"Where?"

"Why, that I don't know, sir. Perhaps it would be best if you spoke with Mr. John O'Neil."

"No, I reckon I can find my wife," said Lem angrily.

"Why, I didn't know Miss Hawke was married," said the clerk.

"Maybe she's forgotten it too," said Lem. He turned on his heel and left the hatters, Morgan chasing after him.

"Where did he say Mama was?" asked Morgan when they were back on the street.

"Some fancy hotel," said Lem, scowling. "Let's get Hammerhead and go a-lookin' for her."

"I bet she's lookin' for us, too," said the boy. Lem looked down at his son. Morgan was probably as bewildered as he was himself.

Lem put Morgan up on the horse, climbed into the saddle. He rode to First Street, turned right. Worthington House dominated one corner of Walnut, its massive columns supporting a stately roof, looming over a wide veranda. Crepe myrtles and roses of Sharon bloomed in the yard. Huge mimosas flanked a magnolia tree that provided shade for the walk and the porch. A small ornately lettered sign proclaimed that this, indeed, was Worthington House.

"What is it?" asked Morgan.

"That's where your ma is supposed to be," said Lem, as he stalked up the cobbled walk. Hollyhocks bordered the bricks, all neatly trimmed, the blooms just starting to fade. Lem and his son climbed the steps. The door opened and a black man dressed in livery stepped out.

"Mistas," he said, "you done come to the wrong do'."

"I'm lookin' for somebody," said Lem.

"You'uns'll have to go around back," said the servant.

"No, we ain't," said Lem, pushing by the Negro.

"But you can't go in there."

Lem ignored him, but he blinked his eyes in the dimness of the foyer. Beyond, down a long hall, he saw a smartly dressed man standing at a podium by a doorway. Lem headed for him, Morgan running to keep up.

The servant trailed after them, his hands uplifted in helplessness.

The man standing on the podium, a small platform adorned with carpeting, turned to face them. He held a large book in his hands.

"What is it, George?" he asked the black man.

"Mista Blevins, I couldn't stop these two. They just busted on by me."

Blevins, the maitre d'hotel, looked down at the man in the linsey-woolsey shirt, the urchin at his side.

"What is the meaning of this?" he asked.

"I'm lookin' for my wife," said Lem.

"Well, she most certainly is not in here," said Blevins, from his haughty perch. His sickly smile stopped just short of being a sneer.

"I was tolt she was," said Lem.

"Well, you have been misinformed. We don't cater to your class here."

Lem glared at the man, then reached out and grabbed Blevins by the shirtfront. He jerked him from the platform and spun him around. With a heave, he shoved the hapless man into George's arms. The two staggered backwards, fell down in a heap.

Morgan stared at the two men in wonder.

Lem walked into the large room. Tables with bright white cloths and set with glasses stood at intervals from one another. Plants helped to break up the expanse of room. Waiters hurried in and out of a pair of double doors at the far end. A few diners looked toward Lem and Morgan as they swept into the room. In a far corner, Lem saw Barry O'Neil sitting at a table by a window. There was a woman with him, but he couldn't see her face.

He headed in the direction of Barry's table. A waiter came toward him, looked at Lem's face and veered off. Morgan's feet thumped on the carpeting as he hurried to keep up with his father.

The woman looked over Barry's shoulder as Lem came up to the table.

It was Roberta, and she was dressed in a fine black dress, her lips and cheeks rouged so that she looked like one of the women in the tippling houses. She held a glass of spirits in her hand.

"O'Neil," said Lem, "what are you a-doin' with my wife?"

"Why, she works for me," said Barry.

"Bobbie, you come on back home with me," said Lem.

"Oh, don't be silly, Lemuel. You have no right to order me around."

Her words were slightly slurred. Lem knew she had been drinking.

"Mama," said Morgan, "Mama, we come to see you. Pa's gonna get me a haircut."

"Is that your son?" asked Barry, turning to Roberta.

"No, it's his son," she said, and her eyes flashed a hidden bitterness. "Leave us alone, Lemuel."

"Yes, I believe the lady wishes you to go," said Barry.

"You comin', Bobbie?"

"For the last time, no," said Roberta. "Get out of here. I never want to see you again."

With that, she leaned toward Barry, slithered an elbow-length glove around Barry's head, pulled his lips toward hers. She kissed him, long and lingeringly, then released him with a flourish.

"You bitch," said Lem.

Barry stood up, pulling his sleeves back.

That's when Lem hit him. He doubled up his fist and drove it straight into Barry O'Neil's jaw, knocking the small red-haired man backward into his empty chair. Barry's eyes rolled up in their sockets and then crossed as he collapsed and sank to the floor.

Roberta stood up and screamed hysterically. She began to throw water glasses at her husband. She threw the glass pitcher at him, splashing water all over the table and carpet. She began to throw silverware, cursing like a dockworker.

"Get out! Get out!" she screamed. "You filthy bastard."

Spittle formed on her lips and her face whitened to a floury mask.

Lem took Morgan's hand, backed off.

"Whore," he whispered, and turned on his heel. The maitre d'hotel and the liveried doorman stepped aside as Lem and Morgan stalked past them. The diners sat frozen, their mouths open, their eyes fixed on the pair who had caused so much commotion on a quiet morning.

"I hate you!" Roberta screamed. "I hate you both!"

Morgan began to cry. Lem knocked the front door off its hinges as he kicked his way outside.

"Son, no need to shed no tears over a woman like that," Lem said as he reached the street where Hammerhead stood hipshot in the shade of a mimosa.

"But she's my ma," whined Morgan.

"Not no more she ain't," said Lem, and he knew they were the saddest words he had ever spoken.

The truth was, he wished he could cry himself.

14

Lem looked at the first snow of winter falling, dusting the hills and fields with flour, the flakes swirling in the rising chimney smoke. Morgan stood with him at the corral where the new horse pranced in a circle, blowing steam through his nostrils. The horse was a chestnut sorrel, gelded, six years old, fifteen and a half hands high. Lem had traded two pair of buckskins and ten bushels of corn for him.

"What should we name him, son?"

"He's sure pretty, Pa."

"Hammerhead's gettin' old. Might not be around much longer."

"He's got gray whiskers, ain't he?"

Lem chuckled. The boy was observant. He looked to be growing tall. It had been two years since they had last seen Roberta. A constable had ridden out one day and served Lem with papers he could barely read. Then, another man had come

162

out and told Lem that his marriage was formally dissolved by the court in Lexington. A year ago Roberta had sent a present for Morgan back with Nancy Bickham, a little coonskin cap, and no word from her since. He had heard the other day, from Calvin Moon, that she and Barry O'Neil had gone to Nashville, Tennessee, to open a haberdashery and sell hats, furs and clothing to a fashion-conscious clientele.

Lem had been numb inside for so long that he seldom thought about Roberta. But, with Morgan's birthday coming up in October, the next month, he had begun to think of his wife again, wondering how she could leave her flesh and blood behind without so much as a fare-thee-well. It pained him to think of Morg growing up motherless and nigh to sixteen years old. He had gotten some schooling from Nancy Bickham and her kids, could read, write his ciphers, knew the alphabet and how to add and subtract numbers, do simple multiplying. That wasn't much, but the boy seemed taken by hunting and fishing more than schooling.

"You go on and name him," said Lem. "Might be I'll let you ride him."

"Can I? Oh, I want to, Pa. When can I?"

"Soon's you give him a name."

"Well," said Morgan seriously, "he looks like a big fox, and his stockings make him look like he's got on boots. I think he should either be called Fox or Boots."

"You call it," said Lem.

"Well, I don't think he's a fox. He's not sneaky or anything and he don't chase chickens. So, I think his name is Boots."

Lem laughed.

"Good name," he said. "You get a bridle on him and I'll help you get on him."

"Oh, bully, bully," said Morgan. He ran into the small barn he had helped his father build. A few moments later, he came out carrying a bridle. Lem held the horse's neck down while Morgan slipped the bridle on, tied it under his chin and behind his ears. Lem lifted his son onto the horse's back, stepped aside.

"Well, you're pretty tall, Morg. Think you can handle Boots?"

"I can handle him."

"Don't run him hard. Just let him get used to you."

Lem watched as Morgan rode out into the snowy field, Friar Tuck barking as he raced to catch up on stubby legs. The horse had three gaits that he knew of, was saddle broke, seemed gentle enough. A wave of sadness, like hearing a fiddle play a mourning song, washed over him. Snow tinked against his face, melted on the sun-leathered skin. He had taken to growing a winter beard and the stubble that shadowed his face was already a quarter-inch long, dark as hog bristles.

Morgan rode to the edge of the field where a rabbit broke from cover. Friar Tuck cut off his pursuit of Boots and Morgan, took after the rabbit, into the woods. Morgan rode the edge of the field, put the horse into a gallop as he cut back toward the house.

Lem smiled as Morgan rode up, grinning wide as a wolf.

"He's a beauty, Pa. I really like him."

"Well, you put out some feed for him and rub him down good. I'll get us some supper."

"Can't I ride no more?"

"Be dark soon and I 'spec by mornin' we'll have us a snowfall. Chores'll take longer."

"Aww."

"Put him up, boy."

Lem turned and walked back to the house. He'd had a fair crop and had given Morgan some coppers to save when they sold the last of the corn. Next month, he might buy the boy a rifle. He was already at work on some buckskins that ought to fit him. Morgan didn't know about them. Lem worked on them late at night after the boy was asleep. Morgan was the only thing that kept him going, but his son could not fill the emptiness he felt whenever he thought of Roberta and what she had done to them.

That night, after supper, Morgan went to bed early. Lem stayed up, working by lamplight on the trousers of the buckskins. He felt like an old woman at such times, sitting there with the awl, sewing like a granny. But, it was something to do; something to pass the time.

———·———

The October hills were dusted with an early snow, the trees gaunt and leafless, the hollows drifted in wavelets from the wind like floury oceans. Lem and Morgan had been gripped by cabin fever during the freak storm, snapping at each other like children, pacing the floor, looking out the window, hoping the storm would break. It had started out as rain, turned to sleet, then hail, then back to rain again. Just before morning, the temperature dropped and the rain turned to snow. When dawn broke, clear and cold, Lem took his rifle, primed it, and told Morgan to bring his new one, the birthday rifle, a lean Kentucky of .41 caliber, with fancy brass furniture, an English lock, blade front sight, buckhorn rear.

"We goin' huntin', Pa?"

"Might be time for you to get you a buck," said his father, slipping his possibles pouch over his shoulder. He wore buckskins, warm enough for hunting with the woolens under them, a coonskin cap like Morgan's. The buckskins he had made for the boy fit pretty well. The sad thing was that he would outgrow them in less than a year. Lem had left some bottom in them to let out, some waist as well, but he couldn't do much about the length and the lad's shoulders would break out the seams in the shirt if he kept growing.

"You got your woolies on, Morg?"

"Yep. Just like you, Pa."

"'Member all I taught you?"

"I truly do. I can shoot me a buck."

"Got your horns and pouch?"

"I'll fetch 'em."

Lem felt a pang of pride at the boy's eagerness. Morgan draped himself in powder horns and hunting pouch, checked the lacing on his boot-length moccasins. He stood there, rifle at his side, as his father slipped some biscuits into Morgan's pouch.

"'Case we get hungry later on. Your rifle loaded?"

"It's loaded, Pa. I ain't primed the pan yet."

"Time enough when we get a piece away from the house. Better put Tut up so's he won't run the deer."

"I got him tied up in the barn," said the boy.

"Well, let's see what we might see," said Lem, smiling.

"Yes sir, let's see what we will see," mocked the boy.

Friar Tuck yelped from the barn as Lem and Morgan stepped outside.

"Pay him no mind," said Lem.

The boy and his father walked across the field, Morgan following the trail Lem broke. They entered the woods, climbed to the top of the nearest ridge. Lem pointed out deer tracks, most of them small, does and yearlings, as they went deeper into the hardwoods.

A startled squirrel chittered from a hickory tree, and the ground was laced with his brethren's tracks. They also saw the tracks of birds, rabbits, fox, and finally, the deep spoor of cloven hooves in a briar thicket.

"There's your buck," said Lem, in a low whisper.

"Big 'un," said Morgan.

"Umm. We got to go careful. You foller, stop when I stop, step real soft. Watch them twigs brushin' against your 'skins. Don't do no talkin'."

"Ought I to prime my pan now?"

Lem almost laughed, but held it in. He nodded, watched as the boy took the small powder horn, jerked the stob out with his teeth and poured fine powder into the pan. Morgan blew away the excess as his father had taught him, closed the frizzen.

"You ready?"

"Ready, Pa," Morgan whispered.

Lem circled the thicket, picked up the buck's tracks on the other side. The tracks were fresh, less than an hour old. Farther on, Lem found a pile of droppings. They were still steaming, had partially melted the thin snow. A doe had left a yellow stain and the buck had added some urine of his own. Lem pointed out tufts of deer hairs stuck to the oaks and hickorys, a fresh rub where the buck had stripped a sapling of bark as he raked it with the tines of his antlers.

Morgan was thrilled at everything he saw. He tried to do everything his father did, step where he stepped, stop when he stopped. He held his breath when they halted to listen.

The buck stopped following the doe and his tracks veered off, heading toward a deep hollow.

Lem stopped, leaned against a tree. He hunkered down and Morgan squatted next to him, a puzzled look on his face.

"That buck knows we're a-trackin' him now," whispered Lem. "We got to get ahead of him or figger out if he's a-goin' to circle us."

"How do we do that?"

"You stay put right here, Morg. I'm going to cut way off and make a wide circle. I figger he'll come back this way to pick up that doe's track. You be ready. Hold on him just behind the shoulder, squeeze off your shot when you got him in range."

"Pa, what if I miss?"

Lemuel put a hand on Morgan's shoulder, looked him square in the eye.

"Son, when you're a-huntin' you don't think about missin'. A deer ain't nothin' but a overgrowed rabbit. You just hold yourself steady and think about that ball a-goin' into his heart."

Morgan crinkled his face in a weak smile. Lem chucked his son on the arm and strode off at an angle away from the buck's tracks. It seemed to the boy that the path his father was taking was all wrong, that he would never intercept the buck. He was sure his father was widening the distance with each step. He watched until his father disappeared. He stood against the hickory tree and blew into his cupped hands. The silence welled up around him.

Lem made a wide circle, keeping the ridge between him and the hollow where the buck had gone. He moved faster than he could have with Morgan following him. He did not intersect the buck's tracks on that side, so he knew it was likely the deer was still in the hollow, perhaps pawing the snow for acorns missed by the squirrels and deer in the fall. When he had covered a half mile, he looped back toward the hollow where he knew it opened onto the flat. He crossed to the opposite ridge, stayed low, near the brush in the thin end of the hollow. He stalked carefully now, stopping every few minutes to wait and listen.

He moved from tree to tree, using them for cover. He scanned the snow for tracks that would show him the buck had come out of the hollow and gone to higher ground. He saw deer tracks, but none that matched the buck's and none of them had climbed up to the ridge.

He moved carefully the closer he got to where he had left Morgan. He leaned against a tree for ten minutes, listened to every sound. He heard the brush rattle, higher up the hollow. Listening carefully, he heard the sounds of a deer working a sapling, pawing at the snow. The buck snorted, and Lem knew he was preoccupied making a scrape, perhaps a rub as well.

"We got us a hot buck," he said to himself.

Lem moved up the hollow, staying closer to the brush than before. He hunched over, stopped to listen at intervals. The sounds of the buck worrying the snow with its hooves, its rack twanging the saplings, grew louder.

Lem knew that if he entered the hollow, he wouldn't be able to see. The buck could run down it, taking the natural escape route, or take either ridge. Or the buck could run straight up the hollow to the saddle that bridged the two ridges. If the deer ran anywhere but down the hollow, Morgan had a good chance for a shot. But Lem had to make a decision. Should he cut the buck off from the downhill retreat by going into the hollow, or should he try to drive the buck directly toward Morgan? He would be working blind.

He would have to take the chance.

Lem slipped down into the hollow, cutting toward the sounds at an angle. It was slow going. The brush was thick, the second growth tangled with thorny briar that could trip a man, grab his clothing like clutching fingers. If he moved careful, the thorns slipped noiselessly over his buckskins. He made less sound than a deer would make, he thought.

Now, he heard the buck, pinpointed his location. The deer was in the broadest part of the hollow, somewhere in a grove of hardwoods. Lem worked his way through the snow-limned brush, staying downwind. It took him twenty minutes to stalk within sight of the animal.

The buck was big, with a majestic rack. It stood under a low-lying limb, pawing the snow out of curiosity, rubbing its back with the limb. Every so often, it would stop, sniff the air, twist its ears to pick up sound. The slight crosswind was in Lem's favor, Morgan's as well.

Lem saw the deer plain, no more than sixty or seventy yards away. He did not move, breathed so that his breath did not show when he exhaled. His blood raced with excitement. It was an easy shot. The buck's flank was fully exposed, his black-tipped tail flicking nervously.

He wished now that he had brought Morgan with him. But he realized that had he brought his son on this track, they never would have gotten so close. No, this was better. Let Morgan get the buck on his own. Let him feel the thrill of bringing down a running buck for the first time. It would be a moment he would remember the rest of his days.

Lem stood up and yelled his son's name.

"Morgan!"

The buck stiffened for a split second before its muscles bunched up and it wheeled away from the sound of the human voice. It hunkered low and broke into a run up the slope, toward Morgan's stand. Lem ran after it, making all the noise he could.

"Here he comes!" he called to Morgan.

The buck's white tail flared like a flag just before it disappeared, flying and bounding toward the ridge where Morgan waited, in perfect position for a running shot. Lem stopped, out of breath, hoping his son remembered to lead the animal, aim for the heart.

———·———

Morgan jumped a foot inside his skin.

He heard his father's shout, then heard the buck crashing through the brush, headed his way. His heart stuttered a rapid tattoo as he thumbed back the cock, waited for the buck to appear.

His mind flooded with thoughts. He tried to picture the buck in his mind, foretell where it would top the ridge. But the sounds were confusing. Time slowed to a bewildering crawl. He thought the buck might be running the other way; then he thought it must be a few feet away, so loud were the sounds of its hoofbeats. Panic skewed his thoughts; his palms slickened with a sudden flood of sweat. His mouth turned dry and a pulse in his throat began to beat out of control.

The buck scrambled up the slope, its russet coat like fire against the whiteness. Snow flew off its sharp hooves as it struggled for footing. Morgan swallowed a mouthful of air, blinked in wonderment. A feeling of calm suffused him as he saw the magnificent buck, its head held regally high, its antlers symmetrically formed, majestic in their sweep.

Morgan's eye fixed on the buck's side. He brought the rifle to his shoulder. The buck saw the movement, bolted away. Morgan had the deer fixed in his mind. He led it in one clean motion from its rump, swinging the barrel past the target spot behind the left foreleg. When the spot disappeared as the muzzle passed over it, he squeezed the trigger and kept swinging. The rifle bucked against his shoulder. A stream of orange flame and sparks spewed from the barrel. A puff of white smoke billowed from the muzzle, blotted out the racing deer. The shot reverberated in the snow-flocked hills, the report so loud Morgan was temporarily deafened by the explosion.

The white smoke hung in the air and Morgan felt wrapped in a cocoon of silence, an emptiness where he could neither see nor hear. Dazed, he stood there, a tendril of smoke coiling out of the barrel, his cheekbone hurting where the comb of the stock had bruised it in recoil.

Then, the smoke cleared and he saw the buck lying in the snow, some sixty yards beyond the place where he had shot it.

Morgan began to shake as if gripped with a fever. He stood rooted to the snowbound earth, unable to move. His hands shook so that he thought he might drop his rifle. His knees trembled and his teeth began to chatter. He saw his father trudge up over the hill and stop, staring at him.

"Morg?"

Morgan squeaked, unable to speak.

Lem looked at the deer, ran to it, his tread slow through the snow. He approached it warily from behind, his rifle aimed at the animal, his finger on the trigger, his thumb on the cock. The buck didn't move. Lem leaned over it, grabbed an antler, lifted up its head. He dropped it with a thunk and slit its throat with his knife to let it bleed.

Morgan swallowed, trying to free up the lump in his throat.

He saw his father trotting toward him, but he was still frozen there, quivering in every muscle.

"What's the matter, boy? Got you the buck fever?"

Morgan tried to shake his head. Nothing moved. He lowered the rifle slowly; swallowed air. He began to breathe normally again as his father came up to him.

"That was a fine shot," said his father. "Wish't I could have seed it."

"Oh," said Morgan, the squeak fading.

"When did you start to get the shakes?"

"A—after I saw it. Dead. The blood . . . Pa . . . I . . ."

Lem put a hand on his son's shoulder.

"Better you get it afterwards, son. Same thing happened when I killed my first deer."

"It did?"

"Sure enough. Took me a half hour to quit a-shakin'. Come on, let's gut him out. You got yourself a fine buck."

Morgan took a deep breath, smiled wanly.

"Yeh," he said. "I did."

Lem and Morgan reached the fallen buck. Lem took out his knife.

"You watch me do this, so's you know how next time you make meat."

Lem knelt down, stuck the blade into the deer just in front of the genitals, slit back to the anus. He reversed the blade and sliced from aitchbone to breastbone, up the buck's belly, heard the carcass sigh as steam belched from its bloody cavity. He worked the knife past the breastbone and up to the neck. Always, he worked the cutting edge of the blade away from him, in case he slipped with the knife. He squeezed the bladder gently, since it was full, and emptied it of fluid. He cut around the anus to clear the intestines from the pelvic arch, the aitchbone. He reached down into the loins, drew yards of entrails into the body cavity.

Morgan watched in fascination, his eyes glittering. He was no longer cold. The quivering had passed.

Lem turned his head slightly to avoid the fecal stench, drew a shallow breath before continuing to gut out the deer.

Lem probed inside the deer's abdomen at the breastbone, cut the membrane, freeing the innards. He was careful not to slash the stomach or intestines. He cut the windpipe and esophagus, jerked downward, pulling the mass of cartilage and gristle down into the mid-section. He took out the heart and liver, set them aside. Then, he turned the deer over and shook the innards out into a gut-pile. He propped the deer's loins apart with a stick.

"We got to carry it back to the house, hang it up, skin him," said Lem.

"Can I tan the hide, Pa? I want to get me a couple more and make my own buckskins."

"You've really growed up all of a sudden, ain't you, Morg?"

Morgan grinned.

"If you say so, Pa."

"We'll take turns a-draggin' him back. He'll weigh out to a hundred and fifty, I reckon."

"I feel real good, Pa."

Lemuel looked at his son. He felt the pride glowing in him like cherry coals. Morgan did not resemble his mother so much anymore. He was growing tall, filling out. There was a sureness about him that had not been there before. It made Lem feel old. Why, Morgan was nigh as old as he was when he married the boy's mother. A few more years, he might be taking a wife of his own. He hoped Morgan had better luck. His pride turned to bitterness when he thought about Roberta. He shook out the images in his mind, took a deep breath.

"I know how you feel, by God," said Lem. He grabbed a tine and began dragging the buck. "Best load up again whilst I'm haulin' this here deer. Never know what we might see twixt here and home."

"Yes, Pa. I'll spell you when you want me to."

"Well, that won't be too long. Buck's heavy all right. Got him enough points you might want to save his horns."

"Oh, I do, Pa," beamed Morgan.

That night, they both skinned the deer by the light of the lantern. Lem could not help notice that the top of Morgan's head just came nigh up to his pa's shoulder. The boy would be tall, sure enough, taller than his pa.

Morgan sawed the antlers off the buck himself. He took them inside the house that night, put them at the foot of his bed where he could look at them.

Lem said good night and took to his bed. He blew out his lamp, lay in the dark, thinking.

What would happen to him, he wondered, when Morgan grew up and went away on his own? What would happen to him? Where would he go? What would he do?

The sadness came on him again. A different sadness this time. This one smothered him, drowned him. He had lost his wife; he could not bear to lose his son. The night, he thought, was not as dark as the darkness in his heart just then. He turned over, cursing Roberta, cursing all women, cursing them until sleep pulled him down below all thought, all feeling.

15

Morgan Hawke crept up to his favorite tree, sat in the hollow of the earth he had made himself by sitting there so much and leaned back against the oak, his rifle across his knees. He looked down toward the den tree, waited for the light to come. He had made little sound coming through the woods, but even if he had, he knew the squirrels had short memories. Pa had taught him that. Fifteen to twenty minutes. He had tested it himself. If he made noise coming into the woods, the squirrels would all run up their trees and hide. But, if he sat still for fifteen minutes or so, they would come back, forget all about him.

It was a warm morning, the warmest of the spring, and he wanted to bring in at least four squirrels before helping Pa with the chores. He had already set out grain for Hammerhead and Boots, fed Friar Tuck, the chickens, slopped the hogs, brought in the eggs. He could do a lot in the dark, but he had used the lantern this morning because he wanted to get up to the hardwoods before the sky lit up.

From his perch, he could see the house and road. It made him feel like a king to look down on the fields and the house that way, to watch the long road that stretched to the back parcel of the Bickham place.

He saw smoke rising from the chimney at Bickham's. He heard a sound, the scratch of claws on bark. His father had taught him to shut out everything when he was in the woods, just to lean against a tree and become part of it, sit there so long you just became part of the forest and once you had gone into it, you would see and hear things nobody else could hear.

A squirrel stuck its head out of the hole in the den tree. It gave a bark. Then, it was quiet for a while. Morgan closed his eyes and listened. He heard an answering chitter from another part of the woods. The squirrels were waking up. The sun began to peach over the land. A thin scar of cream appeared like a rent in the sky. He liked to watch the woods wake up, see the trees and bushes light up slow and see the leaves take on definition. Stumps and rocks took on color, were no longer blobs of shadow.

The squirrel inched down the trunk of the tree, its tail twitching, its eyes peering everywhere. Morgan sat very still and waited. He had not hunted this tree since last fall and he knew there were other squirrels inside.

Morgan watched as the squirrel leaped to the ground, then rustled through the leaves as it ventured forth in search of food. Another squirrel peeked out of the den hole. Mist began to rise in the valley as the sun rose in the east. The first squirrel came toward Morgan, oblivious to his presence.

The second squirrel scrambled out of its den, scampered down the tree.

Morgan put the rifle to his shoulder. He held the trigger in slightly so there would be no click as he pulled back the cock. He tracked the squirrel with the sights aligned until it stopped on a fallen log. When it sat up, he held his breath and squeezed the trigger. The rifle slammed against his shoulder, spewed flame and white smoke out of the barrel. Morgan didn't wait for the smoke to clear, but stood up, grasped his powder horn. He poured an estimated 30 grains down the barrel, tamped the stock, reached for a patch and ball, seated them on the muzzle. With his short starter, he shoved the ball until it was flush with the barrel end. Quickly, he cut the surplus patch away, then rammed the ball six inches down the barrel. He snatched his wiping stick out and seated the ball on the powder. He primed the pan, started looking for the second squirrel. It had scrambled back up the den tree, was clinging to the bark next to the hole. Morgan cocked his rifle, took aim.

He fired again, saw the squirrel twitch, then fall to the ground.

Morgan let out a breath. He picked up the first squirrel next to the fallen log. The other was still kicking at the foot of the den tree. He picked it up by its hind legs, dashed its head against the tree.

Deftly, Morgan gutted out the two squirrels, stuffed their warm carcasses in the back of his loose shirt. He started to walk up to the top of the ridge and hunt the other side, when he saw a rider emerge from the mist below. Curious, he stood there, gazing downward, as the man and horse slowly made their way up the road. He wondered who could be coming to see them at this hour of the morning.

There was something peculiar about the man. He wore an odd hat, something odd on his head, anyway, that might have been a hat, and his buckskins were decorated with bright colors. As the sun rose behind him, the rider seemed illuminated in the ground fog. Morgan stared at him transfixed, wondering who he was and why he was riding up their road. There was a bedroll, or pack, on the man's saddle, and a rifle in a buckskin stocking laid across the man's lap.

Morgan forgot about hunting squirrels and made his way slowly down the slope toward the road. He caught occasional glimpses of the rider through the trees, which had not yet begun to bud. As he drew closer to the road, he hid behind a tree so that he could observe the rider more closely. As the man loomed larger, Morgan's pulse began to race.

The horse was old, swaybacked, its hide scarred, its winter coat marred with bare patches. Morgan noticed that the horse wore no shoes and made very little noise. The man riding the bony horse had no face. It was hidden behind a brushy beard that was streaked with white slashes. He was a thin man, as bony as the horse, but fearsome. Morgan blinked to clear his vision, for he had never seen a man dressed as this one was. His buckskins had swatches sewed to them that were blue and red and yellow, black and white. Morgan wondered whether they were made of cloth or painted leather.

Morgan huddled tight against the tree as the horse got close enough so that he could hear its hooves on the ground. He drew his arms in close to his sides, held the rifle straight up and down.

"You, boy, I know you're ahind that tree. Come on out where we can get a look at you."

Morgan's heart seized in his chest.

He peeked from behind the tree. The rider sat his horse not twenty yards away.

"Well, come on, son. I ain't a-goin' to bite ye."

Morgan blinked sheepishly, stepped out from behind the tree.

"Hello, sir," he said. The man was even stranger up close. His buckskins were white as snow and his moccasins had those same colored patches on them. They, too, were white, and the most beautiful he'd ever seen. The man's hair was long, past his shoulders, and his beard was so bushy it was hard to see his eyes. He wore a tomahawk and a knife on his belt and a pistol jutted from his wide belt. He looked, Morgan thought, like some kind of warrior. His hat was made of the shiniest fur, red and golden and russet, and it had an animal's face on the front, all squinched up. But he could tell it was an animal from its eyes and ears. He thought it might be a fox, but he was shaking inside so much he couldn't tell for sure.

"Sir? My, ain't we the polite chile? What's your name, son?"

"M-M-Morgan, sir. My pa taught me to address older men that way."

"Oh, he did, did he? Morgan, you say? Now, Morgan's my name, boy. Don't seem likely they'd be two with the same name in the same spot, does it now? You don't reckon somebody stole it from me and give it to you?"

"That was the name my pa give me."

"Then I reckon he's the one what stole it."

"My pa don't steal," Morgan said, a hard edge of defiance to his tone.

"Who's your pa?"

"Lemuel Hawke."

"Well, I'm Silas Morgan and I'd sure like to talk to this Lemuel Hawke what stole my name. That his hut yonder?"

"Uh huh. It ain't no hut, though. It's our house."

"Well, take me to him, young Morgan. We'll just talk to Lemuel hisself about this business of stealin' a man's name." Silas didn't smile and Morgan thought he was dead serious. "I seed you shot you a couple squirrel up there. You cook?"

"I can skillet fry 'em."

"Well, get to goin' then. I've got a gut thin as a spring b'ar's. You ever et elk?"

"No. I ain't never seen one. What is it?"

Silas Morgan threw his head back and laughed.

"Why it's a most fearsome animal, big as my horse here, with sharp horns wide as a wagon."

Morgan didn't believe him. He snorted and started running toward the house. He looked back and Silas was just jogging along, like before, in no particular hurry. He didn't know what to make of the stranger, but up close he saw that he had little fur tails growing out of his buckskins and those colored patches that weren't cloth and weren't beads. He wondered what they were.

"Pa, Pa, wake up!" Morgan yelled as he ran up to the house, breathless. "Somebody's a-comin'."

The door opened.

"I'm awake, Morg. What're you hollerin' about?"

"There's a man says you stole my name from him. He's a-comin'. He was telling me about a elk. He eats 'em."

Puzzled, Lem stepped out of the cabin. His face was lathered with soap. He was bare-chested, his cotton trousers dangling a pair of galluses. He held a straight razor in his hand; his face was half-shaven. Morgan pointed to the man on horseback.

"Don't seem in no hurry, does he?"

"Better get your gun, Pa. He says you stole my name from him."

"Well, if he's who I think he is, I did steal your name from him."

"You did?"

"Did he tell you his name?"

"He said his name was Morgan too. Silas Morgan."

"Well, damn me for twenny seconds in hell, if that ain't your namesake, Morg."

"Huh?"

"That's the galoot I named you after. He taught me more'n any man alive, I reckon. Boy, your ma sure kicked up a fuss when I called you that."

"How come, Pa?"

"Oh, your ma didn't like Silas none. She thought he was the devil's own son."

"Is he?"

Lem started to wave at the rider. Silas waved back.

"Huh?"

"Is he the devil's son?"

Morgan walked over to stand beside his father and peer out at the oncoming Silas Morgan.

"Why that's just a sayin', son. Look, I got to finish parin' my face. You tell Silas to light down and bring him on inside."

"Truly, Pa, I don't know what to make of that man. He looks like a pirate or a murderer."

"Well, he ain't neither. You make him welcome."

His father disappeared, leaving him alone outside with the rapidly approaching man on horseback. He heard the door slam shut.

"Well, was that yore pa?" Silas asked as he rode up.

"Uh, yes sir. He said to—to . . ."

Morgan froze as Silas fixed him with a beady stare. He thought of the devil and wondered if his ma wasn't right about the man looking down at him. He looked right fearsome. He expected fire and smoke to spew out of his nostrils if he looked at him too long. As it was, he was sure, in his imagination at least, that Silas' eyes were shooting sparks right at him. Sparks straight out of hell.

"Well, spit it out, boy. What'd yore pa say?"

"He said, uh, tolightrightdown'ncomeinthehouse." With that, Morgan turned on his heel and went inside the house.

Behind him, he heard Silas laugh and it made Morgan's face flush hot with shame.

Lem finished wiping off the last of the lather from his face. He slipped into a wool shirt and slid his galluses over his shoulders.

"What's got into you, boy?" he asked. "Where's Silas? You should have tended to his horse."

"I reckon he can take care of his horse, all right. He come this far by hisself, Pa."

Lem looked at his son, wrinkled his nose in puzzlement.

"You don't like old Silas? Why he's my best friend."

"He eats elks," said Morgan, unsure of himself.

"Why that's just an animal. I heard of 'em plenty."

"I don't know what to say to him. He gives me the fidgets.'

"Well, you just come outside and stop actin' like a damned fool, 'cause Silas is a sight for tuckered eyes."

Morgan followed his father outside, still suspicious of the strange man.

"That you, Silas?" His father's voice was reassuring.

Silas had dismounted, was looping his bridle reins around a hitch post Lem had sunk into the ground.

"It ain't Brown the tax collector," cackled Silas. He turned, flashed a grin through his thick beard. He walked over to Lem, slapped him on the back. "Boy, I been ridin' a month of hard Sundays to find you. Never thought you'd still be a-farmin'."

"Silas, I got to take your word for who you are," said Lem. "You done hid your face from me. Or are you a-wearin' fur to keep the cold winds from burnin' your pretty cheeks?"

"Haw. I growed me a beard for that very reason and you just as skinny as ever. Got you a pup, too. Mighty skittery, ain't he? What's he sulled up for?"

Lem looked at his son. Morgan's face was as dark as a thundercloud.

"Morgan, shake hands with Silas."

Morgan just stood there, transfixed. Silas held out a hand toward him.

"Lordy, I do believe he thinks I'm goin' to bite him," said Silas.

"Morg, shake the man's hand," ordered his father.

Morgan crept out from behind his father, tentatively stretched out his hand. Silas took it, shook it vigorously, as a man would shake another's. Morgan tried to keep his teeth from rattling. He thought Silas was going to wear out his arm or pull it from his shoulder.

"There now, warn't so bad, was it?" Silas smiled.

"He's pleased to meet you, Silas. And, I'm mighty glad to see you. Come on inside and set. I can burn some vittles for you. Do you take coffee? I got me some beans that are some ripe."

"Well, now, Lem, I could chew me some meat and swaller some coffee bean juice or p'izen."

Lem looked at Silas's skins, touched the colored patches that had dumbfounded Morgan earlier.

"What're them?" he asked.

"Quillwork. Porkypine quills. Inyun gals mash 'em up, twist 'em, and paint 'em. Right purty, ain't they? Some of 'em uses beads and I got me some mokkersons what's got the purtiest colors you ever seen."

"What are them little furs?" asked Morgan, regaining some of his courage.

Silas lifted up a long slender piece of fur, tweaked it.

"Ferrets' tails, some of 'em. Some of 'em's minks."

Silas followed Lemuel inside the house. Morgan almost stumbled trying to keep up. He didn't want to miss a word that Silas Morgan might say.

"Got somethin' to show you by and by," said Silas as Lemuel pulled a chair out for him.

"How'd you find me?"

"Ran into Roberty down to Nashville," said Silas, and there was a silence in the room dark and heavy as a rain cloud. No one spoke for several seconds. Lem stoked the firebox in the stove, cleared his throat. Morgan stood stock-still, his mouth open like a frog's fly trap.

"How—how's she a-doin'?" Lem asked, trying to act unconcerned about it.

"Pore gal is kinda peeked. She tole me you warn't hitched no more and I let it go at that. I asked her where you was and she tole me. Figgered I could find you. No need to bother the pore woman no more." Silas paused, hacked at something in his throat.

"Poor woman?" asked Lem. "Hell's fire, Silas, Roberta wa
livin' high on the hog when she left here, workin' for tha
damned hatter, Barry O'Neil, swilling down whiskey in fancy
tippling houses like a sow. Wearin' clothes more dear thar
anything I ever seen." Lem looked at Morgan apologetically.

Morgan stiffened, tried to fix the wan smile on his face.

"She ain't wearin' fancy clothes no more. She's workin' ir
that hattery all right, sniffin' that glue what makes you crazy
Warn't no fancy tipplin' house I seen her in last, neither."

Lem sat down at the table opposite Silas. He was as rigid a
Morgan a few moments before. Morgan sucked in a quick
breath, stood there hanging on Silas's silence like a boy on a cliff

"She ain't no model or nothin'?"

"Nope," said Silas. "She works same as the other gals there.
makin' hats out of beaver." He turned to Morgan. "Son, kin you
go out and bring me that blanket roll on my saddle? Go
somethin' to show you."

Morgan blinked, then wheeled, ran from the room as if he'd
been hurled from a sling. He dashed to the horse, untied the
leather thongs, freed the heavy bundle from behind the cantle.
He carried it triumphantly into the house and laid it on the table
in front of Silas.

". . . went to see for myself, talk prices with Barry O'Neil,"
Silas was saying. "Ah, thank you, young Morgan." Silas unwrapped the plain woolen blanket. Morgan hung close to the
table, eyes big as a great horned owl's.

"What you got there, Silas?" asked Lem.

Silas did not show everything inside the blanket roll at first.
He extracted an oilcloth from the folded blanket, unwrapped it.
He held up a shiny dark pelt.

"This here's the reason I come to Kentucky," said Silas.

"What is it?" asked Lem. "Groundhog?"

Silas laughed.

"This is a prime beaver pelfry, Lemuel. Caught him myself up on the Wind River, a mighty powerful place in the Rocky Mountains, a place what makes a man feel small and big at the same time. This here's what they make hats out of, makes rich men out of farmers and thieves and the likes of me."

Silas tossed the pelt to Morgan, who jerked back in surprise. But the boy held it and stroked it, turned it to let the morning light drench it in freshets of silver, ripple with shadows and golden threads. The beaver seemed alive in his hands, seemed to radiate a pulse of faraway places, seemed to glow with the promise of sudden wealth.

"Lemme see it, Morg," said Lem, reaching for the pelt. Morgan reluctantly gave it to his father.

"It's so soft," said Morgan.

"I worked on this one special, so's you could see how purty it shines. Beaver don't look like that right after you tan it. Fur's all coarse, hide's rough and slick with beaver grease. Underneath, it's like silk wool, real soft and warm."

Lem examined it, turning it over and over in his hands.

"I never seen anything like this," said Lem. "How do they make a hat out of this?" He looked at Silas's fox-skin hat.

Silas shook his head.

"Nope, not like this fox, though they be some who keep 'em and wear 'em like this 'un. That's personal. Them hatters they go to a mighty lot of trouble to make felt. They shave that coarse hair from the pelfry, then the thick wool. The hatter sells the bare hide to a glue maker, then blows the hair and wool with a little bellows. Got to get 'em separate. He throws away the hair, keeps the wool to make felt."

"What's felt?" asked Morgan.

"Why it's what they make hats out of. Felt stays stiff, not like this fox." Silas took his hat off, handed it to Morgan. "See? Limp as a preacher's pecker at a dunkin'. Felt now, it stays hard and water don't do nothin' but run off it like it does on a beaver."

"How do they make this into felt?" asked Silas.

"I seen 'em do it at O'Neil's in Nashville. It's real interstin' They got this copper cone with a lot o' little holes in it. It spin around and sucks that loose fur up ag'in' it. The gals and feller. pack it down whilst this hot water's a-sprayin' on it. They keep addin' fur to the cone and packin' it until it gets real hard. Whe they got it all done, they take that felt, which looks like a hood a that p'int, and then put it in a mold what shapes it. While the felt's still soft and warm, they got this plunger that shoots shellac into it from inside the mold. Then they take some of the real fine fur and dab it on the hat. They use more hot water to do that Then, at the last, to make it shine real purty, they put the hat on spinning block. Whilst it's a-goin' around, they smooth it all out with sandpaper, irons, velvet and such. It comes out looking rea glossy, glossier'n this here beaver pelfry."

"Sounds like a lot of foolishness just to make a hat," said Lem Morgan's face reflected his rapt fascination with the story.

"Well, they's people who will pay to own a fine beaver hat. A course all that glue and shellac makes them hatters plumb crazy. Addles their brains."

"Is that what happened with Ma?" Morgan blurted out.

"I reckon," said Silas sadly. "Most of them hatters walk around like they been into the hard cider."

"I'll stay with the farming," said Lem.

Silas looked at Morgan, tweaked his beard and smiled.

"Maybe not. I got more to tell you. Lem, I never saw a land such as what I seen out West. A man can't get enough of it, and it fills you up. First time I seen the Rocky Mounts I felt like a ant. And then I swolled up inside until the tears just boiled outen my eyes."

"This is good land right here," Lem said stubbornly.

"Good enough for a little man," snorted Silas.

"Huh? What you mean by that?"

"Man stands on a mountain, he's pretty tall. He goes up short, comes down taller'n any."

"You ain't growed none."

"To me I growed a whole lot," said Silas.

"What else you got in that blanket?" asked Morgan, craning his neck.

Silas smiled.

"I was a-savin' the best for last. Somethin' for you, young feller. Fetch me your powder horn."

"What do you want it for?" asked Morgan.

"Just fetch it."

Morgan looked at his father. Lem nodded. Morgan went over to his bed while Lem stood up, added kindling to the firebox, started to grind coffee beans. Silas drummed his bony fingers on the table, licked his lips.

Morgan laid his powder horn on the table in front of Silas. "That it?"

"That's the horn my pa made for me," said Morgan.

"Well, I got you somethin' better. Made by the Crow Inyuns. They tell me it's got powerful medicine."

"Medicine?" Morgan cocked his head.

"Spirits. Make a man strong. Make him powerful 'gainst his enemies."

Lem poured water in a pot, shook the ground beans into the water. He put the pot on the stove, added a chunk of wood to the main fire. He clanged the door shut, walked over to the table.

"What's this talk?" he asked.

"I brung your boy this powder horn, Lem. I hope you let him keep it. I brung it a long ways. Was goin' to sell it until Roberty told me you had a son. Medicine's better you give it to a young man. Better for me, better for him."

"Let me see it," said Morgan eagerly.

Silas reached into the blanket roll and grabbed something. He drew it slowly from the blanket.

"Aww!" exclaimed Morgan.

Silas held the horn up high. It gleamed like black ivory in the

sunlight streaming through the windows. It was gracefully
curved, slender, with a thick butt, narrow point. Light glinted
from its polished surface.

"There you be," said Silas softly, his voice laden with
reverence. "That be your medicine horn, Morgan."

Morgan reached for it, closing his eyes for a moment as in
saying a silent prayer. He felt strange when he touched it, as if
there was magic in the horn, magic that coursed through him
like the tingle he got sometimes when lightning struck near him.
The hairs on the back of his neck stood up and his arms crawled
with goosebumps.

"My medicine horn," he said, and there was a strange husk in
his voice as he touched the smooth horn with his trembling
fingers.

Morgan Hawke held the medicine horn in his hands as if it was bone china. He looked at the strange markings on it, their indentations whitened as with chalk. It had no powder in it, was light in his hands. It had a wooden peg at the pouring spout, a wooden butt that was flat, inset, and varnished to a dark sheen. There was something mystical about the powder horn, something ancient and timeless and mysterious.

"What do those markings mean?" asked Morgan, his voice cloudy with rapture.

"Them is Crow sign. Some calls 'em the Blue Bead People. Bear Foot, the Inyun what give it to me, said they was a heap of power in 'em. I don't rightly know what they mean exactly."

The coffee pot boiled. Lem rattled a pair of tin cups, set them on the table.

"What you want to eat, Silas?" he asked as he poured the cups full. The aroma of boiled coffee beans filled the room.

"Boy there got him a couple of squirrel."

Morgan's face rippled with surprise.

"Oh, I forgot." He reached behind his back, felt the squirrels inside his shirt. "I'll skin 'em right away. Got me two of 'em, Pa."

"That ain't hardly enough to feed a hungry man, let alone two and a boy," said Lem, but there was approval in his voice. Morgan reluctantly laid down his powder horn and scampered out the door. It closed behind him, but there was a fresh cool in the room.

"Mighty fine lad you got there, Lemuel."

"He's a-growin' fast."

"Wisht you two 'ud come out west with me. I got to make tracks, get to the mountains afore the snow flies."

"I don't know, Silas. We're pretty much settled and all."

"I seen a heap of country," said Silas, reaching into the blanket roll once again. He pulled out another oilcloth, unwrapped it. He handed Lemuel a fine beaver hat burnished to a glistening black. It was round and had a bill made of beaver tail, cured and shellacked until it was hard as a tortoise shell. "This is for you, Lemuel. To 'member me by."

Lemuel took the hat, held it at full length as he admired it.

"Why, it's a mighty fine hat, Silas. I thank you."

"Try it on your pate."

Lemuel put the hat on. It felt alien to him, but was soft inside, fit right.

"I don't know where I'd wear such a hat, Silas."

"In the mountains, that's where. Plenty more where that'n come from."

"I ain't no animal trapper."

"Easy as sin. Lord, it's a life, Lemuel. I seen sights and Inyun gals purty as any you ever did see, and b'ilin' streams churnin' white and foamin', trees bigger'n anything back here, taller, straighter. Everything a man needs can be found in the big mountains."

"They have towns there?"

"No, an' that's the beauty of it. Forts and such along the Missouri and up the Yallerstone, along the Platte, most ever'where a man goes. They's wide places and small, but room for a man to move 'thouten people gettin' in his way."

"You make it sound like . . . like I don't know what. Paradise. The Garden of Eden."

"Waw! That's just what it's like, Lemuel. Ye gods, you got to see it just once. You don't like it none, you come on back to your plow and hogs."

Morgan returned with the two squirrels, cleaned and wet down, heads and feet cut off, ready to fry.

"I'll get the skillet hot," said Lemuel, taking off his hat. Morgan stared at the hat in awe. "Morg, you better fetch some deer meat from the springhouse."

"What's that?" asked Morgan.

"A pure beaver hat," said Silas.

"Did you catch it?"

"I trapped him up on the Yallerstone last winter. Two of 'em jest alike. I sewed 'em together so's you can hardly tell it. It sure do shine, don't it?"

"You bet a shilling it does," said Morgan. "Can I touch it, Pa?"

"Sure, put it on, Morg," said his father. He banged an iron skillet on the stove. "Get them vittles in here real quick now."

Morgan picked up the hat, put it on. It fell over his eyes. Silas and Lemuel both laughed. Morgan took off the hat, rubbed his hands through the soft fur.

"It's beeeyoutiful," he drawled.

"Deer meat," said Lemuel, smiling.

"I'll fetch it," said Morgan and he was gone again, leaving the two men alone.

"What're you tryin' to do, Silas?"

"Seeds, Lemuel. Plantin' seeds is all."

"My boy and me, we got us a good life here. I aim to see him grow to be a man on land I bought and paid for."

"You own this land?"

"Not yet," Lem gruffed. "But I aim to buy it."

"Boy's nigh a man already. He might think different."

"He won't think no different. I'll learn him what he needs to know."

"'Pears he's already learned a lot."

"What're you aimin' at, Silas?"

"Nothin'. I notice he fetches right well. Probably does the chores right good, too."

"You leave us be, Silas. I got plans for that boy."

"Wal, I reckon," said Silas, and took out his pipe and a tobacco pouch made of antelope hide. He filled the bowl. He walked over to the stove, took out a small firebrand, touched it to the tobacco. He drew deeply, exhaled blue smoke. "I can see you and the boy are all set here." Silas looked around the room, sat back down.

Morgan returned with a leg and hindquarter of cured venison, gave it to his father. Lem savagely sliced off several large chunks of meat, tossed them in a greased skillet. He poured more coffee for Silas and himself.

"You want to see my dog, Mr. Morgan?"

"What you got?"

"A beagle. His name is Friar Tuck. He's number two. His pop died, but we got a pup to 'member him by."

"After I get some vittles in my innards," said Silas.

Lem cut the squirrels up, added them to the skillet. He banged the pot on the griddle, rattled the iron stove handles. He grinned maliciously as the meat sizzled, spit and hissed. Morgan took his medicine horn over to his bed, sat down to admire it away from the din. There was something different between his pa and Silas and he didn't know what it was. But he felt it. Silas just sat there, smoking quietly, and his pa wrestled with the hot skillet as if he wanted to burn the meat to a crisp and get it over with.

———·———

Silas stayed there for two days, telling Lem and Morgan about the things he had done, the sights he had seen. He spoke of prairies and rivers and game. He told them of seeing buffalo herds so huge it took them days to cross a river.

"I seen elk in herds of two, three hunnert," he said. "I kilt antelope what come up to me out of curiosity, shot 'em dead at less'n twenty yards."

"What about the Indians?" asked Morgan.

"Some is bad and you got to fight 'em. Some is good and will trade with you, let you sleep in their lodges. You got to keep your wits about you, son."

"Morg, you ask too many questions," said his father.

"But, Pa, I want to know what it's like out there."

Lemuel frowned and said nothing, but Silas smiled at the boy and gave him a furtive wink.

When Lem was plowing, Morgan followed Silas around, listened to his stories of Indian fights, trapping, hunting, fishing, running from grizzly bears. He heard mention of Lewis and Clark, of John Colter, Manuel Lisa, Louison Beaudoin, Jacques Clamorgan. To young Morgan, the names sounded strange and heroic.

The morning came when Silas bade farewells. Lem was anxious to see him go. He had seen a change in Morgan that he didn't like. The boy had taken to daydreaming, staying up late at night with Silas, talking of beaver like they was big as cows, Injun nonsense. Morgan was paying more attention to Silas than he was to his chores.

"Well, Lem, I done wore out my welcome, I 'spect, but it were worth it. I got to meet your boy and see how you growed. I'm back to the mountains and the trapper's life."

"Been good to see you, Silas. Thank you for the hat."

"And for the medicine horn," said Morgan.

"Ain't nothin' to that. You change your mind 'bout comin' out west, you look me up in St. Louis. Most ever'one knows Silas Morgan. You ask. I could use a partner. I'd give you traps and such the first season."

"No more talk about that, Silas. Best you be on your way."

"I will and thank ye for the hospice." Silas rumpled Morgan's hair. "Be seein' you, young Morgan."

"Good-by, Silas," said Morgan, surprised at his own boldness in using the trapper's first name. But he felt grown around him. Silas didn't treat him like a kid.

"Silas, you ride careful," said Lem.

Father and son watched Silas mount his horse and ride to the road. The first sarvice trees were starting to bloom and there were flashes of white, like gunsmoke, in the woody hills. The air had a sharp apple tang to it, and the morning wind blew strangely warm. Lem went to the barn to shoe Gideon, but Morgan stood there watching Silas until he disappeared from sight. Only the ring of hammer on iron broke his revery, brought him back to the present. As Silas was riding away, Morgan dreamed that he was going with him, all the way to the far mountains, where the beaver played in deep, dark pools, and elk roamed the high meadows, bugling like lords in the king's forest.

There was a sadness in Morgan when he realized Silas was gone and that he probably would never see him again.

———•———

In the spring of Morgan's sixteen year, the Bickhams' house caught on fire. The conflagration started on the back porch when a spark from a stump Calvin Moon was burning blew into Nancy's washbasket. The spark apparently smoldered for hours while Nancy was busy shaking out blankets and beating rugs and

Mr. Bickham was in town buying mules and new harness. Late in the afternoon, the porch erupted in flames. The wind came up and spread the fire. The Bickhams' house burned before anyone could get a bucket brigade started. Sparks spread to the hayloft and the barn exploded, spewing sparks and fireballs in every direction. The trees along the road caught fire and the wind whipped the fire across the fallow fields and down to Lem Hawke's place.

Before he and Morgan could do anything to stop it, the fire burned the barn and corrals. They managed to get the two horses, with their bridles, out, but the mules burnt to a crisp, their horrible brays chilling to hear. Friar Tuck Two barked until he was hoarse, ran around in circles until he collapsed in exhaustion. The Hawkes got their rifles, powder, ball, possibles pouches, horns and a few other things out of the house before it caught fire.

"You stay well away," Lem told Morgan. "Keep them horses from runnin' back to the barn."

Morgan led them to the field where their few goods lay in a heap. Friar Tuck followed, tail drooping, eyes swollen and red from the smoke. Morgan snatched up his medicine horn and held onto the bridle reins as his father dashed from the well to the house, carrying a bucket of water.

Lem stood on a wagon throwing water on the walls, but the flames scorched him so badly, he had to run to the well and dowse himself. Morgan stood by in the field, tears streaming down his face, watching the house burn to ashes. He held his medicine horn tightly in his hands until his father had to slap his face to bring him out of his sobbing fit.

All around them, smoke made the land dark, choked them. The fire raged into the hills, hungry flames licked at the hardwoods, snuffed out the beautiful white blossoms of the sarvice and dogwoods, the pale pink blooms of the redwood trees. Lem watched everything he owned burn, watched the woods blaze and belch columns of smoke into the sky until the sun was blotted out. The wind hurled the flames in all directions.

"We'd best go," he told Morgan. "Gather up your things and get on Boots."

"Pa, what'll we do?"

"I don't know, son. Better check on the Bickhams first. Then we got to find us a place to stay."

"My eyes hurt and it's hard to breathe."

"I know, Morg. We got to get out of the smoke."

Horatio Bickham met them on the road. His slaves were all huddled together trying to get the children to stop crying. Nancy's eyes were red from the smoke and her face blackened with soot.

"How's it down at your place, Hawke?" Bickham asked.

"All burnt," said Lemuel.

"Jesus."

"Anythin' I can do, Mr. Bickham?"

"Not now. We'll try and build it back someday. But not now. Jesus."

"Yes sir," said Lemuel. "Could I leave Friar Tuck with Calvin? Don't want him runnin' around town."

"I'll take care of it. C'mere boy."

Morgan carried Friar Tuck over to Bickham, gave him the dog. He patted Tut's head, whispered something into his ear.

"I'll be back for him, Mr. Bickham."

"We'll put him up in the empty hog pen," said Bickham.

Lem and Morgan waved good-by and rode into town. People lined the roads looking at the smoke and when they called out their questions he told them what had happened. Soon, people began to load their wagons up and ride out to see the destruction.

That night, Lem and Morgan sat in a hotel room, looking at their few pathetic possessions.

"I got my money outen the house before she went," said Lem. "We can get by."

"Are you goin' back, Pa?"

"Back? To what? A burnt-down farm. A coupla dead mules."

"We could go out west. Try and find Silas."

Lem looked at the boy, saw that he was serious. He shook his head, slumped with a weary resignation. He thought of the hard work that must be done, the money it would cost to buy new lumber, the time it would take to rebuild. He would still have to plow and plant, buy new stock. There was just him and the boy now. When he had begun the farm before, he had had Roberta and the unborn child to think about. He had wanted the farm then. Now, it seemed so useless. Morgan was growing into a man, filling out. He would be a help if he started up farming again.

"What do you want to do, Morg? Want to start up the farm again? Build us a house? It'd be hard. Plumb hard."

"What for, Pa? You don't own the land. It belongs to Mr. Bickham, you told me so. We could find Silas."

"Dammit, leave Silas out of this!" Lem didn't mean to shout, but there were things that fire had smoked out of him and maybe something burning inside him that he couldn't put out so easy. "Just tell me what you want to do."

"I don't want to go back there, Pa."

Morgan took a quick breath to keep from shaking. His father's scorching stare was making his face hot. But he was glad he had said it out loud. Ever since Silas had come to see them, he had been thinking about going out west, been thinking about those big rivers and the prairies and the beaver. He wanted to see what an elk looked like. He wanted to hunt antelope and see a prairie chicken strut when it was mating season. He wanted to see a grizzly bear up close and stand on top of the world and look down at it like the tallest person alive.

"You don't want no more of farmin'?"

"No," said Morgan.

"Why?"

"I don't know, Pa. It just seems like we don't get no place there. We do the same thing ever' year and then a big fire comes along and burns it all up. Don't make no sense to me. I want to see what Silas seen. I want to trap beaver."

"Be hard, boy. Awful hard. Did he tell you about how cold it gets and about standin' in shiverin' water tryin' to set a trap when your fingers is hard and cold? Did he tell you how dangerous it was? There's Injuns and they ain't no fun. I know. I kilt me a couple and it got a lot of innocent people kilt."

"You kilt Injuns, Pa?"

"I did and I ain't proud of it. It was necessary."

Morgan looked at his father with a keen interest. He felt something like pride swelling in him, something making his heart beat faster.

"Well, I'll fight 'em. You ain't got to worry none."

"Brave talk," said Lem, but he was pleased with his son.

"Let's go, Pa. Silas asked us to. Can we? Can we, please?"

"I'll think about it. It's a mighty big chunk right now. A fur piece to go, just on one man's say-so."

"We could do it, Pa. I know we could."

Lem sighed. What was it Silas had said? Seeds? Well, some more had been planted this night. He looked at Morgan, tried a feeble smile. Maybe the boy was right. Maybe they should move on, try something else. He had no close friends in Kentucky. He had done well, but he would have to start all over again.

"You go to sleep, Morg. I'll study on it awhile and do the same."

"I hope you make up your mind to go, Pa. I truly do."

"We'll chew on it some more in the mornin'."

Morgan grinned.

Later, when he fell asleep, his heart raced. Maybe they would go, he thought. Maybe they would see Silas again and go to the mountains with him.

———·———

In the morning, Morgan woke up in an empty room. It took him several moments to realize where he was. And then he remembered the fire.

"Pa?"

There was no answer.

He felt a tug of fear, a queasy swirl in his stomach. What if his father had left him? The room was strange. He scrambled out of bed and dressed quickly. He walked down the stairs and through the lobby of the hotel. Out on the street, he looked both ways, hoping to see his father.

There were a few people on the street. A two-wheeled cart lumbered by. Somewhere, a dog barked. Morgan's heart sank like a stone.

Then he saw his father emerge from the livery stables down the street. He was leading Hammerhead and Boots, and they had new saddles on their backs. Well, they were not new, but Morgan had never seen them before. His heart soared. He ran to meet his father.

"Where we goin', Pa?" he yelled. "Where we goin', huh?

Lem smiled.

"Why, we're a-headin' west, Morgan, to see if we can find old Silas. After we pick up Friar Tuck and say our good-bys to the Bickhams."

"Oh, Pa! Oh, Pa!" Morgan jumped up and down. He wanted to do handstands and cartwheels, but he chained his exuberance by pumping his arms up and down and just hopping around like a fool. But he felt real good and he wanted to hug his father and maybe peck him on the cheek.

"Settle down, Morgan. We got a heap to do afore we can

leave. We'll need food and canteens and somethin' to sleep on and under and a whole lot of stuff."

"I know, I know. Oh, Pa, I can't wait to go."

"We might stop by and see your ma, too. Tell her we're goin'."

Morgan fell silent. He had forgotten about his mother. But she would want to know, he reckoned. Maybe. She might not like it, neither.

"Let's just tell her real quick and then go on our way," said Morgan.

"We won't linger none," said Lem, and the bitterness welled up in him again. He was leaving a lot more than Kentucky, he thought. He was leaving a life that had gone bad on him for no good reason. Maybe Morgan was right. Maybe it was time to move on and forget about the past. He had money. He didn't owe any taxes.

For the first time in his life, Lemuel Hawke was beginning to feel truly free.

17

Friar Tuck ranged the post road out of Lexington, sniffing at every clump of grass, peeing on trees, jumping quail out of the thickets, chasing rabbits across wide, fresh-plowed fields, disappearing in the bluegrass that was just high enough to hide most of him. The Hawkes, father and son, left the town behind them as they headed southwest on the post road. The sun spangled the green buds with gilded spray, splashed goldenrod pollen on the winter-bare pastures, laced the ponds with ripples of molten honey. Meadowlarks piped on the fencerows as Morgan and his father, their horses loaded down with bedrolls and saddlebags bulging with foodstuffs, looked one last time at the hills and hollows they were leaving.

Morgan's stomach jiggled with the flutter of butterfly wings. A terrible feeling of homelessness overwhelmed him, but there was another, more elusive feeling as well. He dreaded seeing his mother, not so much for his sake, as for his father's. He had heard his father moan in the night and call her name aloud in his sleep. "Bobbie, Bobbie," his father had called, and Morgan awoke with an eerie feeling that she was in the room with them, come back to lurk in the shadows like a ghost. He had slept fitfully after that, and when they had said good-by to the Bickhams, Mrs. Bickham had broken down and cried, then run away to call her children together and tell them the Hawkes were leaving.

It had pained him to see Mrs. Bickham cry that way and he wondered if his mother would feel the same way when his pa told her about going out to the West.

Morgan slowed Boots some to ride behind his father. He looked at Lem's strong back, his long hair burnished dark by the sun. He knew that his pa still loved his mother. He had often heard him sob in his pillow at night and call out for his lost wife and it stabbed Morgan like a knife to hear his father weep for the woman who had deserted them both. He missed his mother, too, but he kept seeing her with that other man, Barry O'Neil, and the smirk on her painted face, the blurred look in her eyes. He kept hearing her scornful laughter and it tore at him like razors, left him bleeding inside with dozens of tiny wounds that hurt like black locust thorns.

After they had said good-by to the Bickhams, to Calvin Moon and the children, he and his pa had returned to town and bought goods for the trip: fry pans and boiling pots, wooden canteens, powder, ball, extra flints, smoked bacon, sacks of beans and flour, coffee, tobacco, blankets, rope, an axe and hatchet, a few tenpenny nails, some tinder and used cloth for making fires.

They had slept in the hotel one last night, his pa telling him they'd be spending their nights on hard ground once they left Lexington. Morgan looked at the stars a long time that night, standing at the window until his pa had called him to bed. He went to sleep wondering where Silas was at that moment, whether he was still in the mountains or if he had come down to the plains with his furs.

His father turned in the saddle to look at him. Morgan bowed his head for he did not want his pa to see what surely must be on his face.

"You tired, son?"

"Naw."

"Som'pin' wrong?"

"Nope. I was just thinkin'."

"Well, come on up and ride beside me."

Morgan tapped his heels into Boots's flanks, caught up with his father.

"What you been thinkin' on, Morg?"

"Ma, I reckon."

"Well, she might be glad to see you, seein' as how you've growed some."

"How come she to leave us, Pa?"

"I can't figger it. She got sweet on that Barry O'Neil, I reckon."

"You pine for her, don't you?"

"Some," said Lem, and drew in a breath, let it out in a barely audible sigh. "Was a time I thought she was the prettiest thing I ever saw. She was, too. I get to pinin' for them days now and again."

"I don't hardly remember her anymore," said Morgan, but that wasn't what he wanted to say. He didn't remember her as his mother, just as a woman who had been drunk and sent them away so's she could be with another man. Morgan hated her for that. He couldn't remember her touch, or whether she had ever put her arms around him or hugged him. Those were the things he wanted to remember, but he could never summon them up to his mind.

"Sure you do, son. Why, she used to dote on you."

"Did she?"

"On both of us," said Lem, and then he was silent, remembering little things that he had almost forgotten.

Lem thought of those lazy afternoons back in Virginia when he wanted her so much he had to come in from the fields and tease her, coax her into bed. He remembered her shy giggles when he wrestled with her, and burned her cheeks with kisses, smothered her with his youthful lust. He remembered the glow in her brown eyes when he made love to her, and how they lay back and lingered on the beauty of their passion, awestruck at the wonder of it. Her hair smelled of lilacs and her mouth tasted of crushed mint. He remembered how she made him feel good inside, how his awkwardness would go away when she kissed him back as good as he had kissed her. Those were the thoughts that wrenched him now, made him realize how much he had lost when Roberta had left him.

"I hope she's glad to see us," said Morgan, breaking into his father's thoughts. "But, I hope you don't auger none to stay."

"She won't want us to stay," said Lem.

"And we won't anyway," said Morgan, so curtly his father laughed aloud.

"No, we won't stay. Once you cut loose, you don't let nothin' stop you from goin'."

Morgan grinned, rode off chasing after Friar Tuck with a whoop and a holler.

———·———

After camping for one night in the woods and riding half a morning of the next day, Lem and Morgan rode into the Cumberland Valley where the post road intersected another road running east and west through Gallatin. They headed south to Nashville, passing a number of tippling houses, some of them new. They came to the town just after noon. They passed fields planted in cotton and tobacco that butted up to the narrow Cumberland River with its deep brown waters. They looked up, saw small houses clinging to the edges of a bluff like boxes nailed to a wall. Lem put Hammerhead into a trot as the road steepened, rising up above the river. There, atop the high bluff that commanded the wide valley, stood the town of Nashville.

"Small, ain't it?" said Lem, looking at the houses and buildings.

"Not as big as Lexington," said Morgan.

They kept to the main road, looked at the houses lining both sides of the unpaved streets. At the center of town, Lem marked the public buildings as his gaze swept the business district. There had been earthquakes during the winter; they had seen wrecked buildings in Lexington and along the way. Here, the damage seemed worse; they passed brick buildings that had cracked open like eggs, chimney bricks strewn in the weeds beside collapsed houses. In the center of town, there were downed scaffoldings, teetering walls and scattered piles of rubble everywhere they looked. There was a jail, a courthouse, a post office, and a large market house. The side streets were all crowded with people at market, and they had passed two noisy inns just before reaching the square.

At another, the Red Lion on a corner of the square, a man hailed them. His cheeks, nestled in a thick, woolly beard, glowed like cherry coals. He stood outside the inn, holding a fired-clay jug.

"Pilgrims," he called, "light down and wet yore thoats."

The man was dressed in grimy buckskins that were almost orange and most of the fringes had rotted or been torn away. He packed a large skinning knife on his wide belt, and a hunting pouch and a matched pair of powder horns hung from his shoulders.

Lem shook his head, but the man stepped onto the road and blocked their way.

"You farmers?" he asked.

Morgan shook his head. Lem nodded.

"Well, which is it? One is and one isn't."

"We been farmin'," said Lem, holding Hammerhead back with the reins pulling on the bit.

"I been trappin' the Great Lakes and the Ohio Valley, eatin' bear meat and wolf. Good season too, when we wasn't fallin' down from the quake."

"We got to get on," said Lem.

"Not 'thout havin' a tipple with Nat Sullard, you don't," said the man.

"My boy don't drink," said Lem. "And neither do I," he lied.

"That yore boy? Wal, now, Pilgrim, 'bout time he tasted the critter. Me 'n my pard's quittin' the Ohio and headin' west to the big mountains."

"You been there?" Morgan just blurted the question out.

"Nope, but they's a feller over to the market sellin' the purtiest furs you ever seen what he got in a place called Yallerstone. Me 'n him're hookin' up, and my pard's a-goin' with us. Light down and come inside. The boy can have ginger beer, won't hurt him none."

"We got things we got to do," said Lem.

"Pa, can't we? Just for a little while?"

"Why, shore, Pa," mocked Sullard. "Come on and meet some of the trappers. We done sold our goods and we aim to drink Nashville dry afore we set out for the mountains."

"We'll come back," said Lem. "We got business."

"Wal, now, you and the boy come back. Me'n Charlie Pack will be in the Red Lion swallerin' grog."

"Oh, Pa, can't we go in now?" asked Morgan.

"We'll be back," said Lem.

"Promise?" asked Sullard.

Morgan looked hard at his father.

"Promise," said Lem tightly, slacking up on the reins. Sullard stepped aside and the Hawkes rode slowly by him. From inside the Red Lion Inn, they heard a burst of laughter, and someone yelled exuberantly above the noise.

"We'll be back, Mr. Sullard," said Morgan, waving to the trapper, who was already weaving his way back inside the tippling house.

"Morgan, you got a lot to learn," said his father, as Hammerhead broke into a trot.

"Look, Pa," said Morgan, pointing to the big market across the quad. "That's where the other trappers are!"

Buckskinned men sat on bales of furs, or leaned against two-wheeled carts. Clumps of men crowded the makeshift counters out front, pawing through loose pelts, holding them up to the light.

"Trappers," said Lem, riding toward the bustling throng of marketers and fur traders.

Morgan grew excited when he saw a man standing atop a large crate, waving a beaver pelt like the one Silas had shown them.

"They got beaver," exclaimed Morgan, clapping his heels to his horse's flanks. Boots galloped ahead of Lem's horse, heading straight for the trader's market. Men looked at the boy and a constable waved a wooden stick at Morgan, warning him to slow down his horse. Morgan reined up and waited for his father.

A trapper argued with a fur buyer over the quality of his catch. One of the buyers wiped perspiration from his brow with a swatch of broadcloth. The trapper had a faint accent. He was burly, muscular, with a dark shock of hair coiling from under his light voyageur's cap. He was dressed in cotton trousers, wore a bright red sash under his belt, a loose-fitting muslin shirt that bore the grime of a working man. He carried a large knife on his belt, wore moccasin boots that laced to his knees. His most striking feature, however, was that he wore a smile, even though he appeared to be angry.

"But you are cheating me," said the trapper. "Deez are prime fur, you bet. O'Neil, he give me one pound."

"That's my price, Jocko," said the buyer, a reedy-voiced man in his midtwenties. "Barry's bought up. Half a pound."

"Pah! You take dem, you cheater sumbitch," said the trapper, still smiling. "You give me twenty pound."

"Nineteen and the half," said the buyer.

"Twenty."

The buyer sighed, pulled out a roll of banknotes. He counted out twenty and handed them to the trapper. The trapper, still grinning, counted each bill and stuffed them inside his sash. He swaggered toward Lem and Morgan.

Lem swung down off his horse.

"Sir," he said to the trapper, "could I have a word with you?"

"I got no more fur to sell." The trapper smiled pleasantly.

"I'm wondering where I can find Barry O'Neil," said Lem.

"That sumbitch. He don't show his damn face. He send that cheater Wally, eh? O'Neil, he got better t'ings to do."

"Where can I find him?"

"He got a store just down that street." The trapper pointed. "Big store. He buy plenty fur cheap. I go see Big John. He owes me money. Then, I go to St. Louis. No more cheating this damn place."

"You goin' to the mountains?" asked Morgan, his eyes lit up like firebrands.

"You bet," said the trapper. "Ever'body he go to the mountains. Dis be last time I trap those damn big lakes."

"That's where we're a-goin'," said Morgan. Lem gave his son a dark look.

"You meet the Major?" asked the trapper.

Morgan shook his head.

"Come, you follow Jocko to see Big John O'Neil. He owes me some money, eh? Then we go to that Red Lion whiskey store, see Major McDougal."

"Who's he?" asked Lem.

"He works for Missouri Fur. He make you a good offer, I think. Me, too. We go to see that Major, listen to what he has to say, huh? He sell plenty prime fur for top dollar."

"We'd be mighty obliged to go with you to O'Neil's," said Lem. "I got business with Barry."

"Ah, Barry, he ain't no count," said the trapper. "Mighty good bootlicker for his uncle, I think."

"What's your name?" asked Morgan, not realizing it was considered impolite.

"Hah! I'm Jacques Decembre. They call me Jocko DeSam. And you, young feller, what they call you?"

"I'm Morgan Hawke."

DeSam turned to Lem.

"And this is your papa, no?"

"I'm Lemuel Hawke, the boy's pa."

"You're not trappers?"

"No," said Lem. "But we aim to go west, see someone we know."

"This Morgan, he look pretty young."

"He's broke to the plow," said Lem, some testiness in his voice.

DeSam laughed. He slapped Morgan on the shoulder.

"You come with Jocko. We get the business done and see Major McDougal. He make you both a good offer. Plenty of money in the fur, I think, but in Tennessee, they are all thieves. Big John O'Neil's the biggest thief of all."

Lem mounted up. They followed DeSam to the street he had pointed out. Halfway down the block, Jocko stopped in front of a large building. Workers were filling in chinks where bricks had loosened during the winter earthquakes. The big sign over the entrance proclaimed:

TENNESSEE HATTERY
JOHN O'NEIL, PROP.

"Used to be called different," said Lem.

"He big-time hatter now," said Jocko. "He make the best

damn thief." DeSam smiled when he spoke, as if everything was a big joke to him.

The three entered the store, stood peering about the large showroom. Men and women shoppers browsed among the hat displays. Male clerks fawned over the women and Barry O'Neil held a mirror up to a female customer's face while she admired a beaver felt hat. A tall man at the rear of the store pulled down a hatbox, handed it to a man at the foot of the ladder.

"That's Big John back there," said DeSam.

"Me'n my boy'll speak to Barry, that red-headed feller over yonder," said Lem.

Jocko strode toward the rear of the store, making a beeline for Big John.

Barry looked up, saw Lemuel and Morgan. He smiled at the woman, handed her the mirror. He stepped away, waited. Lem jostled a man aside. Morgan followed in his wake.

O'Neil swaggered to meet them, the barest curl of a smile at one corner of his twisted mouth. Morgan felt his muscles tauten as he looked at the man he'd last seen with his mother. He could not help thinking that he was already as tall as the man his father hated.

"Hawke," he said. "It's been a long time. I hope you came to buy a hat." Beneath the overt cordiality, there was a faint trace of nervousness, a slight quivering in O'Neil's voice.

"I come to talk to Roberta," said Lem tightly.

"She hasn't worked for us in some time," said O'Neil.

"You know where she is?"

"Last I knew, she was staying at Miss DuMont's Boarding House. Over on Central." O'Neil held up his right hand, curled the fingers as if examining the nails. He regarded the Hawkes with a diffident air.

"Why ain't she a-workin' here?" asked Lem.

"That's none of your business, Hawke."

"Maybe it is. You fire her?"

"We had to let her go. She, ah, she has a fondness for barleycorn whiskey."

"If she does, you put her to it."

"I think, Hawke, whatever she has, she brought it with her."

"You sonofabitch," said Hawke quietly, a seething hatred in his tone.

O'Neil turned on his heel, took a step before Lem caught him by the collar. He spun the hatter around. Barry's mouth widened in surprise.

"Somethin' to remember us by, O'Neil," said Hawke. He drew back a fist and shot it straight to Barry's jaw. There was a sharp crack and O'Neil's eyes rolled backward in their sockets. His neck snapped backward and he reeled away, crumpled into a hat tree. The tree and O'Neil went down with a resounding crash.

"Golly damn!" exclaimed Morgan, swearing for the first time. "You busted him good, Pa."

John O'Neil, hearing the commotion, broke away from Jocko, sweeping him aside with a brawny arm, headed toward the scene of the ruckus. DeSam, angered that he had not yet finished the argument to his satisfaction, recovered his balance and set off at a strong lope to catch the elder O'Neil.

Barry groaned and pulled himself to a sitting position. Lem braced himself, his hands still balled into fists, and glared at the fallen O'Neil. He did not see Big John eating up floor with long, determined strides.

Big John O'Neil was not the puny spectacle of manhood his nephew Barry was, but an oversized brute with muscular arms, powerful broad shoulders and a neck thick as a nail keg. He stood six foot six in his socks. His massive brow jutted over crisp blue eyes, set off a jaw square as a plumb-bobbed slab of granite. The only resemblance between him and his nephew, Barry, was the thick sheaf of red hair that graced his pate like a lion's mane.

Morgan looked up and saw the giant redhead striding straight toward his father.

"Pa, look out!" he called.

Lem turned around, but not in time.

Big John, for all his size and weight, was quick and lithe on his feet. He grabbed Lemuel Hawke by the scruff of his collar and hauled him toward a ham-sized fist hurtling toward the smaller man's jaw with the impetus of a 16-pound maul. John's fist landed square on Lem's chin, propelling him from O'Neil's grasp and into a woman's bustle. The woman screamed in terror and went down. Lem slid across her rump and into a cabinet stacked with hats.

Morgan threw himself headlong at Big John's legs, tackled him. It was, he thought, like trying to bring down a scaly-bark hickory with twenty-foot roots. Big John didn't budge and lashed downward with one of his gigantic hands. He grabbed Morgan's hair and jerked the boy upward like a kicking puppet.

DeSam waded into the melee with both fists swinging. He caught Big John in the side with a roundhouse left and banged his right into a kidney. It was like hitting a slab of cold beef hanging from a butcher's rack.

Barry O'Neil scrambled to his feet and raced from the store, screaming at the top of his voice.

"Constable! Constable!" Barry yelled, and the store, filled with screaming women and confused men, emptied like a factory at the closing whistle.

Morgan broke free of Big John's grip and fell to the floor.

Big John turned and warded off another of DeSam's blows and slid an uppercut under Jocko's right arm and compressed his chin with a solid, smashing fist of considerable force. DeSam blinked like a snared rabbit and staggered around in a little circle on rubbery legs.

Lem crawled from under a pile of hats and ran back for

another chance at Big John, as the latter swung a bruising fist in Morgan's direction. Morgan ducked and felt the rush of air over his head. The fear that knotted his innards oozed away with the rush of anger that filled his veins with needles. He saw his father jolt into Big John's midsection like a charging bull. Big John, caught off balance, staggered a half-foot off his spot. Morgan saw his advantage and plowed into him, arms flailing like a pair of rug-beaters. His fists grazed Big John's cheek and bounced off his barrel chest. Jocko stepped in, drove a fist into Big John's solar plexus with little noticeable effect. Big John smacked Morgan in the temple. Morgan went down in a heap, but grabbed one of O'Neil's legs. He pulled himself close enough to bite him as Lem and Jocko increased the fury of their twin attack. Morgan bit Big John in the calf and felt the muscle cord up and harden like a chunk of pig iron.

The next thing he knew, Morgan felt a shoe crunch his stomach flat and he lost all the air in his lungs.

Three constables rushed into the store, each grasping a polished bung-starter. On their heels, Barry O'Neil gripped a chunk of two-by-four lumber snatched from the construction platform outside.

Big John went down, to his knees at least, under the onslaught from Lem and Jocko. But, the constables came up on the fight just as both men were about to deliver the *coup de grace* and started clubbing them mercilessly with the bung starters. Barry O'Neil swung his two-by-four club on Morgan, thumping him soundly on the temple. Lem and Jocko went down, blood streaming from their scalps, thickening in their hair, blinding them in a crimson rush.

"Arrest them, arrest them," Barry screamed, and one of the constables shoved him aside and spoke in a thick Irish brogue.

"Sure, and that's just what we'll be doin', Mr. O'Neil, if you'll stop your squawkin' and leave to us the immediate corporal punishment of these divils."

Barry took one more whack at Morgan, hitting him in the gluteus maximus with the flat side of the board. Morgan never felt it. He was out cold, a lump growing on his temple to the size of a darning egg.

Within a half an hour, Lem, Morgan and Jocko were all painfully regaining consciousness in the Nashville jail.

18

Morgan heard the soft tread of footsteps outside the jail cell. Thin morning light streamed ashen through the single high window in the log wall. He shivered in the chill, rubbed his grit-clogged eyes. His pa and DeSam were asleep in opposite corners. His father had moaned during the night, whimpered sporadically in his dreams. The three of them were the only prisoners and no one had come by since one of the constables had turned the key on them the day before, locking them in. No one had fed them and Morgan's stomach rumbled with hunger.

He stood up, his joints stiff from sleeping on the hard dirt floor of the cell. His neck and shoulders ached. A shot of pain stabbed his chest. He peered hard at the woman standing in front of the iron bars.

For a moment, she looked like a statue, or a scarecrow. Morgan felt an odd tingle at the back of his neck, a slender moment of fear that he could not explain.

Roberta stood to one side of the cell door looking frail and emaciated in her loose-fitting cotton dress. She wore a faded bonnet that failed to shield her gaunt face. Her eyes drooped with weariness and resignation. There was no depth in their murky brown pupils; they appeared glazed and lifeless.

"Ma?"

"Is that you, Morgan?"

He walked a few steps toward her, trembling. He felt dizzy, lightheaded.

"I—it's me, Ma," he stammered. The shock of seeing her so close, and after so long, made his throat go dry.

"Come here," she said, "so I can see you."

"Yes'm," he said, and walked a few paces toward her, then stopped.

"Come closer."

He stepped up to the bars, quaking inside with that nameless tingle of fear still probing his spine.

"My, look at you. Nigh full growed." She paused, looked at him oddly. "I was beautiful once," she said.

"Yes'm," he said, looking down at his feet. He felt her eyes scouring him from head to toe. He thought it was strange for his mother to say that. He remembered her as being beautiful. She still was, in a way. There was just something peculiar about the look in her eyes.

"What has your pa done to you?"

"Nothin'."

"Fightin' and such. The whole town's talkin' about it."

"That Barry O'Neil, he started it. Then, his uncle got into it and them constables come in and started hittin' us. Throwed us in jail."

"What does your pa want in Nashville? Have you seen my mother? She was not beautiful. No, not in the least, I tell you." A savage tone crept into his mother's voice. Morgan swayed back on his heels, but he did not move away.

"We come to say good-by to you," said Morgan. He looked

up at his mother, then. She reached through the bars and touched his hair. He drew back. His pa stirred at the back of the cell.

"Lemuel," said his mother, looking past her son.

Lem moaned. Morgan turned, saw his father rise to his feet, sway on wobbly legs.

"Bobbie? That you?" Lem's voice rasped and he cleared his throat, wobbled toward Morgan.

"It's Ma," said Morgan, some of the fear going away. His pa walked up, stood beside his son.

"Come to gloat?" asked Lemuel. "That chicken gut O'Neil got us into this fix."

"Well, Lemuel," she said softly, "you and the boy turned out as I expected. A couple of common ruffians."

"Bobbie," said Lem, pulling himself up straight. "We—we come to see you, say good-by."

"Is this the way you do it? The whole town's talking about the way you and Morgan attacked Barry and John. You never saw me, Lem. I was there, but you couldn't see me like I was. Like I really was."

"What the hell you talkin' about, woman?"

Morgan heard a sound, looked over his shoulder. Jocko was awake, but his face was a lumpy mass of dried blood and his hair was matted with dark tangles. His lips were swollen and cracked and his eyes were just slits behind puffed mounds as if he had been stung by a swarm of hornets.

Morgan's father looked just as bad, with a tattered and bloody ear, black-and-blue eyes, his mouth crooked and lumpy as unkneaded dough. Lem's shirt was torn and his face stippled with dark bristles.

"You don't know, Lem," said Roberta. "You just don't know. You never did. I wasn't in the dirt. I was in the trees like a beautiful bird. You just couldn't see me."

"I just come lookin' for you," said Lem, awkwardly. He wondered what Roberta was talking about. She sounded crazy.

Roberta stepped closer to the bars, looked down the hallway. She spoke in a deep whisper.

"Well, Big John wants to put all three of you in the stocks. I've come to warn you. Can you pay your fine? I've already spoken to Constable Parkhurst. If you pay five pounds apiece, he'll let you go. Barry is a murderer. He will murder you."

"I ain't afraid of no O'Neil," said Lem loudly.

"Shh! I'm serious, Lem. If they put you in the stocks, someone will sneak up on you after dark and put a bullet in each one of you. Barry plowed me like a field. He dug everything up and then—then he squatted on me and left a smell. He—he scattered all my seeds. He will put you in the stocks and squat on you."

"You think so?" Lem didn't know what to make of Roberta. One minute she seemed sane, the next she drifted off and made no sense at all.

"I heard talk of it," she whispered. She narrowed her eyes and lowered her head. "There are skulls buried out there."

"Pa, let's pay the money and go on out west," said Morgan quickly. He, too, knew that his mother seemed touched in the head.

"You're going west?" asked Roberta.

"We are."

"Then, you'd best be on your way quick," said Roberta. "Before he robs you, too. He will take everything away. He taketh, he taketh." Her eyes rolled in their sockets and she swayed on her feet as if about to topple backwards, but she recovered from her spell and glared at her former husband and her son.

"We'll pay," said Lemuel. "And we thank you for warning us."

Morgan breathed an audible sigh.

"Good," said Roberta. "I'll tell Mr. Parkhurst."

She turned to leave. She stopped, looked back toward Lem and Morgan.

"They'll all burn in hell, Lemuel. All of 'em."

"Wait," said Lemuel. "Can we talk some place?"

"No, it's best you leave town. Your horses are in the Pine Street livery. I'll say good-by now. He loved to touch my breasts and we drank champagne and we lived in clouds, in dark clouds. It was smoky and we floated all over."

She looked at Morgan, drew in a deep breath.

Morgan winced at the sadness he saw in his mother's eyes. She was whispering something and it made no sense. He listened to her words and knew that she was mad. He saw the sugar-hot light in her eyes, the flare of lightning when she talked of strange things she saw in her mind and he knew that she was addled. He did not understand why or how, but he knew she had gone mad as sure as he knew a rabid skunk when it came hunting chickens and spraying the night air with an acrid foulness that stung his nose and blistered his eyes until they watered with unwilling tears.

"Godspeed," she sighed.

Before Lem could stop her, Roberta was gone. He heard voices and a few moments later one of the constables came down the hall. He carried a key attached to a large ring.

"You got the money?" he asked.

"Fifteen pounds," said Lem.

"Twenty."

"I thought—"

"Make up your mind, me bucko. It's twenty pounds. Be higher if you make me wait."

Jocko rose to his feet, lurched toward Lem and Morgan. He reached into his belt, extracted a wad of notes.

"Just open up that door, turnkey," he growled. "We pay you the damned money."

Lem took off a moccasin, pulled out some bills. Morgan watched the two men in fascination as they counted out the banknotes.

"Let's see that key go in the door first," said Lem.

The constable opened the cell door. Lem and Jocko slammed money into his palm, brushed past him. They walked through the office and out the door into the feeble sunlight. Jocko blinked and winced in the glare. Lem squinted.

"Point me to them stables," he told DeSam.

"I don't know who that woman was, but she knows Big John and his damned nephew," said Jocko. "Them two work real good in the dark."

"You heard what she said?"

"I did, sure."

"You goin' west, then?"

"Soon as I can get my traps," said DeSam.

"Maybe we'll meet up with you," said Morgan.

"You know the way?"

"We do," said Lem. "It's a fur piece."

"Maybe I see you in St. Louis," said Jocko. "You go down this street to the next one yonder and turn right. Stables be back of Blevins Dry Goods."

"Thank you kindly," said Lem.

DeSam flapped an arm in farewell, plodded off in the opposite direction. Morgan watched him get smaller and smaller, then realized his father was already walking away in the direction Jocko had pointed.

Within an hour, Lem and Morgan were finished with Nashville. They heard talk of war with Britain at Blevins's store, where they bought extra shirts and a coffee pot. The clerk mentioned a man named Andrew Jackson, who was recruiting a militia, and Blevins himself said they ought to go over to the courthouse that night and hear a young lawyer named Thomas Hart Benton talk about defending the southwestern frontier of

Tennessee. Lem had told both men they were leaving the country, heading for Missouri Territory. Morgan noticed the odd looks as they carried out their goods.

"How far to St. Louis, Pa?" asked Morgan as they rode along the Cumberland River.

"'Bout three hunnert mile," said Lem.

"How do you know the way?"

"A long time ago, Silas told me about it. I guess it plumb stuck in my craw all this time."

Morgan beamed.

"I'm glad we're goin'," he said. Neither of them wanted to mention that they now had another reason for leaving. Morgan kept thinking about his mother and the scary things she had said. He knew his father was thinking about her too. He was as solemn as a preacher.

"You tell me that next week, Morg. Silas said St. Louie was just about the hardest place to get to he ever seed."

"How come?"

"Well, you just can't go straight to it. We got to ride the Natchez Trace to the Mississippi River. What I hear, it's a fearsome wilderness. We'll have to keep our eyes peeled and locks primed."

Morgan's face glistened in the cool wash of sunlight. He touched the medicine horn slung on his shoulder and felt a surge of excitement. With the horn and his rifle, he was ready to face the most horrible dangers he could imagine. He looked forward to anything that would stop him from thinking about his mother and her madness. He hardly noticed when his father turned southwest, heading, it seemed, in the opposite direction of where they were bound.

———·———

After waiting five days in Natchez for a boat to carry them up the Mississippi, Lem and Morgan Hawke thought they'd never live long enough to see St. Louis. Morgan did not mind the slowness. He loved the feel of the rolling river, the tide surge of the mighty waters that made the deck rise and fall. He felt a sense of power watching the land go by and when he saw game, mostly deer, he took imaginary aim as if holding his rifle and squeezed off a killing shot. They learned, from others who waited, that they could have ridden post roads from Tennessee across Kentucky and up into Illinois and saved a lot of miles. But, Lem did not rue the trip. They had seen a lot of country, had no trouble with Indians or robbers, and now, at last, they were in Missouri Territory.

They unloaded the horses at the small settlement, sniffed the garbage piled in the street along the waterfront. A clutter of whitewashed buildings shone like disheveled swans in the sun. Beyond the foul-smelling sandy levee, the rolling countryside sprawled invitingly toward the distant horizon.

Stevedores wrestled cargo on the docks, swearing in French and English. Boats of all sizes bobbed at anchor or jostled for position at one of the wharves, and the gulls wheeled above the fishing boats like papers fluttering in the wind.

"Where do we go now, Pa?" asked Morgan.

"Find us a place to bed and board, I reckon."

"Will we look for Silas?"

"I reckon." Lem's bruises had faded and most of the stiffness had gone, but he still had a few aches in bone and muscle. He had gotten sick on the boat, but Morgan had scampered about like a swashbuckling pirate, calling out each new sight as if he was Christopher Columbus. Sometimes, Lem thought, the boy's enthusiasm was downright disgusting.

The long trip had hardened Morgan's muscles. His hair had grown thick as a mane and his handsome face was bronzed by the sun. He would be seventeen in October, and he was almost as tall as his father, though not as muscular. They unloaded their gear, packed it aboard Boots and Hammerhead, rode past Front Street and up Olive to the center of town on Fourth Street. They found a stone building that housed a hotel, whitewashed like the others, on Fourth and Laurel, and a stable at the end of the street where they could board their horses. They shared a small second-story room at Lescoulie's Hotel; two cots, a small table and two chairs, a small highboy dresser. There was a privy out back and for sixpence, they could bathe in a wooden tub in a back room on the first floor. Pierre Lescoulie told them about the stables, owned by his brother-in-law, Emile DeBalaviere. Board was a shilling a day.

"It's better you pay in coin," Pierre told Lem. "They's some as will take banknotes, English not American, but most all will take Portagee coin, Spanish bits and pieces, French, too."

"We got mostly coin," said Lem.

"Best get the paper changed," said the innkeeper. "You talk to Emile."

Emile, a stocky Frenchman from New Orleans, had been in St. Louis since 1803, when the Louisiana Purchase made it part of the United States. He had visited the city before, when the Mississippi was a dangerous river, infested with cutthroats and pirates. Emile's father, Etienne, had participated in *L'Anee des Dix Bateaux* (the Year of the Ten Boats) in 1788. The crews of the boats had traveled upstream from New Orleans and met the pirates in savage combat, driving them from the river.

"Since I come here," Emile told them, "ever'body he make a lot of money from the furs. But, there is always much trouble on the levee, the fighting and killing. *Mais,* there are many fine and beautiful homes here, even so."

Emile told them where they could change their pound notes into hard coin. Lem had no American money. Paper currency issued by the Continental Congress had been worthless since it was first issued in '92.

"Where might we find a trapper by name of Silas Morgan?" Lem asked Lescoulie.

"Ah, I know this Morgan. He drink at the King's Boar and he eat at Spanish Jack's. These places are on Third Street. They stink. Too close to Bloody Island for me, eh? Too many men killed there."

"Bloody Island?"

"That whole levee, the waterfront. They call it that. They fight the duels, they bet the cards, they fight the cocks. Gamblers, the freebooters, adventurers, they like cats at night. They look for fights and trouble, no? Eh, I tell you what they say. They say they can do anything they want. God he don't never cross the Mississippi, they say."

"You know Silas Morgan?" Lem asked.

"He work for Missouri Fur. He trap the mountains. So many now. Yes, I know him. He part Indian, I think, part bear. He stay too long in the mountains. Go there too many years."

Emile walked away from them, shaking his head, still talking to himself.

Morgan smiled.

"Let's go find Silas," he said to his father.

"We'll look for him, I reckon," said Lem, hitching up his worn trousers. "Maybe we'll eat supper at Spanish Jack's, ask about old Silas."

Morgan grinned wide enough to make his eardrums pop.

———•———

Spanish Jack's, on Third Street, was crammed between a jumble of other buildings. Lantern light spilled onto the dirt street, buttered the wooden platform that served as an entrance step.

Lem and Morgan stood out front, listened to the clank of metal plates, the tink of clay mugs, the rattle of eating utensils, the low hum, and occasional eruption, of multilingual conversation.

"Let's eat," said Lem.

"I'm sure hungry, Pa."

The two entered the eating establishment, blinked in the yellow-orange light. Heavy tables crisscrossed the room, benches and tables stood near the walls to accommodate larger parties. A serving wench looked up at them, a waiter whisked away through a doorway in the back. The aroma of food assailed Morgan's nostrils and he felt a tug in his stomach.

The waitress cocked her head toward an empty table.

"Pa? There's a table over yonder."

Lem didn't move. Instead, he stared at a man seated with another in one corner of the room.

"Pa?"

Lem stood there, transfixed, looking into the eyes of a man he believed dead.

19

Morgan looked up at his father, saw the startled expression frozen on his face. He tugged at Lem's sleeve. The serving girl waved an arm at the empty table while continuing to stare at the elder Hawke.

"I'm lookin' at a ghost," said Lem.

"Huh?" Morgan followed the path of his father's stare. He saw the man at the far table with that same look in his eyes.

"We got to get out of here," choked Lem, but he remained rooted to the spot, unable to move.

"Who is he, Pa?"

"Someone who's dead."

"He looks alive to me," said Morgan.

The man at the table rose up and Lem's face blanched like an early morel. The man's chair scraped as he pushed away from the table. He started walking toward Lem and Morgan, head cocked to one side, an eyebrow arched in puzzlement.

Lem made a gurgling sound in his throat.

"G-get away from me," he croaked.

"That you, Hawke?" The man hunched over, peered intently at Lem's face. "Aw, shore, it is you, Lemuel Hawke."

Lem gulped in air. His eyes popped from their sockets as the man drew closer. He seemed changed, but there was no mistaking that face. It was older and more cragged than he remembered. But it couldn't be. The man with that face was dead, long dead. Dead and gone.

"Haw, it's me, Dick Hauser. 'Member? Hell, you got to recollec' me. Back when you kilt them two Injuns? When we was all a-goin' to Kentucky, huh? Me and Ormly skelpt 'em, took their rifles."

"No," said Lem and he struggled to lift his foot, but he couldn't force himself to turn his back on the apparition that stalked him.

"Haw, now, Lemuel. I didn't get kilt. Did you think them Injuns kilt me and Ormly?"

"Jesus," rasped Lem. "I plumb thought you was dead. I just knew you was." In his mind, Lem saw the bodies of those who had been killed. The women and children, the men. All of 'em. Ever' damn one of 'em.

Dick Hauser stepped up close to Lem, clapped him on the shoulder. Lem didn't faint, but he felt giddy. Morgan braced himself to fight the stranger. For some reason his pa was afraid of him. Had they been in a fight? Did his pa think he'd killed this Dick Hauser?

"Pa, want me to hit him?" asked Morgan.

Hauser looked, then, at the boy.

"This one of your'n? Looks some to resemble you, Lemuel. Come on, I'll buy you a cup and tell you my tale. It's long and fearsome, but I got out alive and stand here fit and hearty to tell about it."

"Christ, Dick," said Lem, shaking his head in disbelief. "I surely thought you was dead. I mean—"

"I know. They kilt ever'one, my poor wife and kids, and Ormly's family. Come on, set with us. The boy might like a good story. What's your name, son?"

"Morgan Hawke."

"Good name."

"Come on, Morgan," said Lem, recovering his composure. "We'll set with you, Dick. If it's really you."

"It's really me. Luckiest son of a buck what ever walked this earth. C'mon."

Puzzled and curious, Morgan followed the two men to the back table. The serving girl gave the boy a funny look and shrugged. When they reached the table, the other man looked up at Lem Hawke without smiling.

"Doc, this here's Lemuel Hawke, the one I told you about. Some older an' I hope not much bolder, but here he be."

The man at the table scowled. Morgan took him to be likkered up. His breath reeked of strong whiskey and his eyes were red-rimmed. He was dressed in simple clothes, like Dick Hauser. He wore a shabby linsey-woolsey shirt, the cuffs dirty. His eyes were pale blue and he had a mole on the tip of his bulbous nose.

"Well, well, well," said Doc. "The big brave Indian fighter. Never mind that you cost the lives of a dozen people, mister. You got your stinking scalps and left behind a lot of women and children to rot like carrion."

"Haw, he don't mean nothin'," said Hauser. "Doc's just drunker'n six pounds and six bits. He come off his first year of trappin' and he's still trying to thaw his pizzle. Gets damned cold a-settin' traps in them high mountain cricks." Hauser paused. "Set, Lemuel. You too, Morgan."

Lemuel was not appeased. He sat down, glared at the man

called Doc. Morgan sat down eagerly. He looked at Dick Hauser and Doc in a new light. They were trappers. Dick wore a dyed linsey-woolsey shirt, heavy trousers, and boot moccasins. He packed two lean Spanish pistols stuck inside a beaded sash tied around his waist. A large knife with a massive handle dangled from his wide leather belt. He had deep-sunk lines and scars on his face, a patch of hair missing in the front. He had combed over it, but Morgan could see the pink circle where hair had once grown. The man was lean as a slat.

"I kilt them Injuns in fair fight," said Lem to Doc, "and I gave the scalps to Dick here, or Ormly one. They was only two and I didn't know the whole damned tribe would come huntin' them folks. Lord knows I tried to warn 'em. Them two was a-tryin' to sneak back and draw more blood, that's for damned sure, mister."

"'At's right, Doc. Fact is, Lemuel, givin' us them scalps was what saved our puny asses. Them Injuns thought we'uns was the ones what kilt their brothers and onliest reason they didn't kill us was to show us off to their kinfolk. Hell, they paraded us around their camp like we was high-kickin' prize mules. They let the women beat hell out of us and the kids crack us with sticks and th'ow rocks at us, but they was proud to capture us, they was. The bucks treated us like we was heroes."

The serving girl came over to the table with a slate in her hand. She sailed it onto the table. It landed in front of Lemuel. The girl scrutinized Morgan, made a slight moué of her mouth. She was dressed in a one-piece cotton dress, gray, high-bodiced, with a black apron. Her hair was auburn, her eyes brown. She looked to be about nineteen, with a fresh-scrubbed face, a ribbon threaded through the bun where her long hair coiled at the back of her head. She wore no rouge, nor charcoal. Her eyes sparkled like shiny beads.

"Eat, drink or both?" she asked.

"Bring my friends here whatever they want," said Hauser.

"We have ale, whiskey, and whatever's writ on the slate," said the serving girl.

"I'll have ale," said Lemuel. Morgan picked up the slate and read the items: boiled beef or antelope, potatoes, fish, beans, turnips.

"I'll try some of that antelope and some 'taters and turnips," said Morgan.

Hauser and Doc laughed.

"Boy, you don't want to eat any of that antelope," said Hauser. "Tough as a Britisher's boot and tastes like buckskin broiled in brine."

Morgan flushed beet red.

"The beef is right tasty," said the girl, nudging Morgan. "By the way, my name's Willa."

Lem frowned at the girl and grabbed the slate from Morgan.

"Bring him the beef, then," he said curtly. "I'll have the same, 'cept beans 'stead of turnips."

"Bring us more whiskey," said Hauser, pointing to Doc.

"Just as you wish," said Willa, deliberately rubbing her hip against Morgan's arm.

"Looks so that gal's got her eye on you, Morgan," said Hauser. "She 'pears to be sweet as honey on a biscuit."

"He'll have none of that," snapped Lemuel. "Damned women, anyway."

"Why, whatever happened to your missus?" asked Hauser.

"None of your business," said Lem, curtly.

Morgan gave his father a look, then his gaze followed the serving girl as she went to the serving bar, put her foot on the iron rail underneath and leaned forward. Her buttocks thrust tight against her dress. Morgan felt a stir inside him. He had begun to look at women and girls. It didn't make any difference how old they were; they fascinated him. There had been a girl about his age on the boat that brought them up from Natchez. She was about sixteen and shy as a titmouse.

One day, when he was sitting on the pitching deck, holding onto a davit, she came up behind him and sat down next to him. She asked him if he'd ever kissed a girl. He told her he hadn't. She asked him if he'd like to kiss her. He had become embarrassed and stricken with a sudden case of the tongue-tied.

The girl had suddenly leaned over and thrown her arms around him. She found his lips and planted a wet kiss on them. She wouldn't turn loose and they were like that when his pa had come up on them. He grabbed Morgan by the ear and pulled him out of the girl's arms. She gave a shriek and jumped up, scrabbled across the wildly tilting deck. Morgan got to his feet to avoid having his ear pulled clean off. He glared at his pa.

"Don't go messin' around with trash," his father had snapped.

"Pa, she was just a girl. We wasn't doin' nothin'.."

"All women are trouble," said Lem and he had stalked away, leaving Morgan with a stinging earlobe and a considerable amount of his pride damaged. The boat had rolled just then and Morgan had to grab the rail to keep from going overboard.

While his pa hadn't mentioned it again aboard the boat, he kept a watchful eye on Morgan and the girl kept her distance. Morgan thought of her now as he looked at the serving girl.

"Ain't much to St. Louis," said Lem, looking around the room.

"It's small, but wild," said Doc. "Easy place to get killed or skinned."

"Keep away from the Masons and the Choteaus," Hauser said to Lem.

"Huh?"

"Free trapper. Onliest way to be," said Hauser.

"'At's right," echoed Doc. "You'll starve a lot quicker that way." His speech was slurred and he had trouble focusing his eyes.

"What you drivin' at?" asked Lem. Morgan stopped looking at the girl. He was getting uncomfortable with his thoughts. He kept wondering what she would look like without her clothes on.

"Masons is tryin' to organize here and get in on the money," said Hauser. "Them Choteaus got a company, Missouri Fur, and got 'em a store. They want to hog it all just like them damned Masons. They might not make you an offer first time out, but you bring in furs, they'll want to put cash in your pockets and give you traps you'll pay dear for when you come down in the spring."

"Who are the Masons?"

"Bunch of secretive pilgrims," said Hauser bitterly. "Hard tellin' who's one and who ain't. I just ask and if they's Masons, I don't sell to 'em or buy from 'em."

"And Choteau?"

"They's a bunch of 'em. They got money. Auguste, anyways. Young Cadet, he's the smart one. Pierre. He got him a license to trade with the Great and Little Osage. Didn't do too well, but Pierre's pa, Auguste, is the Injun agent up there and he did the Mandans a favor once't. You got to get thick with the Injuns, you wantin' to trap, but you got to be careful."

"You do all right, did you, Dick?" asked Lem.

"Not at first. We had some fights with Hudson Bay trappers and with Missouri Fur time and again. Arikaras tried to take our mules, traps, guns and hair once't. You learn."

"But you make good money?"

"You work hard for it," said Hauser.

Willa brought the ale and drinks. Men kept coming into the eatery, buying drinks at the bar. The conversations, in French, English, Spanish and Portuguese, sometimes in German, rose to a noisy pitch.

"War's broke out," said Willa.

"Huh?" asked Hauser.

"They're talking about it. Andy Jackson's gone to New Orleans to fight the British."

"Don't say," said Hauser. Willa shrugged, glanced at Morgan and smiled.

"I'll fetch your vittles," she said to Lemuel, who had that look in his eyes that Morgan dreaded. "A lot of men are goin' to fight in the war," she added, before she left the table.

"Well, I ain't a-goin'," said Hauser. "I've had my fill of the States."

"Fuck the British," said Doc, swilling down a mouthful of whiskey.

Lem didn't say anything and Morgan wondered what his father was thinking. Morgan didn't know what war was, but there had been talk of it back in Nashville and in Natchez. Some said the Mississippi was going to be a mighty busy river.

Willa brought the food and when she served Morgan, she leaned over him so that her breasts rubbed against his back. Lem didn't notice it, but Doc did and he winked at Morgan. Morgan's face felt hot and he knew it was red. He felt the burn of her breasts long after she had gone. He ate in a daze, trying not to think of Willa's breasts, listening to his pa and Hauser talk about trapping in the mountains.

"You got money, Lemuel?"

"Some."

"Might be you could buy some traps cheap from Eshelman. Whatever you buy here in St. Louis is a heap cheaper than what you'd buy up in the mountains."

"I don't know much about trappin'," said Lem, wolfing his food.

"Ain't many gonna tell you much, neither," said Dick. "I learnt from the Injun, some Ojibway I met up north after I got away from Chief Yellow Roach's Tuscarory band of cutthroats. Learnt more when I got to the Rocky Mounts. Beaver's dumb, but they got good noses and you got to fool 'em."

"How do you get to the mountains?" asked Morgan.

"Wal, now," said Hauser, "you can walk, ride or go up the Missouri in a bullboat or such. Easiest way is by water, but you got to lay down more coin on the barrelhead. They's a way through Taos, but you got to watch out for Mexican so'jers and bandits. Lots of Injuns and thieves 'twixt here and yonder, but it's short and straight."

"Anyplace I can get maps?" asked Lem.

"You can get 'em, but don't trust 'em much. I got lost first time I used one I got here in St. Louis. Damned near got kilt."

Hauser ordered more drinks from Willa. Lemuel cleaned up his plate, belched loudly. Morgan still toyed with his food and when Willa brought the drinks she brushed up against him again and he felt his blood heat up and boil up to his neck and face.

"There are some dangerous rivers to cross," said Doc. "It's a long hard way and the Indians might not want you riding through their lands."

"You'd best carry least two rifles apiece," interjected Hauser, "and keep a brace of pistols loaded and primed. Carry a big knife and take lots of powder and ball. You'll need pack horses or mules for your traps and such."

"How long a trip?" asked Lem.

"Ridin'? Two months, maybe three. When you get to the high country it'll take you two, three days to get your breath. Ain't no air up there some places."

Morgan's eyes brightened.

"Me'n Doc here, we take the river. Stay to the forts and stay alive, I say."

"Crowded up where you go?" asked Lem.

"Gittin' thataway," said Hauser. "But them mountains is plumb big and wide. We was workin' up on the Yallerstone and back up in the Absorkas. Run into a brigade now and again. Some places they's trappers run in packs."

"Like wolves," said Doc, his eyes blearing. He took out a twisted cigar, bit off the pointed end and stuck it into his mouth. He reached behind him to another table and grabbed a candle. He touched the gnarled end of the cigar to the candle and his cheeks sank to hollows as he drew air through the tobacco. He put the candle back and sucked the cigar until the end glowed orange.

"Like goddamned wolves."

"You haven't said nothing about your friend Ormly," said Lem, after a silence.

"Ain't seen hide nor hair of him." Dick took a swallow of whiskey, beckoned to Willa, who was across the room. "He had him a little red maid he was sweet on. When we got to the point where we knew we could excape, he said he wanted to bring Little Thrush along. I told him we'd never make it. I had been savin' up powder and ball for when we could run off. Injuns sent me out to hunt, give me one ball. I'd take it out, cut it in half, hide the other half. They never caught on to it. When they gave me powder, they poured it in my hand. I always tucked back a mite and never did use no full load. Ormly did the same, I reckon. They kept us apart, but we got so we could use numbers and some sign to tell each other what was what."

"How'd you get away?" asked Morgan.

"One day Yellow Roach said we had to move. They was Rangers in the woods somep'n. I gave Orm the high sign and he nodded. We knew what direction them woods-beaters were a-comin' from, so when the tribe started to move, I run toward 'em. Ormly and I split up when some of the braves started to chase us. I had one on my tail, waited until he come up on me and I let him have half a ball in his heart."

"You shot that good?" asked Lem.

"Surprised me, too. That half ball went straight."

"And what about the other feller, Ormly?" asked Morgan.

"I heard some shots, but I didn't stay with that dead buck to find out what was what. I just kept a-runnin'."

"Did you run into the Rangers?" asked Morgan.

"Never saw 'em. I made my way up the Ohio and just kept a-movin' north and west. I worked some settlements, got me a poke and went to trappin' up in the north country. I run into a bunch of Americans in a town called Vincennes on the Wabash. A woman there told me about a trapper name of Lisa what had gone to someplace called Mound City in Missouri Territory. That's right here. I come out in aught-three. Then Lewis and Clark come through and come back and I listened to all the tales. Heard about the mountains and rode with some fellers in a keelboat up the Missouri. That was in aught-seven, I reckon. Not many trappers then. I went up there with Manuel Lisa, John Colter and George Drouillard. We didn't get up until late and they started to build Fort Raymond up where the Yallerstone and the Big Horn rivers joined up. Lisa went into Crow country and Colter went somewheres, up in the Wind River country, I reckon, and I come on back. It was too late to trap."

"Then what?" asked Morgan eagerly.

"I got them mountains in my blood. I come back the next summer and roamed around. They was startin' to build tradin' posts along the Missouri. Lisa had been tradin' with the Crow and such. I run into some other lookers and we trapped that winter and I made a few dollars. I stayed away from Drouillard and them. I heard he was a killer and maybe Lisa, too. Them companies. You got to do what they say or . . ."

Morgan sighed.

Willa brought more whiskey and Lem joined in the drinking. Hauser talked of the mountains and Morgan hung on every word like a moth at a lamp chimney.

Doc seemed not to get any drunker. He drank more, but he kept his wits about him. He smoked his cigar down to ash and made dry comments from time to time. Men came and went, talking of the war. Willa rubbed against Morgan every chance she got and their eyes met more than once during the conversation at the table.

Morgan got up to relieve himself. He walked out the front door onto the street, looked for a dark place. He peed against one of the buildings and as he was walking back, Willa met him.

"Uh, hello," said Morgan.

"I come out to talk to you," she said. Her face was in shadow, but the light from the lamps in Spanish Jack's made her hair glow.

"I got to get on back."

"I like you," she said. "I've got a room upstairs. Would you like to come up? I get off in a few minutes."

"I don't know," he said.

"Please. There's some stairs out back." She moved close to him and he stood there, wondering what to do. She touched his hand, ran her own up his arm. She kissed him and it was not like kissing the girl on the boat. Willa sent sparks through him, made his lips warm. He felt a stirring in his loins, an embarrassment because she was so close. "Ummm," she moaned and put her arms around him. She kissed him harder and he put his arms around her. He closed his eyes and the heat from her body warmed him, warmed him all over and she was soft, so soft, she made him giddy.

Morgan strangled on words of protest, choked them down because he did not want to say them.

She took his hand and led him to the back of Spanish Jack's. She pointed to the dark stairs.

"First door on the left," she whispered. "Go on up. I'll meet you there in ten minutes."

"God, I don't know."

"Yes, yes," she said, and he knew he would go up the stairs.

She touched the part of him that was hard and he knew he would go up there and wait for her.

She left him there, scurried around the building. Morgan took a deep breath and started for the stairs. His feet were leaden and he cringed when the board on the first step creaked.

He walked up the stairs, counting the seconds in his mind, wondering why time went so slowly now.

20

Morgan opened the door to Willa's room. Stepping inside, he closed the door quietly. He groped in the dark until he found a chair. He didn't dare light the lamp, didn't know where it was. The chair creaked when he moved and he was sure that people downstairs could hear him. Gradually, the dim light of stars seeped through the window, gave fuzzy shape to the objects in the room. Pale outlines of a bed, a table, a dresser, began to appear. Morgan sat on the chair, listening to the ripple and thrum of voices filtering from below up through the flooring. He heard the clink and tinkle of glasses and plates, the ebb and flow of laughter washing through the walls, rising and falling like waves on a sea of air.

Morgan stopped counting the seconds and waited for the slow minutes to pass. Every time he heard a sound, his heart jumped and a throb of fear pulsed at his throat. Finally, he heard a footfall and his blood seemed to freeze in his veins. He saw a light flicker under the door. The door opened and Willa entered, carrying a candle on a pewter saucer. She moved toward him, in shadow, and the light splashed her pretty face, made her eyes glitter like obsidian beads. She slid the chimney up on a lamp, turned the wick up. She touched the candle flame to the wick and the oil burst into flame. She adjusted the intensity of the blaze and blew out the candle. A thin tendril of smoke lingered in the still air of the room. Willa walked back to the door and slipped the bolt through its slot.

"Hello, again," she said, a thrill to her voice, a lilt that made his heart jump.

"Hello," he said, a thick husk in his voice.

Willa took off her black apron, tossed it across the room, toward the bed. She fluffed her hair and moved toward Morgan. He rose from his chair and took her into his arms. She embraced him eagerly and he felt the softness of her hair brush his chin.

"Mmmm," she breathed. "You don't know."

"Huh?"

"The kind of men who come here. They paw me and try to lift my dress. They're crude and smelly and mean."

Morgan said nothing. She looked up at him, small and comfortable in his arms. He pressed close and his manhood stirred, began to swell.

"I-I ain't n-n-never done nothin' before," he stammered.

"You'll learn," she whispered, and pulled his head down toward hers. She kissed him and her tongue streaked across his lips. He felt a stab in his genitals and the lump hardened, strained against the crotch of his pants.

She rubbed his back with eager hands, stroked him as she moved her lips against his. He wanted her then, wanted to plunge into the heat that he knew was there, wanted to bury himself in the heat, inside her and he lost all reason in that moment when tumescence peaked in his manhood. The heat blinded him and made his brain swell and the other swelling made him want her bad.

"Oh God," he breathed when she broke the kiss and he felt her hot breath against his face.

"Yes," she said. "I feel you. Do you want me?"

"Yes."

"The bed," she told him. "Let's lie down and take our clothes off."

He followed her dumbly across the room. She slipped out of her dress so fast he wondered how she had done it. Her breasts were beautiful in the lampglow and she stooped slightly to take off her panties and then he saw her, saw the dark thatch between her legs and the nipples on her breasts. He saw all of it and felt the wonder of her womanhood, the mystery of her sweeping through him like a storm. There was a pride in him that she let him see her and it was like being in a dream or in a trance because he had never seen a naked woman before and he was so close to her he felt faint.

"Hurry," she said, and he fumbled with the buttons on his shirt and his fingers lost their deftness so that she had to help him. She peeled his shirt off and her hands dove to his pants and she slid his trousers down and he blushed because he stuck out and she could see the hard bone of him jutting out and leaking the clear fluid of desire.

She pulled him onto the bed and slid beneath him. He looked down at her and swallowed. Her hips were dotted with small bruises the size of thumbprints. Her breasts, too, were blotched with yellow-purple blemishes. His breath came in short gasps as he touched a breast, roamed his hand over it, touching the nipple and feeling the little brown bumps around the dark aureole.

"Does it hurt?" he asked, an almost reverent tone in his voice.

"No," she said. "It feels good. Kiss me. Touch me between my legs."

He leaned down, kissed her on the mouth. His hand crept to her leg, slid into the wiry thicket of her sex. He felt her body quiver and he probed the soft lips between her legs, felt surprise at the delicate sponginess of that part of her. She pushed upward and moaned.

"Do it to me," she said, moving her head to break the kiss.

"I—I don't know what to do," he said, but he knew; he was just afraid to do it wrong.

She opened herself to him and drew him into her. He shuddered and closed his eyes. It was like being suddenly hooked up to a lightning bolt. Phosphorous explosions lit up his brain. His body coursed with savage pulsations, electric jolts that rendered him mindless. It was all over in a rush, but in that brief moment, universes opened to him, ecstasy suffused his body, a great mystery dazzled and tantalized him. He rode the bright heavens and strode the earth like a god. Just for that one fraction of a second, he knew the awesome power in his loins, felt the magnificence of creation when his seed burst forth in a mighty spume like some divine fountain.

————•————

Lem was getting drunk. Not roaring drunk, but drunk enough so that his vision wavered and his tongue thickened. He looked at the cracks in Hauser's hands, around the knuckles, wondered about them.

"Cold water, hot sun, dry thin air," said Dick, holding his hands up as if he was wearing rings. "Got the same thing when I used to milk cows back in Virginny."

"It looks like you've got leprosy," said Doc. His hands were smooth, the flesh around the knuckles tight.

"How come yours ain't that way?" Lem asked Doc.

"He rubs 'em with grease ever' night," said Hauser. "He still thinks he's a surgeon."

"You a real doctor?" asked Lem.

"None of your business," said Doc. Dick gave Lem a look, shook his head slightly.

Lem drank another swallow of whiskey, felt its glow as it went down. He looked around the room.

"Hey, where's Morgan?"

"He went outside," said Dick.

"Oughta be back by now."

"I wouldn't worry none," said Hauser. "He looks like he can take care of himself."

Lem drew a deep breath, drew himself up straight to correct the slump of inebriation.

"Damn kid," he said.

Doc got up from the table, headed for the door. He was surprisingly agile and gracefully dodged a drunk who teetered into his path. He seemed more sober than any man in the room. Lem watched him cross the room and marveled at Doc's ability to hold his drink.

For a moment, Lem forgot about Morgan. He turned to Dick after the door closed behind Doc.

"What's he got in his gullet?" he asked.

"Doc?"

"Yeah, him. Damned sourpuss barber."

"He ain't no barber, like a lot of 'em," said Hauser. "He was a surgeon, a pretty good one I hear tell. He don't do no cuttin' no more, but he carries them sharp tools around with him. I only seen him use 'em once, when he got a Ree arrer stuck in his leg. Took 'em out and cut out the arrerhead 'thout ever blinkin' a eye. Salved it up and bound it. Them Rees was mighty disappointed. So was Doc, I reckon. I guess he blames hisself for when his wife died."

"Huh? How'd she die?"

"Way he told me, she had a busted appendix. He went to cuttin' on her and she up and died. Broke him right in half, he said. He quit surgeryin' and come west to try and drink up all the whiskey he could get his hands on."

"How come him to go a-trappin' with you?"

Hauser fixed Lem with a blistering eye, keen as a Spanish dagger.

"Well, Doc just don't care no more about hisself—I reckon he wants to die, but is too God-fearin' to take his own hand to it. He don't much favor one way over another, neither. Just so's it's hard and real painful like his wife done."

"Jesus," said Lem, momentarily sobered. "No woman's worth that."

"This'n was, 'cording to Doc."

Lem said nothing, but he was thinking about Roberta and the alcohol fueled dead thoughts, made them swirl and boil in his mind like rocks and sticks caught up in a whirlwind. And then he thought about Doc and the thoughts got all tangled up and driven by the fierce winds of his own personal hatred. Doc's wife had died and even in death she was tormenting the man, wouldn't leave him alone. A woman was trouble, sure enough, and had been since Eve gave Adam the apple in God's own garden.

"What's Doc's real name, anyways?" asked Lem, trying to break out of the foul mood brought on by his dredged-up thoughts of Roberta.

"Henry McIntire," said Hauser, "but you'd best not call him that 'lessen he asks you. He don't want to be nobody."

"Damned women," snorted Lem and he would have gone down into his dark thoughts again, if he had not seen movement out of the corner of his eye.

A man in his late thirties, wearing a grimy apron and carrying a wooden tray came up to Hauser's table.

"You gents need anything here?" he asked.

Hauser nodded. "Three whiskeys," he said.

Lem looked up at the man, brought him into blurry focus.

"Hey, where's 'at gal what was here? Wilma."

"You mean Willa Montez?" asked the waiter.

"Willa, Wilma. Gal 'at was a-servin' us," said Lem.

"She's gone upstairs to her room. She's off at ten of the clock, and it's a good quarter past that." The waiter was very polite, with a northeastern accent. He looked out of place in the room full of rowdy, rough men. His hair was neatly slicked with grease and trimmed, his shirt pressed.

"She live here?"

"She has quarters upstairs, as do I," said the waiter. He glanced at Hauser. "I'll bring your whiskeys promptly, sir."

The waiter left. Dick finished off his cup and banged it on the table.

Lem's brows wrinkled in thought. He swept the room again with a searching glance, contracting his pupils to bring faces into focus. He looked at the door as it opened. Doc was just coming in, listing slightly to one side, but he straightened and wove his way to the back table.

"Ah," Doc said, as he sat down, "a muggy evening, with the scent of raw piss on the air, the stench of rotting fish and yesterday's garbage disgusting as ever. St. Louis is a stink hole. No wonder we go to the mountains and endure hardships beyond human bearance."

"Aw, Doc," said Hauser, "you ought to go east where you belong."

"Never," said Doc, emphatically. "To live back there is to die slowly of indolence and boredom. I much prefer to meet my end in an adventurous way. I'll hie back to the mountains and pray for the swifter death from the Rees' hatchet or the grizzly's violent hug. If we stay here, we'll suffocate in the fecal atmosphere of an open-air latrine."

Lem didn't understand a word Doc had said, but he knew what was bothering him. He lurched to his feet, extended his fingers to the table for support. He swayed there until the room stopped spinning.

"I'm goin' to look for Morgan," he announced, and when Dick put a hand on his arm, Lem tore away from him and staggered toward the bar.

"The man's looking for trouble, I suspect," said Doc.

"He's carryin' him a load," said Hauser.

"I know exactly what you mean," Doc said, and his stare went vacant. He sat there, soundless as stone.

Lem saw the stairs, aimed himself toward them. He took the first step, faltered as a strong hand squeezed his arm.

"That's as far as you go, pilgrim," said a faintly accented voice. "There is nothing up there for you. Piss outside like everyone else."

Lem turned around, looked at the man who had stopped him.

"I aim to find that gal Wilma," Lem told the man.

"She's occupied."

"Occupied?" Lem asked drunkenly. "Occupied? What the hell's that mean?"

"That, *señor,* is none of your business."

"And, who in hell are you to tell me my business?"

"I'm Jack Montez and Willa is my daughter."

"Well, she'd better not have my son up in her room with her," said Lem and pushed Jack backward with a flathand slam to the man's chest. With that, Lem took four steps in a single bound and disappeared at the top of the stairs before Spanish Jack could stop him.

Lem tried each of the four doors. All were locked. The last one had a glow of light seeping from under the door. He pushed and banged on it. The door wouldn't give. Spanish Jack appeared at the top of the stairs, started toward him. He carried a bung starter in one hand.

Lem banged on the door again. He heard the soft pad of footsteps. The door opened. Willa stood there with a nightgown held against her naked body. Lem saw Morgan on the bed, pulling at a pillow to hide himself.

Jack Montez raised the bung starter overhead and charged Lem. Lem ducked low and sailed his right fist into Jack's gut. Spanish Jack doubled over and gasped for breath. He waddled backward on the heels of his boots as Lem swept Willa aside and entered the room.

"Pa!"

"What the hell are you doin' with this woman?" asked Lem.

"Pa, don't start no trouble now."

Willa went to her father, put her arms around him.

"Papa," she said, "let me talk to the man."

"Aquel hijo de mala leche," swore her father in Spanish. She pushed him back, pleading with her eyes. Then she reentered the room.

Lem turned to her.

"You slut!" he spat. "What did you do, you harlot?"

"Please," said Willa. "We don't want any trouble, sir."

"I'll give you trouble, you fornicating bitch."

Morgan watched in horror as his father lunged at Willa. She staggered backward to avoid his rush. Spanish Jack came into the room, still carrying the bung starter, as his daughter spun away. Willa screamed as she crashed into the bureau. Lem followed after her, yelling at the top of his voice. Morgan dashed up just as Spanish Jack brought the bung starter down hard on Lem's head.

As Spanish Jack's momentum spun him around, Lem accidentally struck Willa in the mouth. Blood spurted from her lips. She screamed again and Lem turned to fight off Spanish Jack. Morgan leaped into the fray, naked as a frog, trying desperately to reach his father, pull him away from the fight. Jack tried to hit Lem with the bung starter again, but he was too close. Lem cracked the Spaniard on the jaw with a crossing left. Spanish Jack's knees buckled. Morgan grabbed his father. Lem stiffened his son with a straight right to the temple. Morgan collapsed, his eyes rolling backward in their sockets.

Willa screamed and started flailing Lem's back with her fists.

Lem turned on her and pushed her away. She smashed his nose with a roundhouse swing. Blood gushed from both of his nostrils, ran down his cheeks like the juice of a crushed tomato. Jack tackled Lem and wrestled him to the floor. Morgan struggled to regain his senses. He sat up groggily and watched his father lay into Jack with both fists pumping. Jack went down, blood seeping from a half dozen cracks on his face. The lamplight flickered on his battered features, gave his visage a grotesque cast.

Lem was still beating Jack when Doc and Dick Hauser stormed into the room, dragged him off the unconscious man. Willa whimpered and fell down beside Morgan. Morgan put his arm around her, fought away the fog in his brain.

"Enough, Hawke," said Dick. "You already done enough." He steadied Lem with an armlock around Hawke's neck.

"That two-bit slattern," growled Lem. "She done guiled my boy."

Morgan looked at his father in bewilderment. Hauser forced Lem to his knees. Lem lashed out ineffectually. Doc stood in front of Lem, fists balled, ready to put Hawke down by force, if necessary. Spanish Jack groaned, but he was still out.

"Pa," Morgan said, "you . . . you hadn't ought to have come up here. Now look what you done."

"What did you and her do?" Lem croaked.

"It don't make no difference," said Hauser. "What was done was between him and the girl. Now, steady down or I'll have to choke you, drag you out of here like dead meat."

Morgan, keeping a wary eye on his father, got up and slipped back into his clothes. Willa, still sobbing, wiped her face and breasts with a towel she retrieved from a nail by the bureau, put her dress back on. A couple of curious men looked into the room, then left hurriedly.

"Let me up," said Lem.

"You aim to leave this be?" asked Dick.

"No more trouble," said Lem.

Hauser and Doc exchanged looks. Doc nodded. Dick released his grip on Lemuel's neck. Doc knelt down next to Spanish Jack, felt for the pulse at his throat. He began to gently slap Jack's face.

Lem kept looking at Willa. Morgan saw the look, shuddered inwardly. There was hatred in his pa's eyes, an intensity he'd never seen before. Something cold balled up in Morgan's stomach and made him sick. He looked at Willa. There were streaks of tears she had missed with the towel.

Morgan's muscles were stretched taut with tension. The adrenaline still raced in his blood. Confused feelings stormed his thoughts. He had never seen such a rage in his father, such a killing rage. Willa stood there, trembling, in a paralyzed state of shock. She looked at Doc, who was trying to bring her father back to consciousness. She looked at him with a doll's dead eyes and she shook ever so slightly that Morgan wondered if she was not on the verge of going into a fit. It scared him and he wished he could do something to comfort her. But he would not touch her again while his father was in the room.

"He goin' to be all right?" asked Dick, looking down at Spanish Jack.

"Might need some salts to bring him around," said McIntire. "Concussion, maybe."

Lem said nothing. He kept staring at Willa.

"You got any smellin' salts, Doc?" asked Dick.

"No. You'd have to find an apothecary."

"Hell, don't know if there is one in St. Louis."

"Probably not," said Doc. He peeled back one of Jack's eyelids, bent over to look at the pupil more closely.

Willa broke her gaze, looked at Morgan. He caught the movement, met her glance.

Lem saw it and something broke in him again. He saw the look and he thought of Roberta and Willa became his wife, turned into her in the soft light of the flickering lamp, turned into the girl he had married, the woman who had deserted him. He roared, uttered terrible sounds that sprang up from his throat and shattered the stillness of the room.

All of the pent-up anger of the months and years rose up in Lemuel Hawke and he bunched his muscles, gritted his teeth and charged Willa, snarling like some wild beast.

Hauser reached out to grab Lemuel, but his grasp fell short. Willa screamed and dashed toward Morgan. Morgan pushed her aside and braced himself for his father's charge. Lem crashed into his son and the two fell toward the lamp on the small table near the bed. The lamp went flying, smashed against the wall. Particles of fiery oil sprayed in all directions. The glass chimney shattered. Fresh oil splattered on the bed, the floor and the wall. Little patches of fire turned into tongues that raced along the splatter-path. In an instant, the wall and the bed erupted in flames. The dry wood floor exploded in a wall of flame.

Doc tried to lift Spanish Jack up, but the man's dead weight was too much for him. Lem grabbed Morgan and hauled him away from the burning bed. Willa crawled toward the door. Hauser's shirt caught on fire and he began beating his sleeve with the palm of his hand.

"Get out!" yelled Lem, dragging Morgan toward the door.

Willa ran to her father, grabbed his feet. Hauser put out the flame on his sleeve and went to help Doc and Willa. The flames surged upward, devoured the wallpaper. The small table burst into flames. Wood crackled and popped as the hungry fire lapped new fuel. The room became an inferno. Smoke billowed from every corner and seared the lungs of everyone in it.

Lem and Morgan shoved Doc and Hauser toward the door. Morgan broke away from his father and he snaked an arm around Willa's waist. Doc and Hauser staggered from the room, choking and gasping on the smoke.

Lem turned and pulled at Morgan's shirt, hurling him toward

the open door. He stepped aside and shoved Willa and his son outside.

Doc yelled. "Fire!"

He and Hauser staggered down the stairs. No one in Spanish Jack's moved.

"Fire!" Hauser choked, and the people in the eatery saw the smoke clinging to the hall ceiling, wisps curling around the corners. The room boiled with men jumping up from tables, scrambling for the front door. The bartender and waiter both yelled and ran into the melee. Men packed together, fought to get out as the fire burst from the room and filled the hall with smoke and flames.

"Papa!" screamed Willa and Morgan had to shove her down the stairs.

Flames licked at Lem's back. His shirt caught fire and he grimaced in agony. He shoved Morgan and Willa ahead of him down the stairs.

"There a back door?" he yelled above the din. His skin had turned black from the flames.

Willa nodded.

At the bottom of the stairs, she turned to the right and Morgan followed her.

The men in the restaurant milled and shoved. Their weight pushed part of the wall surrounding the door away and they streamed out into the night.

Willa opened the back door. She and Morgan fled outside, followed by Lem. He dashed past them and threw himself on the ground. He rolled to put out the flames. Behind them, the fire raged.

"Oh, Papa," Willa wailed.

Lem put the fire out and stood up, smeared with dirt. The back of his shirt was burned away and blisters started to form on his flesh.

"I'm sorry," Lem said.

"My papa's in there," said Willa. "Can't you do something?"

Morgan started to go back in, but Lem grabbed his arm, restrained him gently.

In seconds, the entire building was engulfed in flames. The three of them backed away from the heat, powerless to do anything. They heard shouting from out front.

"Get buckets!"

"Form a brigade!"

With a deep sense of shock, Lem realized that the other buildings could catch. But he stood there, rooted to the earth, watching Spanish Jack's burn. The fire roared and sent tongues of flame up into the blackness of night. It rouged their faces and illuminated the stark horror in their eyes.

Willa collapsed in a swoon and Lem stooped to grab her, break her fall.

Morgan knocked his father's arms aside.

"Don't you touch her," Morgan said. "Don't you ever touch her again."

Lem winced as he saw the look in his son's eyes.

It was a look he would never forget.

21

Lem sat on the edge of the bed, slumped forward, his head in his hands. He was covered with soot, his face smeared with dirt and ash, his clothes laden with grime. He could not get the smell of smoke out of his nostrils, the sickly sweet stench of burning flesh. He and the others had worked for hours to put out the blaze, keep it from spreading to the other buildings next to Spanish Jack's. In the excitement, no one noticed when he had finally slipped away and come back to the room. He had not seen Morgan or Willa after leaving them in the alley, but Morgan's things were gone from the room. His possibles pouch, his rifle, his bedroll, the medicine horn—all gone. Lem felt as if something had been wrenched out of him, some part of him stolen and lost so that he could never get it back.

So, the boy had come back, and he had gone off somewhere with that girl. She had started it all, damn her. If it wasn't for her, none of this would have happened. Now, he had to live with it, by God, but he was right about her. About all women. They

253

were the source of man's troubles, had been since the beginning of time. The Bible even said so.

He was sorry about Spanish Jack. He hadn't meant to hit him that hard. The damned fool. Him and his daughter, two of a kind. She hadn't ought to have jezebelled Morgan that way, the little trollop.

Lem straightened up, lay back on the bed, too tired to wash up. He lay there, his mind squirming with thought, wondering what to do. The knock on the door jarred him out of his tormented reverie. He leaped from the bed, opened the door.

"Morgan. . . ."

It was Dick Hauser, and he looked like an apparition from hell. His face was black with soot and his eyes red-rimmed. His hands looked like lumps of coal.

"Gotta talk to you, Hawke."

"I thought you was Morgan," Lem said lamely. "He's done picked up and gone."

"That's what I come to talk to you about. You got any squeezin's?"

Lem shook his head. He closed the door, waved Hauser to a chair. The last thing he wanted was whiskey. His mouth tasted of rust and rain water; his stomach was knotted and raw. A distant throbbing in his skull reminded him of the whiskeys he had had earlier.

"No matter. Look, Lemuel, you done me a favor once't and I figger I owe you. I ain't got much but advice to give you, but it's good advice."

"What's on your mind, Dick?"

"Well, they ain't much law in St. Louie, none at all, I reckon. But Spanish Jack had him friends and they're talkin' about puttin' a ball in you or makin' you a rope collar. Was I you, I'd make tracks for somewheres right quick. Bunch of 'em is drinkin' at the King's Boar right now and decidin' how to make you join Spanish Jack in the local cemetery. Word ain't got to the town yet, but it'll spread by mornin'. Best leave the country, go somewheres until this blows over."

"Where's my son, Dick?"

"Him and Willa is safe. Nobody blames them for what happened. But Morgan don't want you to go lookin' for him. The gal's pretty broken up. All she had was her pa. Her ma died five year ago and she ain't hardly over it yet. She didn't have much of a life, but she put a fair amount of stock in her pap."

"Christ, I'm sorry Dick. I just—"

"Hell, I know you didn't mean nothin', Lemuel. But, folks is folks, and they's some as got blood in their eyes. You'd best pack out of St. Louie right quick."

"Where would I go without Morgan?"

"Likely he'll get over his mad someday."

Lem tried to hold it back, tried to stay the ache in him that made his eyes crinkle up and start to leak tears. He couldn't help it, though. He thought of Morgan, that last terrible look he had seen in his son's eyes, and he broke down. He rolled over onto his belly, put his head in his hands. His body shook with sobs, his throat boomed with the wrenching sounds of his weeping.

Dick rose from the chair and left the room quietly. He did not say good-by.

Lem didn't hear him go.

———·———

Emile DeBalaviere shook his head.

"The boy, he take his horse last night. He did not say where he was going, *non*. But, he had no girl wit' him. He was alone, eh?"

Lem sighed, finished tightening Hammerhead's cinch.

"I'll need me a mule or two," he told the Frenchman. "Some advice about trappin' the mountains."

"Ah," said Emile, eager to provide information. "I have the best mule, eh? The Mexican, he make the best."

"How much?" asked Lem.

Emile squinted at an imaginary ledger in the palm of his hand. He scratched a spot just behind his right ear.

"One mule or two?"

"Two, I reckon. I got to carry traps, grub and such."

"*Oui*, two of the mule. You have the coin?"

Lem nodded.

"Silver?"

"I got silver."

"I will sell you the mule for thirty Mexican pesos apiece, and you can buy traps and trade goods from Eshelman."

"Trade goods?"

"If you want to buy the bevair from the savage, you must trade him the pretty things, *non?* You buy the ribbon, the little mirror, the beads and the cloth. You must take the whiskey and the axe, the skinning knife, eh? Eshelman, he tell you what to take, I think."

"Look, Emile, if I give you some money, will you give it to my son? To Morgan?"

Emile scratched his head again. It seemed a ponderous question to him.

"I don't know if I see him, eh? He don't tell Emile where he go."

Lem was almost certain Emile was lying.

"But you might see him?"

"Eh? Maybe."

Lem counted out the silver. He did not have enough pesos, but he had shillings and Spanish silver.

"This is for the mules," he said.

"You will have to buy the pannier to pack the goods, *non?* Eshelman have the good ones, I think."

"This is for Morgan," said Lem. "You tell him I'm a-goin' up to them Rocky Mountains."

Emile's eyes widened at all the coins.

"I will do this," said the stableman. "Ah, if I see the boy, that is. Now, we get the mules, eh?"

Lem led the two jacks up to Eshelman's on Fourth and Market as the sun was just clearing the levee. There were a few people about, but they paid him no attention. Dogs searched the edges of buildings for scraps, roaming in and out of the shadows of morning like skulking robbers. He hitched the mules and Hammerhead to the rail out front of Eshelman's. He knew the store. This was where he had changed his money.

Eshelman and two clerks were stacking blankets as Lem entered. Another clerk was rolling a barrel out of the back storeroom.

Lorenzo Eshelman nodded to Lem.

"I will be with you soon," said the storekeeper, a German with only a faint trace of a Pennsylvania accent.

Lem started toward the back of the store.

Two trappers stood at the counter looking at jars full of trade beads. They were attired for the trail, possibles pouches slung over their shoulders, knives on their belts, pistols jutting from their sashes. They wore light clothing, tattered and patched, boot moccasins. Both were young and bearded. Lem had not seen them before, but he walked toward them now. Eshelman continued to separate and stack blankets on a square boxlike table along one of the aisles. The store was lined with shelves, crates and tables stood in rows facing each other. One small section of wall served as a display for traps, knives, hatchets, tomahawks, lanterns and other hardware. Behind the counter, prominently displayed, a sign painted on a flat section of two-by-twelve proclaimed NO CREDIT.

The clerk who had rolled the barrel in finished positioning it next to the saws and double-bit axes in a corner and walked behind the counter as Lem came up alongside the two trappers.

"Mornin' gents," said the clerk, young, dough-faced, with jutting ears and pomaded hair that glistened like sweat on a black horse. "See somethin' you need?"

"Need a dozen six-inch candles and two dozen of flints," said one.

"Gimme a gross of them blue, red and yaller beads," said the other man, "and ten pound of middle fine powder, a chunk of lead, say ten, twelve pound, three dozen assortments of them buttons."

"Surely," said the clerk.

Lem cleared his throat.

"You goin' to the mountains?" asked Lem.

"No, we're goin' to a Sunday picnic," said the candle-and-flint man. He was chunky, with a moon face lumped with fat, a little cherubic mouth and tiny blue eyes swallowed up by puffy cheekbones. He looked as wide as he was tall and his legs were as bowed as barrel slats.

"None of my business," said Lem, "but I'm headin' there myself and need to know a good way to get there."

"You ridin' or floatin'?" asked the bead man. There was something familiar about him. Lem knew he had seen the man before. He was only slightly less chunky than the other trapper, but taller, with apple-round cheekbones, crafty hazel eyes, sandy hair still tangled from sleep. His clothes had more patches on them than a quilt. His hands had scars like those he'd seen on Hauser's.

"Ridin'. I got me two mules and a horse."

"They's a whole lot of mountains," said the first man, "and a whole lot of ways to get to 'em. Fust time me'n my brother Leo come here in aught-seven, we follered the Missouri clear up to the Yallerstone. Next year, we follered the Osage to ther South Platte and follered it on into the mountains. Last year, Leo and I trapped south of here on the White and my brother drownded in a flood. You ain't agoin' to get lost if'n you foller the Injun trails, head toward the sunset and stay close to the big rivers."

"But not close enough you get in any one's way," said the other trapper, the one who looked familiar. Lem was trying to place him.

"What?" asked Lem.

"He means huntin' Injuns," said the first man. "Say, what's your name, pilgrim?"

"Lemuel Hawke."

"I'm Bill Letterman and this year's Nat Sullard. He don't say much 'ceptin' when he's drunk."

"He don't look the same sober, neither," said Lem, grinning at Nat Sullard.

"Do I know you?" asked Sullard.

"You offered me a drink at the Red Lion in Nashville," replied Lem. "You said you was with a man name of Charlie Pack."

Sullard squinched up his eyes and regarded Hawke with a scathing look of interest. Recognition flickered in his eyes.

"You 'n the boy," said Nat. "Farmers. Hoo boy, you got a good mem'ry. Me'n Charlie was out to drink up all the whiskey in that tipplin' house."

"Wasn't you the ones got into a fight with Big John O'Neil?" asked Letterman.

Lem winced inwardly. He cocked his head in assent.

"Nat tolt me about it," said Letterman. "I was there. Finally got him an' Jocko and Charlie convinced to come out here and trap the Rockies with me. The Major is takin' a brigade up in a day er two for Missouri Fur."

"MacDougal?" asked Lem.

"You know him?" asked Nat.

"No. We met up with Jocko DeSam and he said I ought to meet MacDougal."

"Meanest bastard you ever saw," said Bill. "But he knows them mountains. Chouteau puts a lot of stock in the Major."

"You might be able to get on," said Nat.

"No, I reckon I got to go my own way," said Lem.

Evidently the two trappers hadn't heard about the fire the night before, the death of Spanish Jack. It was just as well. He didn't know how he could explain such a thing. It was still unreal to him, like a bad dream.

"Free trapper, eh?" said Bill. "Mighty hard. You can't get credit and you got Britishers and British-bribed Injuns after your scalp. Mighty hard."

"I got to try," said Hawke lamely.

The clerk finished packing up the goods the two trappers had ordered.

"Anything else?" he asked.

"That'll do 'er," said Letterman. He turned from the counter, called to Eshelman. "Lon, what're you gettin' for your traps now?"

"Four dollar," said Eshelman without batting an eye.

"Whooee," said Letterman. He turned to Hawke. "They was a dollar seventy when I first come out here and that was in the Injun territory. Last time, it was three dollars American. Be five or better at the forts."

Lem's heart sank.

"How many traps you figger a man needs?" he asked Letterman.

"You can run a line with half a dozen, but you better square that, just in case."

"Two dozen would be better, still," interjected the clerk.

Eshelman walked over. He was a burly, drum-chested man, with a thick black moustache, black hair and neatly trimmed sideburns. He had a wide forehead, a sturdy, though crooked, nose and deep-set brown eyes, fleshy lips. He looked darkly Teutonic with his square, determined jaw and muscular build.

"You get a price on four dozen," said Eshelman. "Three eighty-five the trap."

"Well, Lon's going to sell you the store, Hawke," said Letterman. "We'll be goin'. Pay the man, Nat."

Nat plunked down coin.

"Before you go," said Lem to Bill Letterman, "would you know a man by name of Silas Morgan?"

"I knowed him," said Bill.

"Is he dead?"

"No, I reckon not. Seed him over the winter, up on the Yallerstone."

"Would he be in St. Louis?"

Letterman laughed.

"Nope," he said. "Old Silas, he got him a Crow squaw. He's been livin' with 'em. Part Crow hisself by now."

Lem was crestfallen. Silas living with an Injun woman? It didn't seem possible. Silas was—was, well, he was a dyed-in-the-wool bachelor, he was. Always had been.

"Are you certain sure?" he asked Bill.

"Sure as I'm a-standin' here, Hawke. Silas got him a squaw purty as any I ever seed. They call her Blue Shell."

Bill laughed again, slapped Hawke on the back and the two trappers left the store. Lem felt more alone than he had since he'd left the room at Lescoulie's hotel. He hadn't a friend in the world and no son anymore. It was enough to break a man's heart and mash it into pulp.

Lorenzo Eshelman took charge of Lem, showing him the various breeds of traps, axes, beads, cloth, blankets, knives and "necessaries." Lem bought two sturdy panniers and some rope.

"I'll need a good pistol," said Lem. "Cheapest you got."

"I got 'em from two dollar on up, Spanish breed, or Portagee, English or Pennsylvania-made."

"I'll look at the Pennsylvanias," Lem told him.

He ended up looking at all of them. He wanted one that had a sturdy lock, would not fail him when he needed it. The Spanish locks were big, brutish, and the English locks not much better.

He finally settled on a Pennsylvania-made road pistol in .58 caliber. Eshelman said his brother, living in Lancaster County, had made it. The lock was tight, the workmanship better than any of the others he had looked at. It had a heft to it and a good feel to the walnut grip. The stock was all of a piece, the inletting precise and smooth.

"You made a wise choice," said Eshelman. "Those pistols do not stay long in stock."

The merchant sold Hawke a hide-vial of castoreum for two bits and by the time Lem left the store, he was down to a few dollars American with which to buy food staples. But he left with something even more valuable than money. Lon Eshelman had copied for him a crude map showing the trails, the rivers, the major fords, the forts. The fords would change, Eshelman told him, as rivers always changed.

"Likely you'll run into trouble on the upper Missouri," Eshelman told him. "Manuel Lisa left early this spring, prepared to do battle with the British agents who are stirring up the Indians. You look out for the Blackfeet and the Gros Ventres."

"Are them tribes of Injuns?" asked Lem.

"Devils," said Eshelman, and Lem had left with his thoughts, his doubts, his considerable worries about Morgan. It crushed him to leave like this, an outcast, a murderer.

At LaValle's River Market, Lem bought flour, beans, coffee, buffalo jerky in thick, lumpy strips, half a smoke-cured ham, sugar, and salt.

Marcel LaValle and his wife, Denise, chattered like French magpies as they filled his order. In English, they mentioned the terrible fire and asked him if he was heading west. Denise said that he was so young and it was so dangerous in the mountains. Marcel asked Lem if he was with one of the fur companies. He was a sprightly man, thin as a beanpole, with dark Gallic features, a pince-nez perched on his aquiline nose, ears that jutted from his head like jug handles.

"Nope," said Lem. "I'm goin' alone."

"Which way you go?"

Lem had already decided to go to St. Charles and follow the Osage River to the Platte.

He told LaValle.

"Ah, that is a very dangerous way," said Denise in her precise English, the vowels soft and drawn out. "And you go alone. Tss, tss."

"Well, I think some go alone and do not come back," said Marcel, "but some go with other men and some of these do not come back, either. So, you go with God, young man, and I hope you can shoot straight."

"You tell us your name and we will wait for word of you," said Denise.

Hawke told them his name, feeling very itchy about it. They both smiled as they talked and the talk was light, but their words gave him an uneasy feeling, nonetheless.

After fiddling with his packs longer than necessary, graining the mules and Hammerhead until they could hardly walk, Lem set out from St. Louis with a heavy heart. He looked long and hard at the map again and decided against traveling up the Missouri. It was a longer way and the Platte, either South or North, looked like an arrow pointing to the mountains. He headed north to St. Charles where he knew he could pick up the Osage River, heading southwest.

He kept wanting to turn back and look for Morgan, but he knew his son was filled with hatred for him. Maybe it was best this way, he thought. Morgan could find his own way. He was almost a man, sure enough.

A bittern, startled by the horse and mules, jumped up from the shore of the Mississippi river, flapping ungainly to gain altitude. It flew downstream, screaming in protest, crying out so forlorn Lem felt as if the bird was talking to him, expressing what Lem felt inside. The echoes of the bird's scream lingered in Lem's mind and the silence only deepened the numbness of his grief, a grief so complicated and deep he couldn't explain it to himself.

Lem's heart was stone heavy and hurting as he followed the river, the well-rode prairie trail north to St. Charlies. Beyond, to the west, lay an unknown land, the future. He kept looking back, every so often, but there was nobody there and the emptiness inside him kept widening like the blue sky, the endless sea of grass that stretched to the west, to the distant horizon.

Morgan sat in the chair that leaned against the wall. He ran his fingers over the medicine horn, just the touching of it was a comfort to him. The feel of the hard polished surface somehow soothed him. He looked at Willa lying there on the bed in the small, bare room in Emile DeBalaviere's house. There was no table, only a single chair, a long box made into a chest of drawers, a small stool fashioned from a nail keg. Emile was at the stables, but he had come up to the room that morning, given him the money his pa had left for him. At first he had wanted to refuse it, but he didn't have a shilling or a note to his name. Willa hadn't even awakened when Emile had come. She had not awakened since she fell to the bed, exhausted, and cried herself to sleep.

And Morgan was too keyed up to sleep. His thoughts raced and darted like tadpoles in a pond.

He could not stop looking at Willa, thinking about her. She was still a wonderment to him. There was something so beautiful about her form as she lay there. Like a fine woodcarving, graceful and smooth like his buffalo horn, but more than that, more mysterious, more puzzling. Her dress clung to her thighs and legs and he imagined her naked underneath, imagined being with her all over again. But his imagination would only carry him so far. He remembered only parts of it and it seemed like dreaming, as if he had dreamed some of it, or all of it, and when he tried to think of being inside her, of exploding his seed inside her, he couldn't remember how it had been. But his flesh remembered it and he wanted her again, wanted to go into her and become part of her, sink into her until his senses drowned and soared at the same time.

Willa stirred and Morgan's breath caught in his throat. He felt guilty, a-spying on her like that, lusting for her when she was asleep. Wanting her when her pa was dead and his pa had caused it. He got mad every time he thought of his pa coming up there and hitting her. He had no right to do that. He shouldn't have done it. Look what had happened. But that, too, was like a dream.

Morgan stood up, walked over to the bed.

"You awake?" he asked.

Willa groaned and her eyes fluttered. She blinked, then her eyes opened.

"Where am I?" she asked.

"Emile, he give us this room."

She shook her head, sat up, her dress falling back, snugging wrinkled against her thighs.

"I remember," she said. "Oh God, I feel awful."

He sat down, tried to put his arms around her. She pushed him away.

"What's the matter?" he asked.

"I don't want you to touch me," she said, and there was anger in her voice, loathing in her tone.

"Why? What'd I do?"

"What'd you do?" she asked, and her voice rose in pitch, hovered on the edge of hysteria. "My papa's dead and you ask me what did you do?"

"Willa, I—I'm sorry, really sorry, but I didn't have nothin' to do with that fire."

She laughed harshly, swept her tangled hair back with a violent rake of her hand. She fixed Morgan with an icy glare and her lips curled in a contemptuous sneer.

"You bastard," she said. "When I look at you, I see your goddamned worthless father. You're both the same. You even look like him, act like him. Get out, get away from me."

"Willa, don't," he said. "It ain't that way. My pa's done gone and I want to take care of you. I mean you give me somethin' last night, somethin' I ain't never had before and I want to make it up to you, your pa dyin' and all."

She spat at him and Morgan recoiled, startled. Willa's face turned ugly, then, and left him bewildered. Gone was the pretty face of the girl he had lain with the night before. The night-soft contours of her face had been replaced by the hideous visage of a witch.

"You can't bring him back," she said, a snarl edging her voice higher on the scale. "You goddamned dumb pilgrim. You can't do anything right, you stupid farmer. Where's Doc? Have you seen him?"

"Doc?"

"Didn't you know? I was just makin' up to you last night to make Doc jealous. Doc's my man and he—he made me feel bad."

"You mean you didn't want me?"

"Oh, little boy, grow up. I want a man. Like Doc."

The enormity of what Willa was saying sank into Morgan's mind like a lead sash weight. He felt like a fool.

"Did Doc put them bruises on your body?" Morgan asked.

"He's very strong."

"God, Willa, you—you make me sick."

"Is the little boy going to cry?"

"I ain't no little boy. You done me wrong, Willa. You done my pa wrong, too. You was playin' with me. Look what it done to your pa. I felt sorry for you, but I don't no more. You—you just can't do people like this."

"You wanted it. Like a lovesick puppy. Now, get out. I never want to see you again. You and that stupid powder horn."

The coldness of her words knifed through him. He gripped the medicine horn more tightly in his hands. He wanted to brain her with it, wanted to smash her face until it bled. He wanted to lash out and hurt her as she had hurt him. His face darkened and his eyes narrowed to slits. He shook with the repressed violence that gripped him.

"I'm a-goin'," he said. "I hope you and Doc are real happy together. He's a damned drunk and you're nothin' but a whore."

Willa laughed. She laughed at him and that hurt worse than anything she had said to him. Morgan turned, angrily, and grabbed up his rifle, possibles bag, bedroll, all of his meager possessions. He stormed through the door, slamming it behind him. One of the leather hinges ripped apart and the door sagged to one side. Willa's laughter increased in intensity and the sound followed him as he stalked through the house, fighting down his anger.

Neither Emile nor his wife were home. He looked for them, but they were gone. Morgan walked to the little barn where he had hid Boots. The horse whickered when Morgan entered the darkened stable. Friar Tuck was still tied to one of the posts. He started wagging his tail when he saw Morgan.

"Tut, you doin' all right, boy?" Morgan untied the rope. The dog squirmed and groveled as Morgan walked over to the horse. Boots bobbed his head as if he wanted to prance.

Morgan saddled him and rode through town, a purpose in him now. Tut barked at everything in sight, but didn't stray far from

Boots and kept looking up to see if Morgan was still riding the horse. It was nigh noon and there was something he had to do before he left St. Louis.

The King's Boar was an outpost on Fourth and Laurel, a log structure that had been enlarged with wood and limestone. Its shingle creaked on rusty chains, stirred by a slight river breeze. Horses and mules stood hipshot at hitching rings and rails, each with its own pile of steaming droppings. Some of the mules were loaded down with diamond-hitched packs as if ready for a journey. A couple of bearded men dressed in trapper's garb sat in the shade outside, drinking from tankards, smoking pipes. Morgan did not recognize them, but they laughed throatily as he dismounted and stalked to the door, packing only his medicine horn.

"Give you a dollar for thet buffler horn," said one.

"I'll give you two," said the other man.

"It ain't for sale," said Morgan. He entered the tavern, blinked in the smoke, the hazy darkness. He saw only dim shapes of men, a face or two in slanted sunlight that streamed through a pair of partially curtained windows on the sun side.

"Hawke!" called a voice, and Morgan recognized it as Jocko's. He peered through the gloom, saw an arm waving at him. He walked toward it.

Jocko DeSam sat with a couple of trappers Morgan didn't know and the man he and his father had seen outside the Red Lion tavern in Nashville.

"Hear tell your pa's done gone and left," said Jocko. "He no take you with him?"

"Me'n pa had some words," Morgan said laconically.

"I hope you got more sense than him," said one of the men Morgan didn't know.

Morgan felt a testiness beginning to prickle him like a stinging nettle.

"Mister, my pa's got sense enough for bothen of us."

"Now, don't you get your hackles up, sprout," said the man. "I mean looks like he's gone off by hisself up the South Platte and if a man values his hair, he don't take two mules and goods into that country by hisself."

"How do you know this?" asked Morgan.

"Saw him at Eshelman's and LaValle told me that Hawke was headin' over St. Charles way to catch the Osage trail to the South Platte."

"Morgan, set," said DeSam. "This here's Braggin' Bill Letterman talkin' to you, eh. And this here's Pappy Roth, recently down from the north bringing pipestone he stole from the quarry. He makes the good pipes. And this is Nat Sullard what trapped with me up on the Ohio."

Morgan did not sit down, but he looked at Letterman, Roth and Sullard. Roth wore a round bushy beard threaded through with gray hairs. He smoked a pipe that was pink, carved out of a stone Morgan had never seen.

"I recollec' you, Mr. Sullard," said Morgan.

"Why you're the farmer boy, sure," said Sullard. "I saw your pa, too, a-buyin' trinkets and such at Eshelman's."

"I'm a-lookin' for someone," said Morgan.

"Who might that be, young 'un?" asked Letterman, the talker in the bunch.

"Doc. Name of McIntire I think. He might be with a man named Hauser. Dick Hauser." Morgan looked around the room. There was a balcony and he saw silhouettes of men up there, heard their talk and laughter.

"Doc's here," said Pappy Roth. "Hauser, too." He gestured with his pipe toward the balcony. "You don't want to see him, though, I reckon."

"Why not?"

"Drunker'n a hive of smoked hornets," said Roth, "and gettin' him a mean up worse'n a she-griz with pups."

"I don't care how drunk he is," said Morgan.

Roth stood up. "Maybe I better go up there and see how he is," he said.

"You tell him I want to see him," said Morgan.

"I'll do that, son, but you might think on pickin' a better time."

Roth went up the stairs.

"Set, Morgan," said Jocko. "No use you goin' up there."

"Yes, there is," said Hawke.

He started to leave, go up the stairs, but Jocko grabbed his arm.

"Sit with us, Morgan. We're fittin' out to trap for Missouri Fur. I might can get you on, get you some advance monies. We're packin' out today or tomorry for Missouri Fur."

"Ain't int'rested," said Morgan. He pulled away from Jocko. Jocko shrugged. His eyes blinked like an owl's.

"You change your mind, eh, you come see me," said DeSam.

"Hell, Chouteau ain't gonna take on no boy," said Letterman.

Morgan ignored him and headed for the stairs, the medicine horn banging against his side with a dull thud.

The tavern reeked of stale beer and fresh whiskey fumes. Upstairs, the tang was even stronger. Morgan saw that the balcony was really a large upper story, open, with a separate serving bar, benches along the walls and tables where men could drink or play cards.

Morgan looked for Dick Hauser, saw him hunched over in conversation at one of the tables near the side of the room. Doc was with him, and another man Morgan didn't know. Pappy had scooted a chair close to their table. Doc had a small wooden keg in front of him. Dick and the other man held copper tankards in their fists.

Doc looked up as Morgan approached. His face broke into a wan smile that curved into a smirk the closer Morgan got.

"Now, would you look at who's here," said Doc. "Young Master Hawke and he's got blood in his eye."

Hauser rose out of his slump. The other man turned his head.

"Uh oh," said Dick. "He looks mad."

Morgan stopped at the table, his hands balled into fists. He glared at Doc.

"What's on your mind, sonny boy?" asked Doc, with a taunting sneer. "Did your daddy run off with your sugar teat?"

"Easy, Doc," said Hauser. "Go easy on the boy. You got you a snorter full of firewater and it ain't hardly past noon yet."

Morgan felt something harden inside him. He didn't know what it was, but it calmed him down, made him feel strong. He looked square into Doc's eyes and he saw a man afraid, a man hiding in the whiskey, swimming in it, swimming in the hopes he might drown. Willa had said Doc was a man, a real man, but Morgan couldn't see one there. He saw only someone cruel enough to hurt a woman and let another man take blame for something he did.

"I ain't never hated no one before," said Morgan, his voice low and steady.

"Huh? What're you saying, boy?" asked Doc. "You hate me? Why, whatever for? What harm have I ever done you? I don't even know you. Don't want to know you. You're nothing but a pimple on a gnat's ass, still wet behind the ears, still suckin' on a woman's teat. Didn't Willa give you some of that cunnus of hers? Didn't charge you, did she? She usually gets at least six bits for bedding a man and she doesn't care about the color of his epidermis. She told me she was going to give it to you for free."

"You know about it, then," said Morgan. He held back, wanting to make sure. There was time. He wanted to savor the moment when it came. He wanted to feel something course through him that was like when he spilled his seed with Willa. He wanted to feel good about what he meant to do to Doc.

"Knew about what?"

"Willa takin' me to her bed."

Doc threw back his head, roared with laughter.

Hauser frowned.

"I don't like this," he muttered.

Pappy Roth sucked a lungful of smoke from his pipe, let it out like a belching chimney.

"Did you?" Morgan asked again and there was a deadly tone to his voice that made Doc stop laughing. He seemed to sober up in that instant.

"I knew she was making a play for you, sonny," said Doc. "She made it quite clear. She's just a common trollop. One pecker is much like another to her. She was just a receptacle to me, something to piss in."

Morgan drew back his fist then. Doc saw it coming. He made no move to avoid it. He closed his mouth and seemed to brace himself, to stiffen.

Young Hawke drove his fist into Doc's nose. He felt the bone and cartilage crumple under the impact. Blood spurted from Doc's nose like a squashed raspberry. Doc fell backward, still in his chair, hit the floor with a resounding thump.

McIntire didn't move. He didn't make a sound. He lay there like a corpse. Hauser leaned over and looked at him. Doc was conscious, but he didn't move. Pappy Roth rose up and craned his neck to look at Doc, too. He shook his head and sat back down.

"That was for my pa," said Morgan. "He's a damned sight smarter than any of you."

Hauser straightened up, looked at Hawke with something like respect in his eyes.

"Is that it? You just gonna hit him once? Hell, I thought you was mad."

"I'm not mad," said Morgan. "I just hate what Doc done, not only to my pa, but to Willa. She's real sweet on Doc and he done kicked her like she was a dog. Ain't nobody ought to be treated like that. Nobody."

Morgan turned to leave.

Hauser rose from his chair.

"Where you goin' boy?"

Morgan turned. His eyes seemed to burn a hole through Dick's skull.

"I'm a-goin' after my pa. Me and him are goin' to trap them Rocky Mountains."

"Hell, neither one of you got the brains of a turnip," said Hauser.

"Well, you're some such to talk about brains, takin' up with the likes of Doc there. He ain't no man, and neither are you if you call him friend."

Morgan left them there. Dozens of eyes fixed on him, followed his movements as he left the tavern. There wasn't a sound until he was outside and then the talk rose up like a cloud of insects on a dusk pond, a chattering din that shattered the ears of every man in the King's Boar.

———•———

Dick Hauser caught up with Morgan as he was leaving LaValle's River Market with food supplies. It was late afternoon, would be dark in a few hours. Tut rose up from his bed in the dirt under Boots's belly, started barking.

"Morgan, hold up."

"I got to get a-goin', Mr. Hauser."

"Call me Dick. Look, I know Doc's got something a-gnawin' at him. He's a mean bastard. Tipples a mite too much. But, he's got reason."

Morgan packed his goods in his saddlebags. He was anxious to leave. The LaValles had told him his pa was heading for St. Charles, leading two mules. He ought to be able to catch up with his pa if he hurried.

"I got to go, Dick." He turned to Tut. "Stop your barkin'." The dog cringed and backed away, whimpering.

"I know, I know. Look, your pa done me a turn once. I feel

sorry about what happened 'twixt you and the gal and with Spanish Jack gettin' burned up like that. I told your pa it might be best if'n he got clean away from St. Louis. Jack's got kin, a brother down to New Orleans. I'll see what I can do about settin' things straight."

"That's mighty kind of you, Dick."

"Morgan, your pa is a good man, better'n most. You tell him I sent greetin's to him. And you, you young whelp, keep your rifle clean as a whistle, your tomahawk sharp, carry plenty of powder and ball. You keep your eyes peeled. Act like you was a-sneakin' up on a deer. Injuns got a way of sneakin' up on you when you're plumb tuckered or busy at somethin'. You and your pa take turns a-sleepin' at night. Don't cross no rivers by a regular ford. Somebody tracks you, you circle around, come up ahind 'em. And, if you get attacked by Injuns, don't stand up. Get off your horse if you're ridin'. If you're a-walkin', get on your knees, lie down, hide ahind a rock or a tree."

"You sound like you know what you're a-talkin' about, Dick."

"Son, I been to the mountains. It's as hard a-gettin' there as it is a-stayin' there."

"I ain't afeard. I got me a good rifle and my medicine horn here." Hawke patted the powder horn. It gleamed black and regal in the sunlight.

"I reckon you'll be all right," said Dick.

Morgan climbed aboard Boots.

Hauser slapped the horse on the rump.

"I'll be seein' you, Morgan, maybe by and by."

"Maybe so," said Morgan. He put his heels to the horse's flanks.

"Just foller the river," yelled Hauser as Morgan rode away, headed north.

Boots stepped out, prancing, flicking his tail. Friar Tuck, tongue lolling, tagged along in the horse's wake, merry-eyed, as if glad to be going somewhere in particular.

Morgan did not look back. He had seen enough of St. Louis to last him a lifetime.

———·———

Morgan caught up with his father at dusk of the following day. He had ridden Boots hard and the horse was weary. He had carried the dog some of the way. Tut's little legs had given out on him and his footpads were cracked and bleeding.

He saw the mules first, then Hammerhead, just over the horizon. A few minutes later, he saw the small fire, his pa hunched over it, feeding it sticks of driftwood. The Osage River shimmered in the glow of the long sunset, its ripples ruddy with the splash of color from the sky.

"Pa!" Morgan called.

Lem stood up. The fire crackled and sputtered. A pair of swifts darted by, streaked across the river, their shadows rumpled on the moving waters.

"Morg? That you?"

"It's me, Pa."

Morgan rode up, swung out of the saddle. Tut squirted out of Morgan's arms and dashed toward Lemuel. The dog leaped up in the air and tried to lick Lem's face. Boots heaved a heavy sigh and switched his tail at the blowflies. Hammerhead whickered a burbled greeting. One of the mules cleared its nostrils, yawned.

"You rode hard, son." He patted Tut's head, pushed him away.

"Wanted to catch up to you," Morgan said breathlessly, beaming a wholehearted grin.

"Glad you did."

"We're still a-goin' to the mountains, ain't we?"

"I reckon so," said Lem, grinning. He put his arm around his son's shoulder. "You hungry?"

"I could eat the south end of a northbound horse."

"Good. Me, too. Strip Boots there and I'll get to fixin' the vittles. You and Tut look plumb starved."

Tut was sniffing every square inch of the camp, mindless of his sore feet, belly full of river water.

Morgan let out a long "ahh" of relief. It was good to be with his pa again, just the two of them, heading west.

That night, they sat on the bank and listened to the river. They looked at the stars spangled in the waters. Lem was smoking his pipe. Morgan tapped on his medicine horn, listened to the tiny reverberations at the spout end, the dull thump at the thick end.

"Dew dust," said Lem, after awhile.

"Huh?"

"Them stars in the water. Heard it called that once. An old man told my pap that when you saw stars in the water, it meant a heavy dew come mornin'."

"You never told me that before, Pa."

"Never thought of it till now."

"It's mighty pretty."

"Sure is. Man in St. Charles told me we got to watch out for the Pawnee. Them are bad Injuns and we'll likely run into them on the Platte."

"You know where we're goin', Pa?"

"I thought we'd take the north fork of the Platte. Got me a map. Looks shorter that way. Feller what spoke of the Pawnee told me about going to a place called South Park. He made a circle on my map where it's at. Said beyond them big mountains, they's plenty of places what ain't trapped out, game aplenty so's a man can live."

"Yes," said Morgan, a dreamlike quality to his voice, "I think that's the best place to go."

Morgan picked up a small stone and chunked it into the river. It made a sound and the water wrinkled the starshine and then it was quiet again.

The two men sat there for a long time, without speaking. But Morgan felt as if they were talking, even so. His chest swelled

with a good feeling and he could hear his father's voice as h
talked about the journey to the mountains. He could see all th
rivers and hear the elk bugling in the high meadows. He coul
see the beaver swimming and leaving wide wakes in peacefu
streams. He saw the immense land in his mind and his father wa
telling him that wherever they went, the land was theirs.

"Seems like you growed some since I last seen you," said Lem

"I reckon I have, Pa."

"You're almost as tall as me."

"Almost." Morgan grinned. Lem grinned back at him. The
looked like a pair of raccoons. The fire died away and coal
pulsed like something alive and breathing.

Later, the moon came up and Morgan knew it was the sam
moon that shone over the Rocky Mountains.

Both of them looked up at the moon.

"Be closer when we get up high," said Lem.

"A lot closer," said Morgan.

The two men laughed softly in the dark.

Their journey had begun.